MW00615952

SEVERED HANDS

BY M.W. GORDON

DEADLY DRIFTS

CROSSES TO BEAR

"YOU'RE NEXT!"

GILL NET GAMES

BARRACUDA PENS

DEADLY AIRBOATS

BARBED WIRED

BLACK FLIES

TOXIC TROUT

SEVERED HANDS

WATERLESS CREEKS –2009

SEVERED HANDS

A MACDUFF BROOKS FLY FISHING MYSTERY

by

award winning author

M. W. GORDON

SWIFT CREEKS PRESS EDITION, April 30, 2018

Most of the geographical locations are real places but are used fictionally in this novel. This is a work of fiction, and the characters are either the product of the author's imagination or are used fictionally. Any resemblance to actual persons, living or dead, or to actual events or locales is unintentional and coincidental.

Library of Congress Cataloging-in-Publication Data
Gordon, M.W.
Severed Hands/M.W. Gordon

ISBN-13 978-0-9989436-1-9
Printed in the United States of America

DEDICATION

to

Gregory Gordon

my brother

Four years my senior, as a youth Greg shared with me all his interests, teaching me to love opera, stamps, tropical fish, and mostly building HO gauge railroad cars, engines, and buildings. He never lost his interest in the trains and after university, military service, and several years in international business, opened his first model railroad store in Simsbury, Connecticut. That was followed decades later by a similar store in the same state in the small town, Collinsville, ironical when one considers that the weapons used in this novel—the machete—were likely made by the world-famous Collins Company Axe Factory, located on the wonderful fishing river—the Farmington.

Over the years I had many friends. But my brother was my best friend.

THOUGHTS ON WRITING

There is nothing to writing. All you do is sit down at a typewriter and bleed.

Ernest Hemingway

Everywhere I go I'm asked if I think the university stifles writers. My opinion is that they don't stifle enough of them.
There's many a best-seller that could have been prevented by a good teacher.

Flannery O'Connor

The writer who neglects spelling and punctuation is quite arrogantly dumping a lot of avoidable work onto the reader, who deserves to be treated with more respect.

Lynne Truss, *Talk to the Hand*

PROLOGUE

Elsbeth's Diary

When I arrived home from my year abroad at Oxford, both Lucinda and Dad had changed. It occurred in some ways by choice, in others by inevitability. Regardless of what we do, the years catch up. My dear friend Sue, who went to Europe with me but spent her year at St. Andrews in Scotland, returned home to Jackson to learn her father had early Alzheimer's. Sue's mother didn't want to tell her until she was home because her mother didn't want her to terminate a year when her letters showed she was thrilled and challenged.

Dad had reduced the number of Montana river guide trips on his drift boat that he would do per week over the season, which he also shortened, and for those fewer days on the rivers, he stopped taking people he didn't know. A client from hell could do more than ruin his day, and Dad was determined not to spend eight hours rowing someone who might make the day less than what it should be, an unforgettable and rewarding experience on one of the country's most beautiful rivers.

Lucinda—to this day I prefer to be incorrect and call her Mom—and Dad were highly regarded citizens both in Paradise Valley and throughout Southwestern Montana and Western Wyoming. Their insights in dealing with the spillage of toxic waste from the old gold mine on Mill Creek made many people realize they had become useful in solving mysteries like the spill and the earlier barbed wired deaths. And even back as far as the shuttle gal killings more than a decade ago.

It was beguiling over the years to watch the two of them deal with cases. Dad slowly accepted the fact that Lucinda was a better crime solver, and Lucinda learned from Dad that while he had done some controversial work over the years for the CIA, including his assassination of the Sudanese terrorist, Abdul Khaliq Isfahani, he was far more in control of his emotions than was Lucinda. She nearly went over the top dealing with the Chinese

1

mining industrialist, Xia Han, who intended to re-open the Mill Creek gold mine. Given the chance, I think Lucinda would have killed Xia, but Dad was able to calm her down. At least, I think that was the case. I have moments when I am sure Lucinda killed Xia as her friend Deputy Erin Giffin once confided in me. I try not to think of that allegation because it carries me back to some other deaths of bad people, to which Lucinda might have been more than a witness. She was relentless in protecting Dad, regardless of what that devotion caused her to do to keep him unharmed.

They were exciting years. I am thrilled with living here in Captiva in the very same cottage that was once south of St. Augustine and was our home before we moved the cottage here two decades ago.

Mostly, I miss not spending time each summer in the log cabin on Mill Creek in Paradise Valley, Montana.

1

MID-APRIL AT THE SNAKE RIVER DRIFT BOAT
LAUNCH AT WILSON, WYOMING

ICE WAS BREAKING UP, SNOW WAS MELTING, AND insect hatches were blossoming on the Snake River in Jackson Hole and bringing trout up from the bottom to feed. Drift boats were beginning to be seen on the five sections for floating between the Jackson Lake Dam and the South Park Bridge. The boats would disappear in a few weeks when the snow melt gathered silt and turned the river coffee and the rampaging water flows propelled the boats at treacherous speeds.

Two unrelated people stood sipping morning coffee next to an old but carefully maintained fiberglass ClackaCraft drift boat on the northwest side of the Wilson Bridge spanning the Snake River a half-dozen miles outside Jackson. They had never met before. One was female; one was male.

The woman wore patched light-weight waders and scuffed felt-soled boots, a jacket with a shoulder patch noting "Simms Guide," a cable-knit sweater, a fishing vest, and a long-brimmed cap that said "Driggs Drifters Outfitting Shop, Driggs, Idaho."

Long, light-brown hair ended in a ponytail thrust through the rear opening of the cap.

She was half-way between five and six feet tall, rail thin despite the bulky clothes, and had a perpetual smile. Her age? If asked, she'd be evasive. If guessed, probably early forties.

Her name was Janice Whittaker, and she lived in a small restored 1920s Victorian house a dozen-miles west over the Teton Pass in Driggs. Her occupation was a fly fishing guide. Any other guide on either side of the Grand Tetons—splitting Idaho from Wyoming—would say she was one of the dozen elite guides in the area and one of the most sought after to spend a long day with fishing any section of the Snake. Or the Teton or Henry's Fork or wade-fishing one of a few nearby less crowded rivers or creeks.

Janice had arrived five minutes earlier towing her drift boat and carrying two paper cups of coffee, one of which she handed to the only other person in the launching area, who walked over to her rig as soon as she parked.

"I'm Janice," she said. "It's chilly but will get warmer in a couple of hours."

"I'm Jorge Castaneda," the young man said, showing a strong Hispanic accent. A scar curved downward from his right earlobe to his chin, which made it hard for Janice not to stare. He was barely five feet and bore a young face. Dark hair showed around the worn front edge of his hood, topping a gray sweatshirt that needed washing. Tight jeans with ragged knee holes from use rather than design, and torn Nikes worn beyond any reasonable expiration date completed his outfit, which Janice viewed as both strange for fly fishing and a little lean for the chilly morning. But his expression warned her not to challenge him.

"If it rains I have raingear for both of us."

4

"Can we get going?" he asked abruptly.

"Sit on that log by the boat and enjoy your coffee. I'll put the boat into the river, park the SUV and trailer, and rig a rod for you. I see you didn't bring a rod. We'll be on the river in ten minutes."

"I ain't got a fishin' rod. I never done this before."

"That's OK. I have extra rods. Have you ever used a fly rod?"

"No."

"Before we get in the boat, I'll work with you on the grass and show you the basic cast. It's a lot easier fishing from a drift boat compared to standing in the river. As the boat floats downstream, so does your fly. You won't have to cast as often."

Castaneda didn't respond, but not because he was looking elsewhere. He had stared at Janice lewdly—back and forth from head to toe—since she arrived, which was beginning to concern her.

After she launched the boat and parked her SUV and trailer, she walked him to the grass and made a few basic casts, explaining the needed principles. Castaneda took the rod, and each cast looked better. He had listened to her, and she felt relieved.

"You're doing great. You've picked up the most important elements of a good cast. A day on the boat and you'll be a pro."

She thought she detected the slightest smile.

"I think we're ready. Let's hop in. Give me your gear bag; I can store it in the back. You sit in the front."

"I keep the bag. It's got warmer clothes than I got on."

Janice held the boat while Castaneda climbed aboard and sat in the bow seat. She gave the boat a shove and hopped on, settling in the middle guide seat where guides always row. That provides the guide a perfect view of the person at the bow.

"We're going to float about eleven miles from here at Wilson Bridge downriver to South Park Bridge."

She wasn't certain what to tie on his tippet; she thought a dry fly plus a nymph dropper trailing by about 18 inches might attract something, but she was concerned with the greater likelihood of wind knots or tangles with the two flies less than two feet apart. Nevertheless, she sensed that Castaneda was good at taking instructions and that she should try the two-fly rig. Perhaps she would have him make his back cast land on the water to the side of the boat toward the center of the river and, when it straightened out, thrust the cast forward toward the bank.

She opened a box of flies and took out a #16 Royal Wulff for the floating fly. It had some bright color that she hoped might attract a trout. For the dropper nymph she chose a bead head Prince, also #16.

After twenty minutes neither fly had gained a trout's attention, and she changed to a smaller Adams on top and removed the nymph below. When Castaneda took back the rod, he made a good cast, and the fly floated into an eddy behind a rock where the first trout of the day struck.

Janice was thankful that Castadeda set the hook and reeled in the trout to the boat where she netted it and handed the net to Castaneda who sat dumbfounded staring at the Rainbow's colors. Janice pulled out a small camera and snapped a photo.

"No!" Castaneda screamed, throwing the trout into the river.

"What's wrong?" Janice asked.

"*No* one takes my picture. I don't like being photographed."

"I apologize. I'll delete it. Do you want to see it first?"

"Yes," he said taking the camera and looking at the photo. He touched the delete button and then abruptly threw the camera into the deeper water in the center of the river.

"Why did you do that?" Janice demanded loudly. "Deleting the photo was enough. That was a perfectly good camera. Not expensive, but it's lasted me a half-dozen-years, and there were a lot of photos on it that I was about to transfer to my computer. I'll have some disappointed clients I promised to send pictures. You had no right to throw it into the river." Her stutter and quivering voice showed her irritation.

"I don't give a damn about your clients. You shoulda asked me if I wanted a friggin' picture."

For the next half-hour neither said a word. Janet rowed as quietly as she could. Castaneda sat motionless facing forward and holding his rod to let the fly drift at its will. He made no casts to improve his chances to catch something. Janice didn't suggest he try.

"Do you want to stop for lunch on a bank with a good view? I brought sandwiches," Janice said quietly a half-hour later.

"No. How much do we hafta go before I can get out and go home?"

"We can do the rest of the float in an hour."

"What's all this land we're passin'?"

"Private land; mostly agriculture or ranching. It's pretty desolate."

"Good," Castaneda said, without more.

Ten minutes later Castaneda pulled his bag from the side and set it on the floor in front of him. Unseen by Janice, he reached inside and removed several pieces of clothing that were wrapped around something. He pulled the final piece off the thing and placed it in his lap. It was two feet long, in a worn leather case. The only part extruding from the case was a cracked, black plastic grip. Castaneda tugged on the grip and slowly a blade pulled free. It was a well-used machete, and the brightness along the edge suggested it had recently been sharpened.

7

Castaneda knew it had; he had honed it himself over and over the previous evening.

"What are you doing, Jorge? Can I help?"

"You don't help!" Castaneda said as he turned around in his seat, the machete—free of the case—resting on his lap.

Janice was partly curious but mostly scared. "Why do you have a machete?"

"I always carry this. I like the feel of holdin' it and runnin' my finger on the blade. It's very sharp," he added, slowly moving his left palm along the blade and drawing blood.

"Why did you do *that?*" Janice asked anxiously.

"To show you how sharp it is. Ain't you never seen a machete this beautiful?" he exclaimed holding the tip of the blade an inch from her face.

"Put it back in the case. Right n. . . ."

Before Janice could finish, Castaneda had lowered the machete and rested the point on the top of her fishing vest. He stood up, smiled, and used all his strength to thrust the blade through her.

A scream broke the silence of the afternoon, but it was not from Janice. A bald eagle circled above the boat and settled on a barren limb of a long dead cottonwood along the riverbank. The eagle glared at the boat as it passed and appeared to be flapping its wings in approval of a perfect kill.

Castaneda leaned over for a moment, seemed to do something to the body, and then tossed the machete to the rear floor of the boat. He pushed Janice off, moved to her middle seat, and rowed to shore. Stepping out, he shoved the boat back into the current and watched it continue its journey downriver.

In a moment Castaneda, the eagle, and the boat carrying Janice's bloody body had disappeared.

Each had gone their separate way.

2

SPRING ON THE SALT FLAT MARSHES OF FLORIDA

THE PIER AT OUR FLORIDA COTTAGE ON THE marshes south of St. Augustine extends from the land's edge eastward through clusters of yellowish-green *spartina* and cord grass. It connects the land and a small dock that is a half-roofed boat storage for our current shallow-draft flats boat. The other half is uncovered for sitting.

My Hells Bay flats boat replaced an earlier Hewes that was burned during the gill net murders. The Hells Bay wasn't destroyed; it was stolen. Now I have a used Action Craft that has the usual features of a skinny water fishing boat including a center console a few feet forward of the modest sixty horsepower, four-cylinder Evinrude outboard hanging over the transom beneath a poling platform. Not once have I ever climbed and stood on top of the platform. Age does not improve balance.

I added the poling platform for my use as a leaning tower and chose the Evinrude partly because its name sounded more American that Yamaha or Suzuki or Honda. That doesn't mean the Evinrude was entirely made in America, but at least I assumed the *nameplate* that says "Made in America" was! I know there must be folks in Sturtevant, Wisconsin, wherever that is, who are pleased that Evinrude is still around. My one reluctance to being seen with an Evinrude motor on my boat goes back to my teens, when I grew up in Connecticut arguing with friends that Johnson was the better motor, just as I favored the New York Yankees over the Boston Red Sox and drank Pepsi rather than Coke. Johnson's gone, and so are some other old favorites like Lionel trains, Pan Am planes, and Woolworth's everything else.

Ten years ago, our first flats boat, the restored Hewes, was set ablaze during one of three deaths that became known as the Gill Net Murders. The boat and part of the dock were replaceable, but the person who died in the fire was not. Charred almost beyond recognition was Hugh Bradford, the much-criticized editorial page head of the *St. Augustine Chronicle*. His hobbies were fishing and beating his wives and kids. Only three people attended his funeral. Few mourned his loss. An assortment of black smudges remain on the dock to this day and remind us of the fire. At times, sitting on the dock and missing my earlier boats, I imagined the acrid smell of burning plastic.

I had never renamed the old Hewes, which had *Much Ado Aboat Nothing* painted across the transom by the former owner. There is an age-old sailors' superstition that a renamed boat is an unlucky one. I hardly consider my Hewes to have been lucky.

The new flats boat is named *The Office*, so I can truthfully tell people who call me during workday hours when I've snuck off to fish that I'm busy at *The Office*.

On the side of our dock that is open to the sky, my alleged wife Lucinda and I installed a frame that holds a double swing that is within inches of the dock's edge, allowing users to pump themselves out over the water.

I say "my alleged wife" because admittedly I have not fully succumbed to Lucinda's claims that we *were* married at a ceremony years ago in Oyster Bay, Florida—a formality I don't totally remember. I've tried without success to find Oyster Bay, including driving to Cedar Key and turning north, but no luck. I can't even locate Oyster Bay on MapQuest.

Lucinda and I often carry a drink to the dock in the evening and gently—depending on how full our drinks are—sit on the swing and propel ourselves back and forth over the water until the sun is down and we're tired of pumping and have finished the drinks, or—more commonly—the mosquitos have arrived *en masse* for their evening slaughter.

Our conversation ranges from what we did that day, how my daughter Elsbeth is enjoying her time studying in England, what we plan for the next day, and what we hear from our friends in Montana where we spend the summer months at our log cabin on Mill Creek in Paradise Valley.

Lucinda is not Elsbeth's birth mother, but we both call Elsbeth "our daughter." Soon after she showed up at our cabin door at the age of seventeen and said "Hello, Dad," she and Lucinda began to bond in a way that makes everyone who meets them believe they are a devoted mother and daughter duo.

"Friends in Montana" is a reference to a life-changing incident close to twenty years ago when I was Professor Maxwell Hunt at the University of Florida law college in Gainesville. My existence abruptly changed after I was beaten nearly to death in Guatemala by an angry man named Juan Pablo Herzog. I was there mainly to give lectures at the Francisco Marroquin law faculty, but Herzog suspected I was working for the CIA.

Some U.S. embassy people in Guatemala City saved me from Herzog and flew me in a private jet to D.C. where I was mostly repaired, partly rehabilitated, and ultimately placed in the Department of State's protection program, which is similar to the Department of Justice's *Witness* Protection Program. I'm not a witness, and the program principally is for good people who have served their country and paid a price.

I was reinvented as Macduff Brooks, a fly fishing guide living in a log cabin on a creek in Montana in the summer and in a cottage on the salt flats of Northeast Florida in the winter. Herzog now serves as President of Guatemala, living in the elegant Casa Presidencial.

That change was the second dramatic alteration to my life. The first occurred only ten years after I began teaching at UF and a decade before my problems in Guatemala. I lost my first wife, El, and our expected first child in an avoidable boating accident on the Snake River in Jackson Hole, Wyoming. That "expected" child, presumed to have joined her mother-to-be in death, was miraculously saved by an older couple who rescued her on the riverbank where the physician wife performed a cesarean. They buried the mother on a mountainside near Encampment, Wyoming, and with the newborn girl continued to their home in Greenville, Maine. For seventeen years they raised her to be a wonderful young lady. Elsbeth learned about her true life when her dying "adoptive" mother in Maine told her the full story, causing her to start a search for me that proved successful.

Integrating Elsbeth into a world far from Maine required some revision of her imbedded dialect. I knew we were in for confusion when the day after she arrived at my log cabin I asked her to drive and pick up the local paper. With a smile she said, "Ayuh, Fathah, may I take the cah to get your papah?" It was a year before she finally said "sure" or "OK" or "yeah" and a year later when I heard the last "ayuh."

"Macduff. . . . *Macduff!*" Lucinda said, prodding me. "I'm being devoured by mosquitos, and you haven't said a word for fifteen minutes. You must be off in another world. Let's flee to the cottage."

"*I* haven't been bitten. Can't we wait until my last sip?"

"I *can't* wait! They hurt!" she exclaimed, jumping down off the swing and running the twenty or so yards to the house, wildly slapping at various parts of her comely body.

"I'm coming. I'm right behind you," I called out, still on the swing sipping.

"It's *your* fault," I could hear her yell as she ran. "You're not taking care of me according to all reasonable expectati. . . ." Her voice faded off.

I let the swing settle and felt the first bites as the mosquitos realized their sweeter target had fled and I was all that was left. Joining Lucinda seemed the wiser move so I dropped off the swing, ran to the cottage, went up to the porch two stairs at a time, and burst in the front door to where she was already rubbing her arms and legs with something showing big "ANTI-ITCH" letters on the tube.

"I've been ravaged by those tiny savages," she exclaimed. "The sun's down. Let's go to bed."

"Sounds good to me, if you're willing to replace those thousands of tiny ravagers with one life-size."

"I can't wait."

3

THE NEXT MORNING

"LUCINDA, I'M GOING TO WALK TO OUR GATE and see if there's any mail. I want to know if we have something we should answer before we leave for Montana. Walk to the mailbox with me?"

"No, but take Wuff. She needs the exercise. She's getting fat."

"*She* needs the exercise! Isn't that the pot calling the kettle black?"

"You're treading on water way over your head and you're about to go under."

"The pot and kettle reference only repeats a proverb tracing back to great literature, in this case *Don Quixote*."

"Oblique literary references get you nowhere with me. You're implying I'm fat!"

"More like adipose or abdominous."

"Don't expect to be forgiven by using deceptive substitutes. You said *fat*."

"I could have said comely or harmonious."

"And instead of saying you were treading on water far over your head, I could have said that you were out on a limb or, closer to home here and more appropriate for us, you were up Mill Creek without a paddle."

By this time Wuff was lying by the door with one paw over her head.

"I think Wuff has to go out," I mumbled, as we two slipped out, pulled the door shut behind us, and unexpectedly stepped off the porch to be confronted by a chilly morning rain. Wuff and I chose the rain instead of dealing with Lucinda and kept walking, stopping at the shed where I kept an extra rain poncho. Wuff had to do without.

The walk to the gate and mailbox on Route U.S. 1, a stone's throw north of the St. Johns/Flagler county line, was about a hundred yards, which we accomplished in two to three minutes. With my head down in the rain, I missed seeing the live oaks, palms, and pines that thrive without the aid of man. That's fortunate. I'm not a gardener, and when I moved to the cottage I walked through our woods and lectured the trees, telling them they were on their own and should expect no periodic trimming or snacks in the form of fertilizers. I do pick up dead branches the first week we arrive each fall, but otherwise it is nature's call.

Our mailman Fred was sitting in his vehicle next to our mailbox sorting catalogs. I forgot his last name, something Polish sounding ending in "ski" or "zyk" that I couldn't pronounce properly and not be embarrassed.

"Hey, Macduff," Fred said, lowering his window, "how's that undersized collie doing? She'll never be as big as her name Lassie suggests. Are you feeding her enough? She hasn't gained much weight over the past few years."

"Wuff's *not* a collie," I said, gruffly. The rain not helping. "She's a Shetland Sheepdog, also called a sheltie. But *not* a collie, and her name's *not* Lassie. She's registered as Piper Woofington of Inverness—that's in Scotland—and we call her Wuff. . . . I'm getting drenched, Fred. So is Wuff. Any mail for us?"

"Yes, this bunch," he said as he reached toward me with a stack but dropped it into an increasing pool of muck forming below the mailbox. "Sorry," he added as he stepped out, picked up the soaked mail, and thrust it at me. I took the dripping bunch and covered it with my poncho. Fred was gone in a few seconds.

Our rush back to the cabin was quicker than two minutes and not because we were anxious to sort through the mail. I could feel the water draining off the envelopes and catalogs under my poncho and soaking parts of my pants not already drenched.

When we opened the door, the greeting from Lucinda was a commanding, "Don't bring all that water into the house!"

Wuff ran to Lucinda and stood and shook water all over her. And then gave a single bark. She was ready for a treat for bringing the mail home. I tried to hold back a laugh. Lucinda took a kitchen towel, threw it at me, and pointed to Wuff.

"I should have locked you two out. Now *I'm* wet."

Dumping the pile of mail onto the kitchen table I picked up the towel and did my best to dry Wuff.

"Macduff," Lucinda began, as she sorted through the stack, "this is all junk! A dozen ads, three useless catalogs, and what looks like two solicitations from organizations we wouldn't give a dime to. But, *hooray*, here's the first copy of our trial subscription to the *Jackson Hole News*. I'll dry it out, and we'll read it at lunch. The headline looks formidable: 'Newly Arrived

17

Salvadorian Gang Strikes Brutally on the Snake River.' It's too wet to open and read now."

"The Snake River? Sounds scary."

4

NOON LUNCH

LUCINDA MADE WAFFLES FOR LUNCH. I HAD learned to like them even though they were made from something called organic whole-grain, which I suspect is part of the myth of whole wheat. I was raised on white Wonder Bread, and I'm alive and content. But I shut my mouth and ate the organic whole-grain and scored some hard-won dietary points with her.

While she concentrated on dribbling a little honey on her waffles, on mine I emptied a quarter of a jar of guaranteed 100 percent Grade A Dark Amber Vermont Maple Syrup.

"Is the newspaper dry enough to read?" I asked, soaking my last bite of waffle in a pool of syrup in the middle of my plate.

"I'll read it to you," she said, delicately pulling apart the stuck pages to the article.

"Oh my God! No! . . . Macduff, this is terrible," she expressed, trembling.

I couldn't understand her she was so disturbed, and I took the paper from her and read it:

Police are searching for members of the Calle Rojo street gang who are believed to have killed Janice Whittaker, a 37-year-old fishing guide who lived in Victor, Idaho, the first town west of Jackson over the Teton Pass.

Yesterday morning Whittaker had driven over the pass to Jackson for the umpteenth time to take her client fishing on a section of the Snake River south of Jackson known as Wilson to South Park Bridge. Her mutilated body was found on her drift boat at 3 p.m.; she had been stabbed in the chest, and her right hand was missing. Police believe her attacker used the bloody machete that was left in the boat. The letters 'CR' were written in blood on each side of the boat.

The Calle Rojo gang originated in Los Angeles two decades ago and is composed mostly of young, illegal immigrants from El Salvador in Central America. The gang has since spread to many areas in the United States, principally large cities such as Washington, D.C., New York, Boston, Philadelphia, Houston, and Atlanta. More recently the gang also has organized in wealthy resort towns, including Aspen, Colorado; Santa Fe, New Mexico; and apparently here in Jackson.

Lucinda was unable to focus on the remainder of the dampened article, which appeared mostly to be promises by Huntly Byng, head sheriff for Teton County, to identify, locate, and arrest the perpetrator. No mention was made of *how* the murderer would be identified and located.

I have known Byng since I arrived in the West about sixteen years ago and enrolled in the Orvis guide school in Jackson. Soon after I began guiding, Byng played an important investigatory role in the murder of retired U.S. ambassador Ander Eckstrum. He was killed on my boat while casting a dry fly to a rising cutthroat a foot off the bank of the Snake River near Deadman's Bar. Someone hidden on the East Shore had used a high-powered rifle to shoot Eckstrum. After re-opening the investigation, Byng concluded that the shooter likely had intended to kill *me* because we were both similar in size and I had been threatened. Also, I had loaned Eckstrum my trademark Stetson hat after he lost his cap overboard. I've never put that hat on again.

Often, I see Byng when I'm in Jackson visiting and fishing with my close friend, guide John Kirby, who has become a prominent figure in Jackson Hole, Wyoming. I've known him for most of my time spent in the West. I met him soon after finishing the guide school and, since then, we have occasionally floated and fished together.

Ironically, I later learned John had been scheduled to be our guide on the fatal float a decade earlier where my wife El died, but the illness of his dad called him to Georgia. A hungover young guide named Steve Brewster substituted, and his errors caused the crash that killed him and El.

John later put me in touch with Park and Kath Salisbury, which led to a bad time when I guided them, and Park bludgeoned a trout on the riverbank. I rowed off with Kath and left Park to walk out alone along the Snake River several miles to Moose. Salisbury came back into my life a year later in a clever disguise when he tried to retaliate and kill me on another float. I admit—reserving the right to rethink the matter—that Lucinda shot him first, saving our lives and that of Wuff, who was hit by a stray bullet. I did get off one shot that hit Park, but Lucinda often reminds me that shooting a dead body doesn't count.

With that kind of background, it may be surprising that John ever wanted to be around me again, but his presence is mesmerizing, and I'd cancel any plans if he asked me to float with him.

"I didn't know the *Calle Rojo* gang was established in Jackson, much less anywhere in the Mountain West," exclaimed

Lucinda, her composure returning. "Macduff, let's call John Kirby in Jackson. We only know what's in this brief article. He must know more."

For John's and his wife Sarah's sake, I hoped the killing of Janice Whittaker was a one-time murder and not the beginning of a vendetta specifically against fishing guides.

When I called, John was at his home a few miles south of Jackson, playing in the yard with his son and the family's dog. He had his cell phone with him, and it answered playing the Georgia bulldogs fight song, sung to the tune of "John Brown's Body." It spells G-E-O-R-G-I-A twice and repeats "Glory, glory to old Georgia" six times, meaning enough times so a Georgia fan might understand it.

"Your song should say 'another year, another loss to Florida,'" I said.

"Be nice, or I'll remind you of all the sports where Georgia beat you last year," John warned.

"I know which sports. But we beat *you* at football, basketball, and baseball. You beat us at bass fishing, horseshoes, and muggle quidditch."

"Where did you learn about muggle quidditch?"

"Where it was invented, in the Harry Potter books. Actually, it's complex. I concede that most Florida football team members wouldn't understand it."

"Did you call me to talk about muggle quidditch?"

"Not really, but it's more pleasant to laugh about than why I called you." I paused, shaking my head, and then began to explain. "Do you know anything about the *Calle Rojo* youth gang and the death of guide Janice Whittaker?"

"I do. Janice was a great, remarkable, tough lady. You learned a lot about fly fishing if you spent a day on her drift boat, including hearing her identify every bird, tree, wild flower, mountain feature along the Grand Tetons, and most insects favored by trout that were flying around the boat or rising to the surface within sight. *You* might even learn to cast properly and set the hook. She was the first female guide in the area and in a few years became a Master Casting Instructor."

"I'll forget about your derogation of my casting and setting or failing to set the hook. . . . Did Whittaker struggle before she died? How many were in her boat? Was it really a machete that was used?"

"It's too early to answer all those," John suggested.

"Was she married? Have children?"

"No and no. She lived with a female companion, an art historian who owns a popular gallery in Driggs. I'll tell you as much as rumor has it here."

"Please, John, I'm also listening. Go ahead," Lucinda added, removing the lunch dishes from the table and sitting down.

"Some of this is unclear. The medical examiner hasn't issued his report. I did have an email from Sheriff Byng that said that, unless he personally knows his scheduled client, each local guide should consider canceling the float until more is known. I don't know exactly what Byng meant. Guides make their living guiding. They can't cancel every committed trip."

"Do you mean Byng thinks the target is guides in general and more may be attacked?"

"Byng said not to panic but to be cautious. I looked at my list of floats for the first week of the spring season. I had booked five clients over the seven days. I knew four of them, all former clients. But I don't know the fifth."

"Are you going to cancel that one?" I asked.

"I already have. It was a young man who came into my outfitter's shop and asked to have me as the guide."

23

"What worried you about him?"

"Mid-twenties. Never floated before. Claimed he wanted to learn to fly cast. Strong Spanish accent. Name was Arturo Toro. Said he was from California. What really bothered me was his shirt was partly unbuttoned and he had some letters across his upper chest. I believe the letters may have spelled *Calle Rojo*."

"Why did that worry you?" I asked.

"It's time to give you a little history on youth street gangs in Jackson and Wyoming in general," John replied.

"I'm all ears. Who told you about them?"

"Last month Sheriff Byng gave local guides a lecture on gang affiliation in our state."

"I knew L.A. had a big problem with gangs, but then L.A. has issues with most everything that troubles large cities," I noted.

"It's been about a decade since the *Wyoming Tribune Eagle* in Cheyenne reported that police there estimated that eighteen identifiable gangs operated in the area. The biggest were two linked to Mexico."

"Were any part of the Cheyenne, Wyoming, youth gangs from El Salvador?" I asked.

"It's not clear. Much of the problem with the gangs has been graffiti and causing trouble at the rodeo and carnival."

"No personal physical harm, such as beatings?"

"That came soon enough. In Cheyenne, a half-dozen years ago a couple of teen gang members fired a gun outside a high school. It injured a fifteen-year-old girl."

"Here we're talking of using a machete to commit a murder."

"The gangs have been getting more vicious. Cheyenne established an Area Gang Enforcement Team. There was a gang-related threat recently by a young man in Casper, Wyoming, to cut off a woman's head if she didn't join a gang."

"Nothing in Jackson Hole until now?"

"Not that I've heard about. Sheriff Byng's office has held two public hearings on gangs. The first was last year. He estimated that there were as many as forty young gang members in Jackson Hole, mostly in the *Calle Rojo* gang."

"Have any been arrested, John?"

"Yes, for drug-related issues mainly, but also some for fighting, usually members of one gang fighting members of a rival group. But a recent issue has arisen."

"More serious?"

"Yes, and Whittaker's death fits the worst of Byng's worries."

"Which are?"

"The *Calle Rojo* gang is dominant here, but there is another gang, *Los Reyes*, that also originated in and is supported from L.A. It's struggling to take over in Jackson. There's a recruiting war going on, each group working to build its strength."

"How does that relate to Whittaker?" I asked.

"It's the way new gang members are inducted. There have been two suspicious killings in Jackson recently that the sheriff's office has linked to *Calle Rojo*."

"What happened?"

"Unlike the Whittaker case, the two earlier deaths were thought to be *Calle Rojo* members killing members of the newer challenging *Los Reyes* gang. Its members are thought to be from Honduras as opposed to El Salvador."

"You mentioned the induction of new members. What did you mean?" I asked.

"The sheriff believes one of *Calle Rojo's* requirements for induction is to brutally murder someone."

25

"A member of an opposing gang?" Lucinda inquired.

"That may have been the case with the earlier two killings I mentioned. But that changed with Whittaker," John added.

"By killing an *outsider*?"

"Yes, but possibly it means only certain targets count."

"A fishing guide seems to count? Why?"

"Fly fishing on the Snake is a big deal in Jackson Hole, as you know."

"What does the *Calle Rojo* gang have to gain killing fishing guides?" I asked.

"Publicity! They thrive on it. The newspapers didn't print much about the gang versus gang fighting. *Los Reyes* doesn't have a foothold, and the way Whittaker was murdered may scare away the more moderate *Los Reyes*. Earlier, the public didn't feel threatened by the gangs, and as far as many Jackson citizens were concerned, good riddance when they killed one another."

"But why kill guides on their drift boats?"

"The *Calle Rojo* gang wants to create a shock reaction of outrage from the public. Most of our local guides are well liked by their clients. Whittaker certainly was. In many ways they're teachers, and teachers—for the most part—are put on a pedestal."

"Why wouldn't the gang go after more than guides? Maybe pick a victim at random. Or some prominent, well-liked person?"

"They may want to hit one kind of person hard, such as fishing guides. A lot of the guides have families. They won't know what to do. Stop guiding? Leave Jackson, at least for the time being? Look for a different job? . . . Macduff, what would you do if the murder had taken place on the Yellowstone River where you take clients? . . . And how do you feel about it, Lucinda?"

"I'm worried after hearing you, John," she answered. "We're not that far from Jackson when we're at Mill Creek. If it happened in Montana along the Yellowstone River or if I thought it might happen, whether or not Macduff would want to leave, I'd get him out of there and back east to Florida, at least until the killings were solved and the murderers caught and punished. . . . John, you've known about our past for years and how Macduff has become a celebrity of sorts for all the things that have happened, in and out of his drift boats. What do you recommend?"

"Macduff is an ideal target. First, don't even think for a moment about coming here to Jackson. If anything, Sarah and I will leave. Right now, we're not at our house, but staying with a friend. If there's another death, we'll go much further. Head to Arizona, maybe Georgia."

"Try Cancun in Mexico. Or go to Hope Town in the Bahamas."

"I thought you were going to recommend Los Angeles."

"I'm thinking about that. Do you speak Spanish?"

5

AN EMPTY WAREHOUSE SOUTH OF JACKSON, WYOMING

"JORGE, GOOD JOB. THAT BITCH DIDN'T KNOW what was happening to her on the drift boat before it was too late," said the person Jorge Castaneda called *Jefe* who sat at an old rusting metal table.

The small building was a stark and dimly lighted deserted Jackson warehouse, begging for demolition. Castaneda stood facing the table. At least thirty persons were sitting in assorted old folding chairs. All were males in their late teens or twenties. They were candidates and members of the *Calle Rojo* gang.

"You know the reason you are here is to be voted on to be a member of the *Calle Rojo* of Jackson?" questioned *Jefe*.

"Sí. Bueno," responded Castaneda, who appeared over-whelmed by the gathering of so many friends.

Several of the young men had removed their shirts, showing a tattoo across each upper chest that had three-inch high letters spelling *CALLE ROJO*.

"You were instructed to kill a person you did not know. Did you do so? Was she the one I instructed you to kill?"

"Todos, sí, I can tell you every detail. You shoulda been there. I was sittin' in front fishin'. She was in the middle facin' me and rowin'. No other boat in sight. The fishin' was kinda fun. I ain't never done it before. I even caught somethin'. I think she called it a Cutthroat trout. Ain't that a laugh? I was about to make *her* a 'cutthroat.' You shoulda seen her when I opened what she called my gear bag, and I pulled the machete out."

"Have you brought the evidence required for initiation?"

"Por supuesto. Of course, *Jefe*. It's right here in this bag."

"Give it to me, Jorge."

Castaneda laid the bag on the table in front of *Jefe* and slowly pulled out a small hand that had seen considerable sun that death had not yet faded. The blood had long drained out, and it was shriveled and wrinkled. The fourth finger bore a sapphire ring. *Jefe* raised the hand for all to see and spoke as though it were a precious object.

"If any person here has any doubt that Jorge should be admitted to the *Calle Rojo* and receive his tattoo, say it now."

There was a silence that gave way to many smiles and nodding heads.

"You have done well, Jorge. You are playing an important role in making the *Calle Rojo* the most feared gang in Jackson. Are you ready?"

"I been ready ever since I was a little boy growin' up in Soyapongo, El Salvador, and got outta there and I came through Guatemala and Mexico and sneaked into California. . . . I am ready to carry out the instructions you gave me, *Jefe*. . . . What do you wish me to do now?"

"Come here for your tattoo. And then join the celebration of your becoming a member."

6

THE FOLLOWING DAY AT THE FLORIDA COTTAGE

" LUCINDA, IT'S THE NINTH DAY OF MAY, AND we're still in Florida. This past winter deposited little snow on the mountains—a bad year for ski resorts. The snow melt was over by late April. The Yellowstone in Paradise Valley is fishing great, but not for long. I think I know why we're still here in Florida. I'm happy to stay until more is known about Whittaker. Are you concerned?"

"Yes, talking to John in Jackson worried me. A brutal murder of a well-known fishing guide strikes too close to home. I know it's been almost two weeks without another incident, but the idea of taking you west to guide hasn't set well with me."

"It was a *guide* who was killed, not the spouse of a guide," I added. "And it took place in Jackson Hole, not Paradise Valley where our log cabin is on Mill Creek."

"Meaning you feel safe heading west?" she asked.

"No. But if we decide to go, we can skirt around Western Wyoming and Jackson Hole by going north and using I-90, well north of the Snake River. . . . I'm flustered, Lucinda. I have to consider that I've booked a bunch of guiding commitments for May."

"When's your first float scheduled?" she asked.

"In ten days. We would barely make that if we left tomorrow."

After a long pause, Lucinda stood in front of me, and pronounced, "*We're not driving west.*"

"Can you make up your mind? You don't want to go west, or you don't want to drive?"

"A bit of both. We *can* stay away. We don't need the money."

"It's not the money."

"Your reputation?" she asked.

"Partly."

"You're only worried about yourself?"

"No, the only reason I didn't pack today is you. . . . But you're not convinced?" I asked.

"Is there some reason you want to leave here other than to keep your commitments?"

"Yes."

"What?"

"I don't want us to stay here in Florida and mope. But also, I don't want us to spend *any* time in Jackson."

"But our cabin at Mill Creek is OK?. . . I'm not sure I follow."

"We can be at Mill Creek, and I can severely limit my floats," I explained.

"I have a better idea. I can think of a better and safer place, but I won't complicate our lives by raising it," she suggested.

"Leaving here but not driving to Montana?"

"Absolutely."

"So we pass on going to Montana this year."

"I didn't say that," she replied.

"Are we leaving here or not?"

"Yes. In a couple of days."

"I think the best thing for me is just to tag along and not ask too many questions," I agreed.

"Good idea. I'd prefer the tagging but with *no* questions."

"You said we aren't driving to Montana. I'm not walking. That leaves bus or plane. The bus might take longer than driving. It must be flying. . . . I'm flying!" I exclaimed, suddenly grinning at the idea.

"I'm not flying if you're the pilot, Macduff. You're not certified."

"Actually, I am, but you should feel relieved. I'm not our pilot yet."

"How do we go?" she asked.

"We drive to Orlando, fly to Salt Lake City, change for Bozeman, and we're at the cabin in half-a-day."

"We'll miss the Great Plains."

"We'll fly *over* them. I'll tell you when we do. You can look down and gloat."

"You know, we've never flown between here and Montana," she attested.

"I'm sick of the boring drive. We've spent so much time in the Great Plains states I dread the thought of crossing again."

"Do you have Stendhal Syndrome?" she asked.

"Yes, I'm overwhelmed by the beauty and rich history of the Great Plains?"

"That must be it," she murmured.

"When we cross, don't you get weak legs and heart palpitations?" I asked.

"Yes. And panic attacks," she agreed.

"That really must be the *Great Plains* Syndrome from the *lack* of culture rather than too much."

"Same effect. Dizziness, delusions, hallucinations. . . . You said we could fly. Did you mean it? Why haven't we flown each spring and fall for the last dozen years?"

"Because of Wuff. And we need an SUV wherever we are," I noted.

"We can leave our SUV here and buy another in Bozeman."

"And put a lot less mileage each year on the SUV."

"It would save five days driving each trip. That's ten each year."

"When do we start?" I asked.

"Maybe tomorrow. I'll book flights."

"And a first-class pet cage for Wuff. Truthfully, I hate to introduce her to Delta."

Two hours later four packed bags were by the door.

"What do we do with the SUV we have here?" Lucinda asked.

"I'll ask Jen Jennings to pick it up at the Orlando airport," I suggested. "Or better would be for her to drive us to the airport. Jen is going to Ft. Myers tomorrow to visit a niece. She'll be happy to drop us off in Orlando."

"What about at the Montana end?" Lucinda asked. "I'm sure Mavis will meet us at the Bozeman airport. I'll call her. But we can take a cab to an SUV dealer."

"I'd like one of those big, square Mercedes G-Class SUVs," I said.

"You probably want four-wheel drive," she muttered.

"Of course."

"I'm looking up Mercedes as we speak. A Mercedes G550 4x4 SUV starts at about $225,000."

"Pamper me. Call it my birthday gift," I said.

"I already have something for your birthday. . . . And how would you feel pulling your drift boat with a Mercedes to park alongside a dozen other guides with their used pickup trucks?"

"But I will be towing my beautiful wooden drift boat *Osprey*, and the others will all have plastic boats. My boat deserves a Mercedes tow."

"One other matter," she said, shaking her head. "There is no Mercedes dealer in Bozeman. The nearest is Billings."

"Oh."

"Is that all you can say?" she asked.

"What do you think we should buy?"

"Do they have a Mini dealer in Bozeman? I'll buy you a convertible."

"No, thank God," I replied. "You wouldn't fit in a Mini. Or Wuff. Or me. . . . I take that all back."

"You better. Is there a Jeep dealer?" she asked.

"You know there is. That's where we bought the one we're driving now."

"I'll even buy us a loaded Grand Cherokee Limited with everything on it you can imagine," she offered.

"All I want is Sirius so I can block out unpleasant voices," I declared.

"I'll overlook that."

"That settled that. It's 9 p.m.," I said. "We have a long trip tomorrow. Don't you think we should go to bed?"

"Have I ever disagreed to that," she said, already crossing the living room, her shedded clothes marking a pathway to the bed.

The next day Jen drove us to the Orlando airport. The terminal was the usual chaos of humanity trying to fly and airlines

34

trying to make it as difficult and uncomfortable as possible. After checking in, the security line took more than an hour.

"Why didn't we think of flying back and forth ten years ago?" I asked.

"Don't ask. I tossed and turned last night wondering the same."

"Maybe we really like driving across the Great Plains. It gives us time to think. Which is worse: facing the Great Plains or facing Delta or American or United?"

"If you are going to miss plodding across the heart of America, we can arrange to take different flights and stay over one night in Omaha," she suggested.

"I'll learn to live with missing the drive."

"Lucinda," I asked, sitting in the Orlando airport and looking at the destination sign above the check-in desk, "why are we in the waiting section for a flight to Marsh Harbour in the Bahamas?"

"The flight to Salt Lake City leaves from the next gate. That waiting area is crowded. It was more comfortable here. . . . I think we need to board."

"I didn't hear the flight called," I responded.

"You need hearing aids."

Lucinda pulled me up and prodded me toward the gate. She handed the attendant both tickets, and we were walking down the chute before I could object.

"We're in 4A and 4B," she said heading down the aisle and pointing at two seats.

I sat by the window; Lucinda, the aisle. The plane seemed small, but I was still groggy from the nap I took as Jen drove us to the airport. . . . I glanced out the window and was shocked."

"Lucinda! We're on the wrong plane! This has propellers, not jets."

"I had to book a short flight to make a connection. I confirmed our flights only last night; there wasn't much available."

"How are we going? Orlando to Tampa, Tampa to New Orleans, then Chicago, Denver, maybe Seattle, and finally Bozeman?"

"Sit back and relax. I did the best I could."

I was tired and dozed as soon as we lifted off. About an hour later I awoke as the plane shook when we began our decent. I looked out expecting the water that I could see must be Tampa Bay. It wasn't.

"Lucinda! We're about to land, but this is *not* Tampa. The water is a spectacular emerald, like we had in the Bahamas. Where are we?"

"We made a little detour. Welcome to the Bahamas!"

7

THE BAHAMAS

"LUCINDA, ARE YOU ABDUCTING ME? IS THIS Abaco? Are we headed to Hope Town?"

"Yes to all three. Do you know what today is?"

"Maybe Tuesday. Possibly Wednesday. With you I never know."

"It's your birthday. This is a special diversion for you. You've been exhausted and overwrought the past few days, and I wanted you to have a few days completely at rest, away from Florida and the Mountain West."

We deplaned. I knew it was Marsh Harbour, where I landed when we retrieved Lucinda from the captivity of Reginald Covington after her eighteen months' abduction and confinement at his Hope Town estate. Covington was a friend of Robert Ellsworth-Kent, Lucinda's abusive former husband from London. Learning that he was killed by a shark near Hope Town, Dan Wilson sent a team to free Lucinda from Covington. I was on that team.

"Come with me, Macduff. I'm going to buy you a Kalik, sit you down, and tell you why we're here and what I know."

We went to the airport lounge and sat in a corner. I had a refreshing Bahamian beer.

"Lucinda, doesn't Covington still live in Hope Town?"

"Yes. I guess he's still living in his mansion where he and Ellsworth-Kent kept me captive. . . . I talked to Dan Wilson at the CIA headquarters in Langley yesterday. I've been slow to tell you, but we both agreed you can't risk going west this season.

"The whole season? I have floats scheduled."

"No longer. I called each of your clients, and every one of them agreed it was best for you to stay away from Montana. Most of them said they hoped to see you *next* season."

"But the murder was in Jackson Hole, not Montana."

"I know," she replied. "As a result the Snake River is closed to drift boats between Jackson Lake Dam and Idaho Falls. The *Montana* Fish, Wildlife & Parks said the problem's effect on Montana drift boat fishing is being studied."

"Don't you think Montana authorities are concerned with our Paradise Valley sections of the Yellowstone River?"

"Of course. But what can they do. I'm glad our plane didn't head to Bozeman. Aren't you?" she asked.

"I don't know what to say except that I worry about the way you function."

"But I'm not a guide," she said. "You're the one who could be a target."

"I'm not guiding full-time anymore. I have time and can afford to be selective."

"It only takes one misstep. And you're well known in both states. At least as much as Janice Whittaker, the one who was murdered."

"Where do we go from here?" I asked.

"We are staying in the Bahamas until the murders stop and are solved."

"Are we staying with your former boyfriend, Covington?"

"You're cute. I talked to Dan Wilson again today when I left you for a few minutes at the airport lounge. He's checking on Covington, who seems to have disappeared, and urged us to stay away from the peninsula north of the town where Covington lives. Dan will let me know soon about Covington's whereabouts. And he made me promise one other thing."

"Which is?"

"Not to kill Covington."

"You agreed?"

"Obliquely."

"What does that mean?"

"*He* thinks I agreed. *I* don't think I did."

"Where are we staying?"

"I rented a house for a week. It's available for longer."

"Where is it?"

"Covington lived north of Hope Town, in the area called 'upalong.' We'll be somewhere in 'downalong,' south of the town."

"How do we get around?" I asked.

"The rental house is on what serves as a main road through what serves as a town. Our first task is to pick up a 20' center console boat I rented. That's to be our main means of getting from island to island. We'll bring the boat back here to Marsh Harbour for serious shopping and some meals. Other meals we'll have on one of the islands to the north, such as Man-O-War, Great Guana, or Green Turtle. The boat will get us to each island."

"What if we pass Covington in a similar boat? He might recognize us."

"Sunglasses and a hat. Always. And we can move well away from a boat that's approaching."

We caught a water taxi at Marsh Harbour and went to the tiny Parrot Cays to pick up our rented boat from Island Marine and then on to a private pier on the east side of the harbor at Hope Town. Our rented house was about the size of our Florida cottage.

"We get sunset views here as opposed to our sunrise views in Florida. Can you adjust?" she asked.

"With time. Do we watch the sun set from bed like we do sun rises in Florida?"

"The sun rose about the time we wanted to get up. It will set here a lot earlier than our usual bedtime."

"I can adjust to an early bedtime if you can."

"Try me," she said, smiling.

8

MORNING IN HOPE TOWN

I WOKE NEARLY AN HOUR AFTER SUNRISE THE next morning, confused about where I was. Lucinda was in the kitchen with Wuff, who must have wondered what was going on. On the trip over from Marsh Harbour, where she was let out of her travel cage, she had to be lifted into the water taxi, lifted out at Parrot Cay, lifted back into the rental boat, and lifted out at our dock. In the rental boat she curled up under whichever of us was at the helm.

When we walked into the cottage, Wuff followed us to the bedroom, jumped up onto the bed, flopped on a pillow, and shut her eyes. Flying *is* exhausting, and we didn't see her until she miraculously awoke at 4:55, five minutes before her dinner was due.

"Call Dan," Lucinda urged the next morning at breakfast. "Tell him we've arrived."

"OK. . . . The speaker is on," I said, dialing.

"Easy trip to wherever you are?" Dan asked.

"I'm still confused. I got on a plane in Orlando thinking I was heading for Salt Lake City and would be changing to a smaller jet to Bozeman. But, when I looked out the window and

41

saw propellers, I knew I was on a very small plane heading elsewhere than Salt Lake City."

"Are you enjoying Hope Town?" Dan inquired.

"How did you know?" I asked.

"I knew where you were going. Lucinda and I talk a lot without you on the line interfering."

"Thanks. Did you approve our coming here?"

"I told Lucinda it was her choice, as long as it's where no one would recognize a drift boat. I know you two love Hope Town. My one reservation is I don't like your being near Covington."

"We will be watching for him and dressed so he won't recognize us," Lucinda added. "No one we know in Montana or Wyoming knows about our affection for this place. Plus, Guatemalan President Herzog doesn't know we're here. It's a matter of balance."

"Don't let the balance tip in favor of Covington."

"How long do you expect us to stay here?" I asked Dan. "We can't stay forever, and I do have obligations in Montana."

"This year is taken care of. If you want to worry about guiding, make it worrying about the following season. . . . When you do go to Montana, look up Will Smith, our Bozeman agent who's your contact. He should be told where you are. Also, the FBI must have a dozen agents in Jackson. And we have two CIA agents assigned there."

"The FBI info isn't comforting. Ever hear what happened to Suzuki, who was the FBI's head in their Salt Lake City office?"

"He's been demoted from heading an area office to being an ordinary agent in a single city," Dan explained. "Unfortunately, that city is Jackson, Wyoming."

"If you talk to him, don't mention me. We had an unpleasant relationship about the FBI's blunders at the Nugget Gold Mine on Mill Creek."

"Didn't you two find a body in a mine shaft there who proved to be an FBI agent?"

"Yes," I said. "His name was Peter Drain. Suzuki probably still thinks Lucinda and I killed Drain. But wishing it and doing it are two different matters."

"What can the FBI do? And why are CIA people in Jackson?" Lucinda asked.

"The second question is easy," Dan responded. "The murderers are assumed to be illegal immigrants from El Salvador. That makes it international and that means us. The first question is always hard since we don't often agree with the approaches to a problem taken by the FBI. We don't agree with how they train, how they operate, and how they manage to lose any semblance of personality when they confront the public. If I had to guess, they are trying to identify all the members of the *Calle Rojo* gang. Maybe find a member who will speak out against what the gang is doing. But don't count on it."

"Are the gang members noted for tight lips?"

"Sealed with super glue," Dan replied. "These are kids who have nothing to go back to in El Salvador. They believe that becoming a member of the gang is a ticket to a more comfortable life, even if that life is supported by prostitution, selling drugs, and extortion, and involves a few murders."

"Do you have any idea how many of these kids are not yet gang members but are determined to join, regardless of what it requires?" I asked.

"That doesn't sound encouraging," Lucinda added.

"Can you imagine there being twenty waiting to join, and each willing, even anxious, to follow instructions to kill a fly fishing guide?" Dan asked.

"That *isn't* encouraging," Lucinda responded quietly.

9

LIVINGSTON, MONTANA

KEN RANGLEY, PARK COUNTY SHERIFF'S OFFICE head and long-time friend, called my cell phone number at mid-day *assuming* that Lucinda and I had arrived at our log cabin in Montana for the summer.

"Can you two join us for lunch?" Ken asked. "Erin Giffin is with me and we are walking into the 2nd Street Bistro in the Murray. We'll wait for you two before we order."

The old Murray Hotel is in Livingston, five minutes from Ken's office and thirty from our cabin. He's a regular lunch time patron.

We all said "hellos."

"Macduff," Ken continued, "you said you'd tell us what you talked about with John Kirby and some other Jackson guides. We have Huntly Byng in Jackson on the line. That makes five of us on the call. Fortunately, there are no other people here for lunch and the speakers on both our phones are on."

"We can't join you for lunch," said Lucinda. "Sorry. But we're listening."

Erin Giffin is Ken's principal deputy in Livingston. Huntly Byng heads the Teton County Sheriff's Office in Jackson.

I whispered to Lucinda, "Cell phones are useful if you don't want people to know where you are. I don't plan to say where we are unless someone asks, and if someone asks, I'll say we're on our way to Montana."

"Where are you two?" asked Erin, one of Lucinda's closest friends.

"Delayed. But were on our way to Montana."

"I miss you two," said Ken. "I'm assuming all of us know some of the details about Janice Whittaker. She died on your turf, Huntly. Why don't *you* update *us*. It's been a week since her death. Your Jackson newspaper reports of the past couple of days have had few details."

"The medical examiner issued his report this morning," Huntly explained. "He concluded that death was caused by a single two to three-inch wide stab in the chest by the machete found with the body. No big surprise."

"Why was the machete left in her drift boat alongside her body?" asked Erin. "Usually a murder weapon is thrown away. One quick toss, and it would have been hidden at the bottom of the Snake River."

"Maybe a scare factor," Huntly replied. "People cringe when they hear about a murder where a machete is used."

"Was anything unexpected found on her body or in the boat?" asked Ken.

"Not really," Huntly quickly replied. "Nothing unusual about her body other than the missing hand."

"Are you sure? *Anything* else?"

"Scribbled in blood on the side of the boat, probably by the killer using a finger, were the initials *CR,* we assume meaning

Calle Rojo. They were quite large, five to six inches for each letter."

"Any DNA on the boat or body?"

"Not finalized. It's being tested. There had to be DNA of Whittaker and almost certainly the killer. . . . Realize that Whittaker took one or two people on each float, and during this part of the season she probably had five to six floats each week. That's a lot of different DNA, unless she scrubs the boat pretty carefully between floats. . . . We hope to know more about any matching DNA in another week."

"What if there were DNA that, if known, came from an unidentifiable illegal alien youth who—maybe—has never been arrested in the U.S.?" asked Lucinda, using knowledge she gained from dealing with the Black Flies murders. "That means there's no DNA match to make."

"I admit," responded Ken, "that there's a chance we will know little more than the killer was probably a *Calle Rojo* gang member. Meaning probably a young school dropout. And probably temperamental and foul mouthed and scruffy and tattooed. Meaning probably unpleasant for most people to be around."

"Not a very nice client to meet and start a float. Wouldn't any guide, seeing someone like you describe, Ken, be wary of the person's real reason to want to hire a guide?"

"After this murder, yes. Maybe Whittaker *was* uncertain and a little scared starting off with the client."

"Was any examination made of Whittaker's vehicle and trailer?" Lucinda asked. "She may have driven the killer to the launch ramp. And he—or she—may have helped launch the boat."

"We examined both. There were lots of prints. But like the issue of finding DNA, if the prints were not registered somewhere, we can't make a match and, therefore, an identification."

"Huntly," Ken asked, "if you do find a name for the killer, is he likely to be found? Would the gang have put him in hiding? Do you have photos of Jackson Hole gangs and their members?"

"We don't know enough about the habits of any gangs. What little we do have tends to be about motorcycle gangs. We've been collecting head photographs whenever we arrested gang members, often when they caused trouble at our local rodeos or outdoor concerts. If we thought they might be gang members, we made them strip and looked for tattoos. You know that *Calle Rojo* members have a tattoo of the gang name across their upper chest, just inside and below the shirt collar. They previously had it on their knuckles or even their brows, but that made it easy to identify them, and so they shifted to the upper chest."

"Where does that leave *us*?" asked Erin.

"Worried," called out Huntly on his cell phone. "Ken, do you have any gangs in Livingston that may provide experience in dealing with them?"

"Yes, but they're bike gangs. One of the main bike gangs in the country—the *Bandits*—has a significant presence here. Started in the U.S. in 1935, it has 200 chapters and an estimated 5,500 members worldwide. They allegedly include contract murders among their activities. But they're not kids, they're not illegals, and they're not from Salvador. What they share is nobody wants *either* gang in their hometown. *Calle Rojo* is a separate group, and I don't know of anything in Jackson similar to the gang existing here in Livingston."

"The *Bandits* and the *Calle Rojo* would have trouble surviving in the same city," Huntly replied. "The *Bandits* are tough characters, but they don't require candidates for membership to arbitrarily murder someone and cut off a hand."

"Once either gang is present, how does a city get rid of all of them?" Lucinda asked.

"Forget the First Amendment and free speech when you deal with gangs. It's like yelling 'fire' in a theater. For gangs, adopt zero tolerance. Do lots of profiling. Give free bus tickets out of town. Better still, build more prisons and don't stop using capital punishment," Huntly offered, sounding more upset with the gangs by the minute. "But don't admit what you're doing, and don't talk to newspapers."

"Why not hang them in the Jackson Town Square beneath the elk antler arches? Every Friday evening to amuse the tourists, like the summer old-time Western gunfights," Lucinda suggested, only half in jest.

"Maybe Friday *and* Saturday evenings," Erin added.

10

EARLY MAY AT THE LAST CHANCE DRIFT BOAT LAUNCH ON THE HENRY'S FORK RIVER IN IDAHO

HENRY'S FORK, NAMED AFTER AN EARLY FUR trader, is considered the best of the best in the West by many a fly fisherman, mainly for its hosting prolific hatches. The most popular drift is through what was once Harriman and Guggenheim family ranchland and is now part of the Idaho state park system.

Dan Goodyear stood sipping morning coffee next to his drift boat at the Last Chance access about mid-way between Island Park to the north and where he would finish the float at Osborne Bridge alongside U.S. 20 and Harriman State Park to the south.

Dan was a fringe member of the Goodyear tire people who, instead of going into the family business, has used his modest inheritance to support himself while pursuing his dream—being a professional fly fishing guide on what he believed was the best fly fishing river in the world. His small, log cabin home at Island Park had photos of his grandfather fishing with his Guggenheim family friends.

Goodyear became a guide nearly twenty years ago and was envied by his peers for his uncanny ability to catch fish in the worst circumstances. But the envy didn't extend to dislike because his personality captured the friendship of everyone in the area who fly fished, male or female. He was a half-a-foot over six feet, which years ago endeared him to his Massachusetts prep school basketball coach. But all through prep school and Dartmouth, Goodyear was not interested in team sports; he fished in the spring, summer, and fall months and skied in the winter. He chose Dartmouth because of its access to fly fishing in New Hampshire and Vermont.

He had a slightly regal look for which he apologized and blamed genetics. He was attractive to women, but his lifetime thus far had not brought him in contact with anyone he thought could be a spouse who also would be his best friend. And who was willing to live with a relatively poor member of the prominent Goodyear family. And learn to fly fish. He became satisfied believing that he'd live out his life alone, and he learned to cherish his privacy.

Goodyear's client this day, whom he did not know, was not from a prominent family. His Salvadorian grandparents and parents survived on meager incomes derived from growing corn and various vegetables a hundred miles from the capital—San Salvador—of their impoverished country.

The client's name was Hector López. He was young and did not want to talk any more than required. Perhaps it was his lack of confidence in speaking a language foreign to him. He told Goodyear he had moved with his mother to Denver. Truthfully, he had fled El Salvador alone after he double-crossed a drug dealer, and he walked, begged rides, or rode busses through

Guatemala and Mexico to ultimately sneak over the border into Arizona.

In Tuscon, López came in contact with members of a youth gang composed almost exclusively of Salvadorians who illegally entered the U.S., often to escape threatening situations at home. Many had initially gathered in L.A. but soon moved on to other less gang-infested cities, including Tucson. But López was uncomfortable in Arizona, being so close to the Mexican border and in a state that he and his friends believed encouraged a hostile attitude towards Hispanics. He moved north to Jackson.

"I'm Dan," Goodyear said to López with a broad smile and friendly manner. "Ready to fish?"

"Yeah, I guess. I ain't done it before."

"I like beginners, especially helping someone new to fly fishing because they often become addicted to it for life."

"Probably not me, but I'll try. A friend in Jackson—he's one of five roommates in a crummy apartment—told me to try it. Some friend!"

Goodyear wondered how López could afford a day fishing with a guide.

"What made you decide to spend a day on a drift boat?"

"There was this outdoor sports fair, and I picked up a raffle ticket from the floor of a bar. The guy next to me dropped it. I won the prize, and here I am."

Goodyear didn't want to ask why he didn't give the guy the raffle ticket he dropped, sensing López was not one to argue with.

"Boat's ready. I'm almost finished rigging a rod for you. Do you know anything about flies?"

"Like mosquitoes. We got lots of them in Salvador."

"Well, that's not exactly what I meant. . . . Look at this, Hector," Goodyear said, handing López a large black stonefly imitation.

"Black bug. So what?"

"I'm tying it on your line. It's been a successful fly here the past couple of weeks. The waters flowing at. . . . " He stopped his own sentence because he realized López didn't care what fly he was using and probably didn't care to be fishing. He thought he'd write this day off and inform his outfitter shop owner he wanted no part of any further clients who had won a a raffle for a float.

Henry's Fork was its usual paradise of gorgeous views, almost as though it were one large spring creek. Goodyear tried to have as little contact with López as possible, and after they netted one 17 inch Rainbow, Goodyear rowed along the edge of the river he thought most unlikely to produce results. That and not rowing other than to keep them headed downriver shortened the time to the takeout.

At noon Goodyear pulled to the shore for lunch and suggested they have it in the boat.

"I gotta pee," said López, soon after they finished lunch and began to drift again.

"Around the next bend is a good place to pull over."

Five minutes later, after López disappeared around some brush, Goodyear wondered what would happen if he left and went on without López. But, by moving downriver without stopping to do any wading, they would finish in under two hours, and his obstreperous client would be gone forever.

When López returned, Goodyear decided he might as well also use the opportunity to relieve himself. He kept the boat within sight, and the only movement he saw from López occurred when he got up, picked up his gear bag, took something out, and set it on the floor.

Afloat again, Goodyear tried his best to draw something positive from of López.

"Who are your roommates in Jackson? Have any of them ever floated like this?"

"They can't afford it. They gotta work or no food and no room."

"Would you do this kind of float again?"

"Screw it, no. This is stupid. I could steal fish from Albertson's if I wanted them."

While López was talking, he turned and set his rod down.

"You OK?" Goodyear asked.

"Yeah. I gotta cramp in my hand from squeezing the rod. I'll shake it out."

"We're almost at a special place. My favorite section of Henry's Fork."

"Good, tell me when we're there."

They floated around a slight bend and entered a run that always seemed to be productive. While López had been off behind the bush twenty minutes before, Goodyear had replaced his fly with a Marsh Brown and added a bead head Copper John nymph.

"Hector, I've put a can't lose combination on your line. Keep an eye out for any movement. If the floating Marsh Brown disappears, set the hook; the trout may be on the dry fly or below on the nymph."

"You really like this crap," López said, scowling and looking angry and bored.

"I do. Maybe in time you'll want to fish again."

"No way. It stinks," he said throwing the rod into the river.

"Hey! You tossed the rod over the side. What the hell do you think you're doing? . . . I'm rowing back for it."

"No you're not," he said, turning in his seat and pointing his arm toward Goodyear. In his hand was a machete. . . . A light came on in Goodyear's head. He had read something about a young gang member in Jackson using a machete on a guide named Whittaker. But he didn't finish the article because it was so gross.

"I don't need no more raffle tickets. You're my ticket to the *Calle Rojo*."

"What's that?" Goodyear asked.

"The toughest gang in the U.S. All we young guys are illegals from Salvador."

"So, what does this float have to do with that?" Goodyear asked, watching the machete which was touching his chest.

"It means this!" López yelled, standing and jamming the machete into Goodyear, who collapsed on the floor of the drift boat, his blood mixing with the puddles of river water that had splashed into the boat.

"I'm in! I'm a member of the *Calle Rojo!*" López called out to no one.

He took one oar and paddled to the eastern shore where he got out and then reached back into the boat to do one more thing with the machete—cut off Goodyear's right hand before dropping the machete into the boat. Then he dipped his finger into the blood dripping from the hand and wrote the letters *CR* on the side next to the guide's seat. He shoved the boat back into the current and jogged the short distance toward U.S. 20, stopping only for a minute, and made a call.

"Come get me. I'll be by the side of the road."

When he got to the main road, a car soon pulled up. Three others hopped out, all without their shirts and each with *Calle Rojo* tattooed across his chest.

"Show us! Show us!" yelled one.

"Look at this," López exclaimed, holding up the bleeding right hand of Goodyear.

"You're in," called out the oldest looking. "You'll soon be one of us."

"It was simple, man. I loved shoving the machete into him. I'd do it again tomorrow if you guys asked."

11

HOPE TOWN COTTAGE

THE WATER SURROUNDING OUR RENTED HOPE Town cottage was so calm that each anchored boat appeared twice, once as the actual boat and a second as the reflection that was only occasionally disturbed when a boat dropped or hauled its anchor or the ferry arrived from Marsh Harbour.

The intense mid-day tropical sun enhanced the iridescent aqua surface. The shallow waters of Abaco allowed the sunlight to reflect off the delicate sandy bottom. I knew that we were in a corner of paradise.

Lucinda and I lounged on separate porch swings, enjoying a break after an energetic morning bicycle ride to the southern tip of the island.

"I'm exhausted and sore all over," I exclaimed. "Especially my rear. Why can't someone make a bicycle seat that's the reverse image of an average rear?"

"Are you suggesting I have an *average* rear?"

"Your seat would have to be specially made."

"Oh! So I have an *abnormal* rear?"

"No one has a rear like you."

"I don't know whether that's good or bad."

"Drop your shorts. I'll take another look."

"And so will everyone in the harbor."

"They'll envy me. I like that."

"Sometimes I rue that cold Thanksgiving Day we met and I invited you into my ranch house in Montana."

"Now *my* rear really hurts, thinking back to that evening when I slipped on the ice you hadn't removed in front of your door, and I landed on my butt just as you opened the door. To add to my pain and embarrassment, you began to convulsively laugh."

"It wasn't convulsive. And I did invite you in."

"And plied me with drink and ultimately seduced me."

"You were so confused. I took advantage of you and enjoyed every minute of it. . . . Can we talk about something else? This is Hope Town. It's beautiful. You could say something more in character with the Bahamas."

"OK, I'll ask you a question. What color is a glass of pure drinking water?"

"I don't know where this is going, but I'll answer," she said. "It shouldn't have any color. It should be perfectly clear."

"Then why are we looking at water that's a beautiful transparent blue-green? The water along the Atlantic coast beaches at St. Augustine isn't like this. It more a murky gray. Why is that?"

"Do you actually expect *me* to know?" she asked. "You're in charge of trivia; I solve murders."

"Listen, and please don't interrupt. The gray is caused by so many millions of phytoplankton and zooplankton in the water at the same time that it becomes cloudy and gray."

"Those are living creatures?"

"Little ones. Wanderers of the ocean. Phytoplankton are pin-head size single-celled plants that have a green pigment we all, including you, know as chlorophyll. Phytoplankton chlorophyll absorbs red and blue portions of light leaving the green."

"And zooplankton?" she asked.

"They are animals rather than plants. Such as the tiniest fish or crustaceans."

"Anything else?"

"Don't forget sand. Very fine sand adds to the dull color and cloudiness."

"Macduff, maybe you're too scientific. I think you're ignoring pollution. It must play a part."

"True. The oceans are becoming a huge landfill, especially for plastics. The trash of thousands of cruise ships drifts on the oceans."

"Does that mean people who live on tropical islands surrounded by crystal clear blue-green water don't pollute," she asked, "but those like us from the more northern and populated areas of the U.S. do?"

"That isn't plausible. . . . And it's untrue."

"Why?"

"It's more complex," I responded.

"Try me."

"In the Bahamas the reefs are barriers and break the force of moving water, such as the currents we have directly off St. Augustine. The waters of the Bahamas, for the most part, aren't churned to the same extent. Around here in Abaco, the green water is inside the outer reefs and barriers. Go out into the Atlantic, and the water is more stirred up."

"Waters around some of the Bahama Islands are clear but have lots of waves. I've seen that around Turks and Caicos."

"Turks and Caicos? When were you at Turks and Caicos?"

"I don't remember exactly. It must have been with Ellsworth-Kent and Covington. I never went anywhere alone."

"Being stirred up has to do with what's in the water."

"And we are back to the more fine sand and living organisms in the water, the more cloudy or less clear it will be."

"Lesson over. Had enough, Ms. Lang?" I concluded, using her maiden name.

"*Doctor* Lang! Please be more respectful. I do have a Ph.D. from the University of London."

"I should have remembered. You're certified to be smarter than me."

"I've been trying to convince you of that for years."

"As you've pointed out, not infrequently, I'm a slow learner."

"Our discussion of emerald water is not over. I think I've heard you say that the greenness is related to the sunlight reflecting off the sand bottom of shallow water."

"That's true, but it's reflecting off the green phytoplankton."

"So I owe my thrill in seeing this beautiful blue-green water mainly to phytoplankton?"

"Mostly. Phytoplankton are alive; they breathe. And they absorb carbon dioxide. Meaning lowering temperature and less global warming."

"I figured you'd get around to global warming. Lesson over, or are you going on? And on and on and on?"

"Lesson fini! Sit back and enjoy the blue-green phytoplankton."

"We bicycled around the southern tip of this island this morning," she commented, apparently finally saturated by the tiny blue-green creatures. "Where to next? Knock on Reginald Covington's door?"

"We can ask him to join us this evening for a drink and dinner to thank him for allowing you to return to me? I do know he likes to drink."

"Do you remember Dan insisted we *not* go searching to find Covington's specific whereabouts?" she reminded.

"Yes, but we need to know to avoid him."

"We know where his house is. That's enough. . . . Should we walk or bike or use a golf cart to explore the north part of the island?"

"Walking is out. I'm tired, and we might run into Covington if he's also out walking."

"The last time you used bikes, near his house you had a crash and knocked on Covington's door for help."

"Forget that," I said. "But if you're working your way toward using golf carts, I concur. There are lots of carts used on the few roads north of the town center."

"When do you want to go?" she asked.

"What about now?"

"Electric or gas cart?"

"Can't we rent a *car*?"

"Not on this island," she affirmed.

"Taxi?"

"None of those here either."

"Motorized skate boards?"

"Forget motors."

"Bikes again?"

"Yes, but the island is about six miles long—north and south—which discourages a lot of people from relying on bikes. We probably won't repeat what we did this morning. You said you were exhausted."

"Can we walk?" I asked.

"*May* we walk? Yes. *Can* we walk? Not me after this morning. From what I see, gas or electric carts have become the most popular way to get around."

"Electric is quieter, but you can go further on a tank of gas than a battery charge."

"Whatever you decide. You're the vehicle freak. . . . What should we wear?" she wondered.

"Covington knows how you dress because you were a guest in his house for eighteen months."

"I wore much the same thing all the time. Short shorts, T-shirt, and sneaks. My hair was longer than it is now."

"Hat?"

"Never."

"Sunglasses?"

"Ellsworth-Kent and Covington wouldn't let me wear them. They said sunglasses prevented them from reading my eyes."

"That's good reason to wear them all the time while we're here."

"Anything else?"

"Wear a hat. Your choice. Something feminine with a lot of brim. Not a baseball cap. . . . What else?"

"I never wore a bra. I wanted to, but Ellsworth-Kent and Covington wouldn't let me. They liked to stare. And feel."

"Me, too. . . . Wear longer shorts; it's too hot for jeans. What kind of tops did you bring other than T-shirts?"

"Not much considering how warm it can be here."

"Wear them, but wear a bra, at least when we're in or north of the town, where Covington is most likely to be seen. But not when you're here at home."

"Anything more? . . . What are *you* wearing, Macduff?"

"I should appear older."

"You are older. You don't need to dress older. It's obvious."

"I'll ignore that. . . . There's no way I can look your age anyway. I won't wear shorts because of my noticeable knee surgery scars. Jeans are hot. I'll wear light weight khakis and one of those belts with designs, like fish or sailboats or signal flags. Topsiders for my feet. Don't let me forget my sunglasses; I don't put them on as often as I should."

We rented a golf cart north of town near the baseball field. Had we rented it south of town, closer to our lodging, we couldn't drive it *through* the town. Even a gate has been installed to discourage that. Fussy rules that add to the island's charm.

Along the road about two hundred yards north of town, Lucinda began to shiver. There was no cool breeze. The temperature had not plummeted. It was something else.

"Are you cold?"

"No," she said in a whisper, looking away from me.

I drove our cart onto the grass and stopped beneath the uncertain canopy of a coconut palm tree.

"You're trembling. Bad memories?" I said.

"I know this road. They took me to town on rare occasions with angry threats of beatings and more if I tried to run. I was always weak from little exercise over the months and couldn't run. Covington's concubine, Candi Treat, was sympathetic and saved me several times. But I always paid a price when we returned to his house."

"Shall we go back and rethink this?"

"No. Give me a few minutes, and I'll be OK. I'm glad we have a golf cart rather than bikes."

63

When she looked at me and nodded a few minutes later, we started off again.

Not more than a hundred yards further, I felt her squeeze my arm.

"I'm not going to look," she whispered, "but Covington's house is on our left. The one with the surrounding wall or fencing."

"I see it. I won't slow down. *Don't* turn your head and stare."

"Do you see any sign of anybody living at the house?" she asked, her hand covering her eyes.

"Yes, when I had a quick view through the fencing, I saw two young couples and three or four children playing with a ball in the side yard."

"That's strange, Macduff. Covington didn't ever have guests, and he *hated* children."

"I know why those people are here," I added as we passed the end of the property without slowing. "There was a sign next to the front gate: 'Vacation Rentals. Short- or Long-Term.' It gave a number. Do you have a pen?"

"Yes."

"Write down '866-8967.' That must be the rental agency's phone."

"Shall we call them?" she asked.

"Yes, when we get back to our rental cottage. What do you think it means? Did Covington sell? You've told me he loved that house."

"Let's stop at the little harbor at the north of this island. Not far ahead. You can buy me conch chowder and a drink."

"Do you think his kept woman, Candi Treat, is still involved?"

"Remember, Macduff, when we flew off from Man-O-War Cay and left Candi, we thought she was going to his home to

64

clean out his safe of cash and secret bank account numbers and get away from the Bahamas. I hope Candi's in Spain or the Caribbean, living life as a wealthy young woman."

"She was smarter than she appeared," I added.

"If you're hinting that applies to me, you're in trouble."

12

AN HOUR LATER

LUCINDA AND I SAT AT CAPTAIN CANDI'S BAR. WE talked and sipped Kalik Light under the welcoming shade of an umbrella. There wasn't any breeze, which elevated the temperature uncomfortably.

Located in North End at the extreme top of Elbow Cay, the bar was about a mile from our rented house in Hope Town.

"Who is Captain Candi?" Lucinda asked the waitress as she set a second bottle in front of each of us.

"My *idol!*" answered the shapely young redhead.

"Why is that?" I inquired.

"You don't know? Actually, she *owns* this place. She's *great.* Pays almost twice what other bars on Elbow Cay pay. Treats us *great.* You don't know about her?"

"Tell us."

"Her full name is Candi Treat. It's actually something else, but when she's here, she wants to be called Candi. A couple of years ago, she was the plaything of the richest guy on the island, named Reginald Covington. He thought she was just another dumb blond he brought to his mansion to be his sex slave for a couple of years and then be dumped overboard off one of the

66

reefs, as rumor says he had done with three others before Candi. But she proved too smart for him. She somehow stripped him of all his assets, including several foreign accounts, whatever that means. She actually ran off with millions, to somewhere in Europe. We guess Spain. . . . You sure you never heard of her?"

"Well, maybe a little. What's she doing now? Still living abroad?"

"She lives *here* on Elbow Cay, in Hope Town. She came back here, bought an old house on the harbor, and opened this bar. She's believed to have another house in Spain, an apartment in New York City, and maybe other places. And she has an airplane! She has sooo much money!"

"Doesn't she worry about Covington?"

"He works for *her!*"

"Doing what?"

"*Anything* she wants. Errands. Yard work. Nothing complex or that uses a brain. Which he no longer has."

"I'm missing something," Lucinda said. "I've heard he was not known as a nice man and boss. But he *was* considered smart and devious. . . . Why didn't he use the courts to get his money back?"

"A combination of damage from an overdose of drugs and a stroke he suffered after he learned that Candi actually withdrew nearly every cent he owned. Anyway, it was almost all stolen or gained from illegal things he was doing. Exactly what I don't actually know."

"Did he have the stroke here?"

"At his mansion, a half-mile south of here. But it's not his anymore."

"We noticed a sign on a big house about vacation rentals, and there was a young family in the side yard."

"Let me go back a minute. Some people came from the U.S. to Hope Town to rescue a woman Covington and a friend of his had kept secluded here for a year and a half."

"Who were the people?" Lucinda asked quietly.

"Candi actually never mentions them by name. But she idolizes them. They saved her because she helped them get the woman off the island. . . . Do you want to meet Candi? She just walked in. She's in the back room."

"Tell her there's a couple who would like to meet her and tell her they were in the Conch Shell restaurant in Hope Town when she was sitting in a booth with Covington. After his two henchmen got up and left, the couple slid into the booth. After a few minutes they all left, too."

"How do you two know about that?"

"We'll tell Candi."

The waitress left, and Lucinda turned to me. "Can you believe this, Macduff?"

"Actually, I want to hear more. You probably. . . ."

"My God! It's *you* two!" Candi was standing by our table and reached to hug Lucinda. "Why are you in Hope Town?"

"I'm Macduff. This is my . . . ."

Candi threw her arms around Lucinda, and the two began to shed tears and laugh. "I know who you both are."

"You helped us," Lucinda exclaimed. "It was a crazy night."

"I watched you fly off in the plane from Man-O-War Harbour."

Candi let Lucinda loose and came over to me and repeated the hug and the tears.

"You won't believe what happened to me right after you guys left."

"Try us. We want to hear every word."

"It's an unbelievable story, but true."

"Start with when we left you and flew off that night."

"I took the boat you left, which was itself scary," she began.

"Ever run a boat before?"

"Not even a rowboat. But I was on a boat with Reggie often. He said he'd kill me if I kept calling him that. I watched how he ran the boat. And I watched you on the trip over from Hope Town because I thought I'd be alone on the way back."

"Did you learn to like boating?"

"You bet. And flying. I've recently bought a 65 foot trawler, and I'm taking lessons on being the skipper. The boat's at the dock in front of my house. I sit on my porch with a drink at night and laugh at what happened. I'm only beginning to believe it myself."

"So, you got back to Hope Town safely that night?"

"Yes. I went directly to Reggie's mansion. I was careful, but he was in his bedroom blotto, and his henchmen were the same in their rooms above the garage."

"Find the money?"

"I think all of it! I was gone in ten minutes. I took nearly a million in cash that was in his bedroom, conveniently kept in large bills in a suitcase taped up under his desk. I found the secret bank account numbers and the ones to open a safe in his office."

"He did have foreign accounts?"

"The bank locations were all listed in a notebook that I took from the safe. One account was in Panama, one in the Caymans, and one in a place I'd never heard of. But now I can even spell it—Lichtenstein."

"Anything else in the safe of use to you?"

"Yes. I don't know why, but there was a power of attorney from him to *me!*"

"Why would he do that?"

"You'd have to ask him. But he had said something at that time about using me for a couple of what he called sensitive activities where I would sign documents and act for him and he wouldn't have to disclose his name."

"He could have woken up and killed you."

"Not likely, he was so drunk. And I took all kinds of pills from his medicine cabinet and stuffed them down him. Then I left. I'm amazed he didn't die from an overdose. But he did have a stroke."

"Where did you go?"

"By boat to Marsh Harbour where I got a charter pilot listed in the phone directory out of bed. For his usual fee plus $10,000 in cash he was at the airport in ten minutes and flew me on his own jet to a private field near Miami where I wouldn't have to go through customs. For another $10,000 he promised to continue to New York City and enjoy a few days of vacation before he returned to work in Marsh Harbour, where he might have to face Reggie."

"Where did *you* go?"

"I took the first morning flight from Miami to the Caymans and emptied Reggie's account, transferring the money to me using my real name and passport. My name was always Jennifer French, until I met Reggie. He made me adopt the name Candi Treat. I'm not sure he even remembered my real name."

"Is there more to this?"

"Two more foreign accounts that I transferred to new numbered accounts. With *my* numbers. Guess what the three accounts totaled?"

"A lot, we hope."

"Just over $300 million! Guess what Reggie was left with, as I learned later?"

"Less than $10 million?"

"Much less. He had the house with a big mortgage and what he had in his wallet. Then the story changes."

"A good change?" I asked.

"For me, yes. For Reggie, terrible. He had the stroke, apparently from the liquor and overdose of the drugs I 'prescribed' for him. They were the wrong drugs for him in quantity and he nearly died. He was in the hospital in Nassau for weeks before they learned he was broke and nudged him out because he couldn't pay."

"No friends to help him?"

"No friends at all. No longer. He was a bastard to all and a friend to none."

"What did he do?"

"Took a mail boat with a sympathetic captain from Nassau to Hope Town and walked to his house. His former henchmen and housemaids beat the crap out of him and turned him into their captive houseboy. But the taxes and costs of running the house went unpaid. The house was taken by the Nassau bank that held a $300,000 mortgage and put up for sale."

"How did you get it?"

"I had friends in Hope Town who got messages through to me with cell phones that weren't traceable."

"You bought his house?"

"Yes, at a bank foreclosure sale."

"Why don't you live there?"

"It's too ostentatious for me and the memories continue to cause me nightmares. I bought a small house on the harbor that was built by some New England loyalist fleeing the rebels who were fighting the English. I didn't like the idea of even setting foot for an instance where Reggie once lived."

"You rent the big house?"

"Sort of. My tenants pay no rent. They are families who have children with cancer and who come for two weeks of free vacation time. I pay for their flights and expenses here."

"I assume the islanders here don't miss Covington and like having you here. Our waitress certainly enjoys working for you."

"I guess."

"What name do you use? What should Lucinda and I call you? It can't really be Candi Treat."

"I use my real name Jennifer French for everything except this bar. Candi Treat's my playtime name. I prefer Jen. But here at the bar they all call me Candi. *You* two can call me *anything!*"

"And what lies ahead for Jennifer French?"

"My net worth is *now* over $400 million. I invested most of the money Reggie 'left' me in stocks of companies that mystified me. Companies started and run by extremely smart people. At least smarter than me, so it meant a lot of companies. It worked. They were names like Amazon, Facebook, and Apple. I'm happy living here. I started and funded a historic preservation charity to save every building on Abaco built before WWII. I've spent about $13 million on that."

"Are you married?" I asked.

"Are *you* available?" Jen replied.

"Wait just a minute," interrupted Lucinda.

"I'm busy," Jen said, laughing. "I'm happy. I don't often date. There aren't many eligible single men on Elbow Cay. A lot of losers looking for an easy ride. They don't get even a second glance. I'm the 'ice lady' to most men here. I like it that way."

There were now nine empty Kalik bottles on our table. Jennifer called to the bartender to get someone to take them away. Two minutes later a disheveled looking hunched over man appeared. He wore a clean apron over old, torn clothing. His hair hadn't been cut in months.

"Yes, Miss French. Yes ma'am."

"Take our bottles. These are some friends. Say hello, Reggie."

The man never looked directly at Lucinda or me. He may have seen her out of the corner of an eye.

"Hi," he whispered, looking down at the table and shrinking away as though he was avoiding a blow. Lucinda was smiling as he left. We were both astonished.

"Why the grin, Lucinda?" asked Jennifer

"I've been dreaming every day since we escaped from that man that I would come back here and kill him. I thought of shooting him, poisoning him, making him bleed, or feeding him to the sharks, but *never* what you've accomplished. It's wonderful. I'm so envious. . . . And I am glad it's over for me."

I was shocked. I never would have recognized Covington. Lucinda never would have forgotten him.

We were looking at the final despondent version of Reginald Covington the Third.

13

THE SAME EMPTY WAREHOUSE SOUTH OF JACKSON, WYOMING

"HECTOR, GOOD JOB. THAT ELITE EAST COAST snob Goodyear didn't know what was happening to him before you destroyed him," said the same person called only *Jefe*, who again was sitting at the old, rusting metal table.

The audience was much the same as at the last meeting, except that the inductee at that meeting was Jorge Castaneda. He was given high fives and head slaps by his co-members. On the table in front of *Jefe*, mounted on a small stand, was a human hand. A small plaque was inscribed "Jorge."

"You know why you're here, Hector. You will be voted on to become a member of the *Calle Rojo* of Jackson."

"I know, *Jefe*," responded López, standing nervously in front of the table shuffling his feet and stared at by everyone in the room.

Many of the several dozen young men had removed their shirts to show a tattoo across the upper chest in three-inch letters spelling *CALLE ROJO*.

"You were instructed to kill a person you did not know. Did you do that?"

"Yes," López said, smirking.

"Was the person the one I instructed you to kill?"

"Yeah. His name was Goodyear."

"Tell us how you did it."

"I didn't like him from the time I met him at the place we put the boat in. He looked at me showing his dislike for the way I looked and was dressed. My Mohawk hair especially bothered him. The bastard! For that alone, he deserved what I did.

"I must tell you that he knew what he was doing on the boat. I laughed to myself when he tried to explain fishing to me. All I cared about was jamming my machete into his heart and having him 'lend' me his hand. I had the machete hidden in my bag by my feet. I was so anxious and excited the whole time I was in his boat before I killed him."

"Did you bring with you what is required to be initiated?"

"I have it here wrapped in paper and sealed in a plastic bag."

"Give it to me, Hector."

He placed the bag on the table, opened it, and carefully laid on the table what was a human hand. It was slightly larger than the one on the stand in front of *Jefe*. But, like the other, it was shriveled. There was a large ring that had a deep blue stone in the center. In letters around the stone was inscribed "Dartmouth University."

Jefe raised the hand for all to see and admire and then set it down carefully next to the mounted hand of the first victim.

"If any person here has any doubt that Hector should be admitted to the *Calle Rojo* and receive his chest tattoo, speak now."

"Silence quickly absorbed the group."

75

"You are to be thanked, Hector. Your act will again confirm us as the most feared gang in Jackson. . . . Are you ready to be inducted?"

"It is the best moment of my life. Gracias, *Jefe*."

"Come and take my chair, and you will receive your tattoo. Then join the others and celebrate your induction."

"Give us a hand!" the group screamed repeatedly.

Hector excitedly turned to face the rowdy gang members and yelled, "Viva *Calle Rojo*!"

14

ABOUT THE SAME TIME AT THE CASA PRESIDENCIAL IN GUATEMALA CITY

"ARE YOU ENJOYING YOUR LUXURY AS FIRST lady of Guatemala?" asked Juan Pablo Herzog, restored as president of his country only weeks earlier. He stood on the balcony of the Casa Presidencial, sipping a glass of his favorite *Ron Zacapa Centenario* and looking at the volcanos Pacaya and Fuego, prominent in the Southwest sky. A whiff of smoke drifted skyward from Fuego, changing the scene from tranquil to ominous.

"Who would have thought a few months ago that I would be here standing here next to you," said the attractive woman next to Herzog, pleased he had his arm around her.

"You mean drinking *Ron Zacapa* once more?" he asked.

"That counts. . . . But I mean living here in Guatemala with you as your. . . *your* whatever. What am I?"

"You're the most important and envied woman in all of Guatemala. Do you want more?"

"For now, that's fine. But I could become the president after you finish your term."

"That's not possible. A Guatemalan woman was elected vice-president just a few years ago but she never became president. She resigned as vice-president and for months has been facing extradition attempts by the U.S. for corruption and bribes received from American importers."

"Has a woman ever been president here?"

"No. And one *never* will be our president. . . . at least as long as I'm alive. . . . Women are not fit to be president. You are not here to be thinking about such things. It is dangerous for you to do so."

Nancy Asturias Ubico Jones, recently known only as Professor Nancy Jones, was a law professor at the University of Florida for all of the twenty years I taught there as Professor Maxwell Hunt. We joined the faculty the same month some thirty-five years ago and for twenty years had adjacent offices. After my wife, El, died in my tenth year at UF, Nancy was a lifesaver. She insisted we lunch together several times a week because she knew I wasn't eating regularly. She coerced me into going to cultural and sporting events because she knew I wouldn't go alone. Year-by-year we became close, more than colleagues.

I was stunned when I heard that Nancy had gone to Guatemala with Herzog, even more so when she appeared to be serving as the closest thing there is to a "first lady" after having added two prominent Guatemalan names to her own: Asturias and Ubico.

She chose the names wisely, and with Herzog's advice. Asturias won the Nobel Prize for Literature and then fled into exile because of his opposition to dictators. Ubico was elected president in 1931 and became a dictator and served until 1944. Nancy

Jones, in her selection of new names, had covered both a democracy and an autocracy.

"What made you come with me?" asked Herzog, turning and admiring her new bouffant hair style and flowered silk dress.

"I was due to retire in a couple of months. But the new dean and I argued, and she made it clear she didn't want me around another minute. I went to my office, told my secretary to donate my books to the library, took all my personal items to my car, and drove off. I haven't set foot on the campus since."

"So you had nothing better to do and came with me?" he said, grinning.

"Don't tease. You made an offer I couldn't refuse. Professor Hunt often told me how beautiful Guatemala was each time he came here. How could I have arranged a better tour guide than you?"

"And when I have personally showed you all of my country, then what?"

"I hope that takes a long time. You're the President. You can travel to most any country and be received with honor. I'll be by your side. When and where do we start?"

"Soon. But today I'll drive us to Antigua, no more than an hour away, and we will stay at my coffee finca."

"I'm ready."

15

ANTIGUA

HERZOG'S COFFEE FINCA COMMENCED AT THE outskirts of the old capital city that was founded in 1527. It was mostly destroyed by an earthquake and deserted by 1773, causing the capital to be moved to its current location, Guatemala City. Reluctant residents of Antigua were forced to move to the new capital.

"It's so peaceful compared to the hustle of Guatemala City," Nancy commented, entering Antigua's cobblestone streets with Herzog. "And far more beautiful."

"After the earthquake Antigua was all ruins of 16th century Renaissance and Baroque structures," Herzog explained. "Most have been restored, less by our government than by private individuals. Antigua gained some protection from the UNESCO declaration a few decades ago as a World Heritage Site."

"Juan Pablo, Professor Hunt used to tell me about this being his favorite place in the world. He said Antigua was the most beautiful colonial city, and that nearby Lake Atitlán had the most dramatic view of a lake surrounded by volcanoes. He also said that the town of Chichi something, not far from Atitlán, possessed the most colorful market in all Central and South America. He never spoke a single negative word about Guatemala. I know you two were once friends but had a falling out that led to your nearly beating him to death at the Camino Real Hotel. The position of the U.S. State Department and the University was that the beating caused his death by a stroke the following day. What caused you to so resent him?"

"He did *not* die from a stroke the next day. The stroke story was pure fiction. You know that. You've told me you believed he survived the beating and was placed in some protection program. You wouldn't be here if I didn't think you could help me find him."

"It's been almost two decades since that time. Why do you still hate him so much?" Jones asked.

"No one has ever treated me the way he did."

"Doing what?"

"When he was here each spring teaching for several weeks at the Francisco Marroquin law faculty, I personally observed him going into and out of the U.S. embassy. With help, I identified some of the people who were with him as being part of the CIA mission in Guatemala. One of them also was acting for the Guatemalan national security force. He was paid very handsomely."

"What happened to him?"

"He is no longer alive."

"Was he killed?"

"We don't need to talk about that. It was not pleasant. Enjoy your rum and the view."

Nancy remained silent for the next half-hour, sipping her drink, frequently smiling at Herzog and rubbing against him, wondering if she went too far by asking about Herzog's hatred for Hunt. She had to move on to another subject.

"Are we driving to those other places Hunt mentioned—Atitlán and that Chichi place?"

"*Chichicastenango.* 'Tenango' means 'the place of.' In this case the place of the chichi refers to the dominant people in the area, the K'iche' Maya. We may visit that part of Guatemala another time and stay overnight on a Wednesday or Saturday to see the market, held only on Thursday and Sunday. Lake Atitlan will easily consume our whole day tomorrow."

The next day they drove to Atitlán and decided to remain for dinner, risking a late drive in the dark back to the capital curving around the winding highland roads.

In the open-air restaurant at the Casa Palopó, they ended their meal with flan. Nancy gently dabbed her mouth after the last bite. Some urge that she didn't fully understand made her ask, "Juan Pablo, you have a niece, Luisa Solares?"

"I *did.* I prefer not to talk about her."

"You mean she died? She was in two of my courses. I liked her as a person, and she was a brilliant student. She earned two degrees, passed the bar exam, and I believe joined a Miami law firm."

"She was everything you say. I knew she was in Miami practicing, and I have assumed she was still there. Miami was the last I knew about her whereabouts. She is tragically missing."

Nancy knew he was lying and that Luisa was in Guatemala.

"Does she like to come back here to visit? I wish I could say hello."

"I don't know where she is," he said, with a tone that told Nancy to back off from asking any more about Luisa.

"If she ever does come back, please tell her I'm here."

He didn't answer her, but his look spoke volumes about his anger at her questioning.

"I think I've had too much Ron Zacapa. I talk too much when I drink," she said, half in apology

"You do. It would be better if you did not raise the names of Hunt or Luisa unless I ask you."

"I don't mean to anger you. You have enough to do running the country without having me upset you."

"Don't do it again. . . . Ever."

16

THE FOLLOWING MORNING

IN GUATEMALA CITY THAT NIGHT JONES SLEPT fitfully. She was unable to fall asleep for two hours and lay quietly, scared she would wake Juan Pablo.

The next morning their few words to each other at breakfast included no mention of Hunt or Luisa. Nancy diverted that potentially argumentative conversation to an issue that was causing the president much effort and grief developing his position on Belize.

"Juan Pablo, I know we're going to the Petén next week for the dedication of a newly restored Mayan site on the road from Tikal to Belize. Are we also going on to visit Belize?"

"We can't. You're an educated woman. Do you know anything about Guatemala's lingering dispute with Belice?"

"I do know that it is always spelled Belice in Guatemala, but the government of Belice says the proper spelling is Belize."

"You must spell it Belice," Herzog insisted. "It is shown on all Guatemalan maps as one of the twenty-three departments, like your states."

Years ago Professor Hunt had told Jones a great deal about that decades old conflict, but knowing Herzog hadn't yet announced his position, she didn't want to upset him after the previous evening's discussion.

"I've seen angry Guatemalan newspaper headlines— 'Belice es Nuestro'—about the seemingly never finally settled Belize conflict," she said, "but because of my poor Spanish, I have not understood the articles."

That was not the truth. She had a very good reading knowledge of Spanish, and since arriving, when she was alone, had read every word printed about the issue. She read not to be enlightened by the vitriolic comments about Belize's demands but to learn to agree with whatever position Herzog would take when he decided to go public. She did not want to challenge that position. Jones knew to Herzog's credit that he didn't want to follow the easy route, which was to denounce Belize and then claim that much of its territory, if not all, belonged to Guatemala. But he knew that was what many Guatemalans expected from their screams of "Belice is ours!"

Jones also believed Herzog was sincere in wanting to help his country escape from increasing control by Mexican drug cartels. He also wanted to reduce corruption in his own government—which he admitted to Jones would never be achieved. He tried to mollify the always agitated army generals—many of whom aspired to be president. And he said he wanted to improve the life of the country's Maya population.

"If you *were* president what would your priorities be?" he asked her.

"Because I know you wish to improve the life of the Maya people, I would emphasize the essential role played by them and concentrate on preserving Guatemala's pre-Columbian past. . . ."

In my brief time here with you, I've worried about the influence of corruption and drugs and how they've have diverted your attention from helping your people. Every presidential campaign seems to speak about ridding the country of corruption and drugs. But the progress has been slow, and I doubt your people are satisfied."

"Perhaps you should be my chief-of-staff."

"I only want to be your number one admirer and your sole bedmate."

"Work on the first. You're doing fine with the second."

That afternoon Jones put on simple clothing and added a head scarf and sunglasses. She slipped out of a rear service door of the Casa Presidencial and walked to the Mercado Central where she was overwhelmed by the intensities and designs of the textiles. She made a few early Christmas shopping purchases for gifts for friends back in Gainesville.

Color was also an essential feature of the clay pottery, especially in the angels and familiar nativity figures, that showed the mark of talented artists. What surprised and pleased Jones most was the food section of the Mercado. In abundance were fruits and vegetables she had never seen, fish she had never heard of, and meats from animals she had never tasted. Food and drink were mainly influenced by Maya and Spanish cultures, but traces of Caribbean favorites added different characteristics.

Jones stopped where food was being served and was surrounded by thousands of flowers that added color and perfumed fragrance of the market. She ordered coffee—Guatemalan of course—and a dish suggested by a local woman standing next to her, a chicken in spicy pumpkin and sesame sauce called *Pepian de Pollo,* which she later learned was the Guatemalan national dish. When she finished she asked for a self-deserved treat, *Pastel de Tres Leches*, a delicious cold desert of cake soaked in three kinds of milk.

When Jones was finished, she wrote several postcards to friends in the U.S., most teaching at various law schools. She mused that they did not know why she had come to Guatemala, why she was living with the president, and what the future offered.

Tiring of writing, she put the cards and pen in her purse and sat sipping coffee and looking at food and craft displays she could not have adequately described in writings to her friends. Nor would they understand the motivations that had brought her to Guatemala. She would not attempt to explain the "whys" of her new life.

Jones wondered what Herzog truthfully intended when he rushed her away from Florida to be his companion as he again assumed the presidency. Was he in love with her? Could he truly love any woman, or did women exist only to serve the intentions of ambitious men? What did he expect from her? To remain in Guatemala as long as he served as president? As long as she served him adequately in bed? Could she realistically be of any help in finding the current name and location of Professor Hunt? Would she even seriously look? And if she learned this information, would she tell Herzog the truth?

Before Jones left Florida with Herzog, she had opened a numbered account in the Swiss Bank of Interlaken, and Herzog had transferred to that private account $2 million, promising an additional $1 million each year she completed living with him.

What she could not tell from Herzog's comments or actions was how much information she had to learn about Professor Hunt. Nor could she guess how long she might remain in Herzog's favor. But she thought that, however much she learned, she would not tell all, but only enough to keep him making his next deposit to her Swiss account and satisfying her own bedtime desires.

Unable to learn anything new about Professor Hunt, she would make something up. She enjoyed the idea of creating a character with a name, an occupation, and a residence that were totally fictitious, as though she were writing a novel.

She would first tell Herzog the occupation she would pretend Hunt had chosen and be certain that it was an occupation found *throughout* the U.S. That might be a high school football coach or an income tax advisor or a car salesman. It would not be something that would help Herzog determine the new name or location of Professor Hunt. She was aware that Herzog had been told Hunt was involved in fishing, but nothing had come of that in a half-dozen or more years, and she no longer considered that information had much truth.

She would not tell Herzog that Hunt had become a ski instructor or a zoo director or a salt water sword-fisherman. Each had limited locations and would narrow the search. Herzog would learn that she had been wrong, which would not fare well for her. She rather liked the car salesman choice since that job existed in every city or town of any size, and the sales personnel often moved from one dealership to another to sell a different make or model in some other city or state.

Nancy thought she might choose to disclose Hunt's current name, if she learned it, but not use something like Friedrich Bonn von Switzer, which may be the name of less than a dozen people in the entire U.S. Instead, perhaps she would use Robert

Smith, considered the most common two-name combination in the country. But even that name has only about 34,000 persons, a significant reduction from including all males in the U.S. when not telling Herzog any name.

Selecting a location was also a thought. New York City would be more difficult to search than Mooresville, Alabama, or Hyder, Alaska, or Gilbert, Arkansas, each with fewer than 100 people.

Jones was enjoying this game. By the end of the first year with Herzog, she likely would have spent countless hours learning of or deciding on Hunt's new occupation, location, and name. She speculated how Herzog would react if she told him Professor Hunt had assumed the name Robert Smith, had become some kind of salesman, and lived somewhere in the Eest.

Her thoughts made her realize she was not and would never be in love with Juan Pablo. She considered herself for the time being to be a very expensive call girl serving a single customer. And she assumed her role not because she loved Herzog, which she was confused about and doubted, but because her tenuous role with him confirmed her undiminished strong feelings about Maxwell Hunt.

"Who is this man I'm living with?" she wondered out loud. "He wants to kill the only man I've ever loved. I look across at Juan Pablo at night, and he seems so helpless that I thought for a moment I could be the one doing the killing. His death would end the life of a man totally devoted to himself who never thought twice about brutally removing an opponent. Only last evening he told me about killing the head of the drug trade in Guatemala years ago, using a chain saw on the tennis court where the man was playing. When he described how the blood drained into and merged with the red clay of the court, he had roared with laughter."

Jones suddenly realized that she was to have joined Herzog thirty minutes ago to attend some official function. He would be livid. She picked up her phone and called him.

"Where *are* you?" he screamed into the phone. "I'm waiting in front of the Palacio Nacional. There are important people here. Get a taxi and meet me at the Francisco Marroquin law building. I'm receiving an honorary degree there in an hour. You'd better show up!"

The phone went dead; he wasn't going to wait for Jones' answer.

Jones couldn't meet him dressed as she was. He would be furious. Were her days numbered? She pulled out a calendar and calculated the days remaining until her next $1 million from Herzog was due and deposited. Far too long! But she would be patient. She thought that, if she held out for a little less than two years, she would have a total of $4 million to add to the modest benefit she had begun to receive from the Florida Retirement System. It went directly into an investment account that should be worth another half-million by the time Herzog paid the second year of what she liked to think of as her workwoman's compensation.

She wondered where Maxwell Hunt was at that very moment and wiped a large tear from her cheek.

17

LATER THAT NIGHT AT THE SAME PLACE

JUAN PABLO HERZOG HAD WOKEN ONLY ONE time that night, during one of the brief times Jones slept. They had more words when Jones never showed up at the honorary degree ceremony. But Herzog surprised himself that he had not struck her when they arrived home. He thought she certainly deserved a beating. But occasionally a soft streak took over his actions toward her, and this was one of those times.

Carefully, so as not to wake her, he slipped out of his side of the bed and walked quietly to his office, out the sliding glass door, and onto the porch that overlooked the president's private garden. It was a peaceful night, but no moon combined with the brightness of the Casa's lights diminished the outline of the nearby volcanos.

After sitting a few minutes, he lighted a cigarette. He was not pleased with himself; his doctor had ordered him not to begin smoking again. This was his first in months.

"Why am I doing this?" he asked aloud.

"I know," he mused quietly. "I'm troubled and frustrated. Why did I bring her with me to Guatemala? First Lady of Guatemala? That's a joke. I am not and never will be in love with her.

But she serves a purpose or for that matter several purposes. The people of Guatemala seem attracted to her. She presents herself well in public. . . . She is attractive, and she satisfactorily fills the other side of my bed.

"Perhaps I brought her because she is part of the longest and closest link I have to Maxwell Hunt. She taught with him for twenty years and believes not only that he survived my beating him, but that he is living somewhere under some name doing something. What I don't know is if Nancy *knows* his current name or location or kind of work.

"If she does not, can she possibly get this information? If she can't, I'm wasting millions on her. If I have any indication she lies to me, she will never live to use those millions. If she tells me what I want, a few million is well spent. Anyway, it comes from public tax revenues and foreign loans, which the public never knows I use for personal reasons.

"I must be more patient. It has been more than a decade-and-a-half since I tried to kill Hunt; I can wait a few years more. By then I will either know Hunt is dead, hopefully at my own hands, or I will know Nancy is dead, clearly at my own hands.

"Life is not so bad," he added, lighting another cigarette and getting out of his chair to pour a tall glass from a bottle of *Ron Zacapa Centenario*.

As he turned, he saw Jones's silhouette in the doorway behind him. She quickly disappeared back into the office.

"What did she hear?" he wondered. Had he murmured to himself so loud she could hear? When he returned to bed after finishing his drink and cigarette, she appeared to be sound asleep. Lying there, he debated if he should strangle her.

To Jones's good fortune, he fell asleep.

18

MID-JUNE AT A SNAKE RIVER DRIFT BOAT LAUNCH

A DRIFT BOAT TRAILORED BEHIND A LONG Dodge Ram pickup pulled up by the log barricade thirty feet up the sloping bank from the Snake River and several hundred feet downstream from the Jackson Lake Dam. A man got out, looked around, removed a fly rod from a long tube in the back of the truck and began to rig it. No one else was in view except a solitary figure wading and casting a spinning rod dangerously close to the dam.

The man rigging the fly rod was Chuck Driscomb. On this warming June morning, he wore little of the usual signs of a guide. He had on khaki shorts, no belt, worn sandals, and a faded blue short-sleeved denim shirt. The brim of his cap said "10th One Fly Contest – 1995." He was a lean six feet tall on tip toes, and his arm muscles verified he spent considerable time rowing.

Driscomb lived in a yurt in the tiny settlement of Kelly, Wyoming, where the Gros Ventre River tumbled out of the Bridger-Teton National Forest. He was married to a brilliant young woman who taught at the Teton Science School. Chuck's friends wondered what she saw in him. She was brighter, far better looking, patient, articulate, possessed more common sense, and had more close friends. She must have liked his body or, what most friends didn't know about, his eight-figure trust fund.

Finished with the fly rod, Driscomb sat on one of the log barriers talking on his cell phone, telling his Chicago broker to sell all the Exxon and IBM stock in his account and buy three thousand shares of Amazon.

"Hey, are you Driscomb?" a voice called out.

Driscomb turned to see a young man walking toward him carrying bootfoot waders and a raincoat. That was wise; rain was predicted for the afternoon.

"I'm Ricardo Colón," spoke what seemed to be an educated voice. "Are you Mr. Driscomb?"

"Chuck, please."

Colón was wearing a new pair of Simms wading shoes, light-weight cargo pants, a long-sleeved plaid shirt, and a hat that read "Grand Teton National Park" on the brim, with "LEAVE NO TRACE" in tiny letters across the brim edge and "Outdoor Ethics" on the side. He seemed too short to carry what was at least 225 pounds. His hair was recently trimmed to a short crew cut.

Driscomb had been concerned about taking a client with a Hispanic name for fear it would be another *Calle Rojo* member. But Driscomb's mother was Mexican, born Consuelo Cruz in the mountainous Chiapas city of San Cristobal de las Casas. She met her husband when she was studying at Iberoamericano in Mexico City and Chuck's father was a Foreign Service Officer at the U.S. Embassy.

Never would Driscomb discriminate by rejecting any prospective fishing client having a Hispanic name, but, nevertheless, he was relieved that Colón didn't fit the description he had of *Calle Rojo* members. He could also see that no sign of *Calle Rojo* tattooed letters was visible on what he could see of Colón's upper chest. But Driscomb didn't know that the tattoo was a reward given only *after* a member was inducted upon completion of the mandatory murder.

"Have you ever fished from one of these drift boats? Or used a fly rod?" Driscomb inquired.

Without a word, Colón took the rod Driscomb had rigged, stripped some line, and made a few decent 35- to 40-foot casts.

"Good. I guess we'll have more fishing than teaching today," Driscomb said, watching with an increasing smile.

Driscomb was pleased with Colón's seemingly perpetual positive attitude. They shoved off in the boat, and Driscomb told an attentive Colón more or less what the Jackson Dam to Pacific Creek section was like.

It wasn't long before Driscomb stared for a moment up among the tops of the trees and, pointing up, said, "Ricardo, look up there! Two bald eagles."

"I've never seen even one," Colón responded, turning and smiling.

Later, after landing three Snake River Cutthroats, Driscomb said, "Look off to the left as we pass the point of land up ahead. There's a beaver lodge, and I think I see a beaver headed that way along the shore."

"I see it. . . . Three fish, two eagles, and a beaver! Quite a day for me, Chuck. Thanks."

"Ricardo, I've got a couple of flies I'd like you to try along the bank to the right. Stay seated. I have to get up and get a fly box from the stern locker. My seat doesn't swivel like yours."

Driscomb rose, turned, leaned down to pick up the fly box, then turned back, and dropped into his seat. He began to tie a #16 Yellow Sally fly onto Colón's tippet when he saw a flash reflection and stared down at the tip of a machete blade."

"Ricardo! Wait. You don't want to murder me. I'm half Mexi. . . ."

He never finished his sentence.

The machete blade had gone into Driscomb's chest smoothly, and he was dead when he hit the boat's floor.

"Like my play acting, did ya? Dumb son of a bitch. You never had an idea I'd be one more *Calle Rojo* member—well, maybe not quite yet a member—to make a hit on a guide."

Colón took the center seat and oars, dipped a finger in Driscomb's blood, scribbled *CR* on the sides of the boat, and rowed to the shore. No other boats were behind him, and he picked up the lunch bag Driscomb had brought, threw out all but a plastic sandwich bag, cut off Driscomb's right hand, put it in the bag, and tucked it in the small knapsack he took from Driscomb's belongings. He hopped out, shoved the boat back out into the flow, and watched it spin slowly around in an eddy. Colón then began a slow jog through the woods toward Route 89, where he knew a car would be waiting.

Colón couldn't wait for the initiation. He'd watched the two previous ones, and this time he would be the star.

He patted the knapsack, felt the hand, and laughed.

19

THE NEXT WEEK IN HOPE TOWN

"Have you heard, Macduff, about Chuck Driscomb?" John Kirby asked before I could say hello on my cell phone. He didn't know Lucinda and I were in Hope Town and not at our cabin on Mill Creek.

"I'm glad Sarah and I left Jackson. We're in our car headed for Canada. A little vacation in Calgary, and I'll fish the Bow."

I assumed the call would begin with some disparaging remark about the University of Florida Gators football team. But this time he passed that by. The call was serious, and I should have known as much by the tone of his voice.

"What about Driscomb?" I asked.

"Did you know him?"

"I knew him," I said. "He was in my Orvis guide school class a decade and a half ago or more. We both wanted to be guides. Chuck coveted getting more than the diploma for having survived the program; he wanted the rarely given certification that he was ready to guide immediately. He was not pleased when he got a diploma and they gave me a certificate. I guided the next day, and Chuck went out again with an instructor.

"We voted Chuck more likely to hook a beautiful bride than a beautiful trout. He was a good looking guy who could find a dozen ways *not* to catch trout."

"Not someone I'd want for my guide," John observed. "But that's over. He's dead. Murdered on his drift boat like the other two. This time on the Snake again."

"You said 'like the other two.' Do the authorities know it was the *Calle Rojo* gang? Chuck was himself half-Hispanic."

"That's probably why Chuck accepted the guy. I assume he knew he was taking a Hispanic before they started the float."

"He must have. He wasn't stupid."

"Chuck undoubtedly accepted the guy as a client because Chuck was half-Mexican and had no quarrel with Hispanics. Maybe if he was suspicious when they shoved off to start the float, he may have thought that once he told his client about his Mexican mother, he would be safe, even if the client was a *Calle Rojo* gang member."

"How do the police really know it was *Calle Rojo*?"

"Not much doubt. Chuck's body was found on his blood-covered boat two miles downstream on the Snake below the Jackson Lake dam. There was a machete stuck in his chest."

"Any more?"

"Big *CR*s were written in blood on the sides of the boat."

"Sounds like *Calle Rojo*. You're persuading me."

"Who else would kill a person and cut off their hand?"

"You've *convinced* me!"

20

THE HOPE TOWN COTTAGE

LUCINDA WAS STANDING OVER THE SMOKING grill on the cottage porch in Hope Town, looking at something she had moved to a platter. It looked like delicious lamb deboned and butterflied. The sides were charred. I love lamb.

"It looks delicious. Is it ready?" I asked.

"Only half done," she said, carrying the lamb into the kitchen where she opened the oven and set the lamb on the center rack.

"It looks cooked. Are you going to blacken it?"

"Don't bother me. I'm concentrating."

She soon took it back to the grill on the porch and after adding a bit of cooking oil to a frying pan, she watched it for what had to be five minutes and then added what looked like eight peaches.

"What for God's sake are you doing? *Peaches* and lamb?"

"Be quiet! I'm caramelizing these, and they are *not* peaches."

She added what I can only describe as this and that. One label did say lemon juice, which is on my list of edibles. But she threw in some grass, which isn't. Grass is for cows.

"What *is* that green stuff?"

"Thyme."

"Of course it's time. You've burned most of the lunch."

"T-h-y-m-e, not t-i-m-e," she said. "Go inside and have a beer."

"I need more than a beer."

She rolled her eyes.

Thirty minutes later, she sliced the lamb, which still looked tasty, but then spread something on the two dinner plates.

"What is that? It looks gooey."

"It's labneh."

"In English, please."

"Well, it's like yogurt. From the Middle East," she added while dropping the slices of lamb on top of the oozing stuff she had passed off as yogurt."

"Well, I'll try it. The yogurt will dissipate. The poor lambs, if they only knew."

"Baa, baa, baa. Poor little lambs who have lost their way," she sang.

Then she turned to the peaches, tearing them into bite size pieces and spreading them on the lamb. I noticed she removed the pits only from *her* plate.

"Take your plate. It's grilled leg of lamb with roasted apricots."

"Apricots! Disguised as peaches?"

"It's good for you. Cures indigestion, constipation, earaches, fevers, skin diseases, cancer, and anemia."

"All of which, and more, I may get if I eat this."

"You are going to eat it, or you don't get the key lime pie for desert."

"Where did you ever find this recipe?"

"It was in *The Wall Street Journal*."

"The purpose of *The Wall Street Journal* is to inform you about what investments you might make, not what food you might cook."

"It has *international* stock recommendations. How can you understand those unless you learn about each country's culture? That includes food."

"Will you tell me tomorrow when you're about to begin preparing our dinner?"

"Yes, but why?"

"I'll be on the outer edge of our dock smelling the mud flats and dead fish. It helps me prepare for one of your meals."

"Someday I will train you to eat decent meals."

"Someday I will be dead."

"Promise?"

21

JACKSON, WYOMING – THE EMPTY WAREHOUSE SOUTH OF TOWN

"RICARDO, COOL, MAN. I HEAR YOUR GUIDE, Driscomb, thought you were a polite young man with your civilized appearance and dress," said the one always called *Jefe*, who was sitting at the rusting table.

Ricardo Colón stood facing *Jefe*, smiling. His hair was two weeks longer and again unkempt. A small piece of metal hung from his left ear; another pierced his left lower lip. He wore old orange sneaks that were torn but comfortable, frayed jeans, and a T-shirt that said "Adios Bitchachos" between a sombrero and the beginnings of a beard. Guide Chuck Driscomb would not have recognized him. Or let him on his drift boat.

The group was about the same as at the induction of Hector López, who was in the front row receiving slaps on the back from the others.

On the table were two small, wooden stands, each with a human hand displayed. The smaller hand had a woman's ring with a sapphire stone set in gold. The other hand displayed a large ring that said: "Dartmouth University." On the first a brass plaque said "Jorge," on the second, "Hector."

"You know why you are here, Ricardo. To be voted on to become a member of the *Calle Rojo*."

"I understand, *Jefe*," replied Ricardo.

Many members had removed their shirts to show the tattoo across each chest that said in large letters *CALLE ROJO*.

"Ricardo, it was your task to murder a person you did not know. Did you accomplish that?"

"Yes, *Jefe*."

"Did you kill the person I designated?"

"Yes, I did. I will tell you about it. He was impressed with me from the time I arrived because I played the part of the nice young immigrant from Latin America who loved living in the U.S. You told me that because of the publicity of the two previous executions by our newly elected members, I had to keep him from believing that I was number three. I did that.

"He was very knowledgeable about fishing, and I must admit I was having a good time. Close to the place where we were to finish the drift, I realized I had to act soon. He had changed my fly and was turning toward me when I jammed the machete into his chest. I don't think he knew what was happening. He collapsed and didn't move. Then I cut off his right hand that had a fancy gold ring on one finger."

"Give me the hand."

"Here it is, *Jefe*," who removed it from a plastic bag and raised it for all to see.

There were cheers throughout.

Jefe raised his hand to quiet the group and spoke.

"If any person in this room has any doubt that Ricardo should be admitted to the *Calle Rojo* and receive his chest tattoo, speak now."

"Immediately, the room quieted."

"Ricardo, because of you, we remain the most dangerous and feared gang in Jackson and now all of Wyoming. . . . Are you ready?"

"I have been waiting anxiously for this moment, *Jefe*."

"Take my chair, Ricardo, and receive your tattoo."

"Give me a hand!" the group chanted.

Ricardo turned to the gang members and yelled, "Viva *Calle Rojo*!"

22

AT THE HOPE TOWN HOUSE

"STOP COMPLAINING, MACDUFF. HERE, READ MY recipe. It's *The Wall Street Journal* article for making charred lamb and apricots. You didn't believe me."

"I'm canceling our subscription and replacing it with *Flying* magazine. That way I'll learn how to fly a jet without worrying about indigestion."

"Buying a jet will not affect my authority regarding what goes on in our kitchen, whether in Florida, Montana, Hope Town, or anywhere else we live."

"Lucinda, you're speaking as though we have three houses."

"Since meeting Covington again at Captain Candi's Bar two weeks ago, I no longer feel I'm here in Hope Town to see him dead. He's close enough, and he's no threat. Maybe we should consider buying a house here."

"Thanks to Candi, Covington is no danger to you. I can't imagine he will change back to his old self. The stroke did him in. . . . Candi is something else," I responded.

"One thing she is not any longer is Candi Treat. We shouldn't call her that except perhaps when we're at her bar. Otherwise, she's Jennifer French again. I heard other bar employees call her only Jennifer or Ms. French. We should do the same."

"I'm not so sure all her employees ever knew her as Candi Treat. I understand why they don't use that name around her."

"Macduff, there's a phone call. Caller ID says it's a local number from a Jennifer."

"Jennifer, hi. This is Lucinda. Macduff's sitting next to me."

"We enjoyed your bar and especially what we learned about you," I added. "*And* about Covington."

"I hope you're pleased with what you learned."

"Overwhelmed! We couldn't be more pleased," Lucinda stated. "We came to Hope Town because we were told to get out of our cottage at St. Augustine, and we both love Elbow Cay."

"You didn't tell me about your being told to leave Florida. Why didn't you go to your place in Montana?"

"That's worse. We'll tell you when we see you. About the latest murders of fly fishing guides in Jackson Hole, Wyoming. I hope we see you again soon."

"How about tonight. At my historic little cottage on the harbor not far from you. You can walk."

"Tonight's perfect. Time?"

"Seven. Sunset behind the lighthouse is about seven-thirty. We'll have a drink on my porch and watch it."

"What can we bring?"

"An appetite. I'm a gourmet cook."

Lucinda looked at me smiling and mumbled something that sounded like, "I hope she serves you fish eyes and conch intestines."

"We're assuming dress is not too formal?"

"I'm not the tight short shorts, no bra, and skimpy halter girl Reggie forced me to be. I'll never dress like that again. But please be comfortable."

We took her comment to mean shorts of any kind, but that halters and T-shirts were out. I got out my red Nantucket light weight pants, pressed a long sleeved blue denim shirt, and opened a new pair of resurrected 1950s style white Keds sneaks. Lucinda wore a thin knit skirt with red and blue mitered stripes and a collared light blue denim shirt. When we arrived, as promised Jen was not in short shorts and a T-shirt. She had on white capris pants and a ruby tunic shirt. When we saw her, we were pleased we had asked about the proper dress.

We walked through the house and onto the porch.

"My house was built in 1779 by a wealthy Bostonian whose two sons fought *against* the British—and were captured and executed," explained Jennifer. "Their father was angry—not at the execution but at the boys' unacceptable loyalty to the rebels. He moved to Hope Town, taking with him his money and his own unwavering loyalty to the Crown."

"It's less ostentatious than Covington's place," noted Lucinda.

"I may tear that house down, fence in the lot, and make it a Hope Town residents' public park. I still get bad feelings every time I go past the house."

"Your porch here is so close to the harbor that it connects directly to your dock."

"Fix yourself a drink—I only provide service at Candi's—and let's sit down on the dock."

Lucinda and I went to the bar on the porch. There were bottles of both Montana Roughstock Whiskey and Gentleman Jack."

"You know what we drink?"

"When Lucinda was kept locked up here and when Reggie wasn't home, I used to go into her room and talk to her. I didn't think she knew I was there most of the time. She sat staring out the window, but occasionally she started talking. One thing she said sometimes was she wanted me to make her a Montana Whiskey or a Gentleman Jack. It took me awhile to understand what she meant."

"I had a few moments of sanity, but I really don't remember babbling to you about drinks," laughed Lucinda. "But I'm glad I did."

"Let's talk about something other than when you were confined here. These are better times. . . . Isn't Hope Town a strange place for you to be in view of your experience here?"

"Agreed. But Macduff and I love it here. By the hours, I used to look out the window of the room I was locked in at Covington's. I fell in love with the green water. It was clean and pure: I was neither. . . . Jen, we needed a vacat. . . ."

"There's more to it than that," I interrupted. "Want to hear our current saga?"

"Every minute of it."

I told Jennifer—often corrected by Lucinda—about the three murders of fly fishing guides and how Wyoming and Montana friends made us "get out of Dodge."

"Out of the frying pan into the Bahamas fire?"

"We hoped that fire was no longer burning. We've been very careful."

"The fire is at best smoldering. Reggie is too far gone to be a threat. I don't worry about him. You shouldn't either."

"Disappointingly so," added Lucinda.

"Meaning?"

"I was planning to kill him. I think Macduff knows that."

"Not fully, but I knew she needed closure. Because of you, she's had it. . . . Consider us here on holiday, to visit an old friend named Jennifer French."

"Perfect. You're staying how long?"

"Until we're told we can go to our cabin in Montana," I said. "If there isn't another *Calle Rojo* murder for a week, we'll go. I had booked about three guide trips a week. I'd like to do as many as possible, but I called and canceled all for the next two weeks—to mid-July. I hate to miss floats with people that I've taken fishing on the Yellowstone or Madison or Snake over the years. They've become friends, and I look forward to being with each of them for a day or two every summer."

"I have an idea for you two to consider," Jen said.

"Tell us," said Lucinda.

"When I saw you two fly off from Man-O-War Cay months ago, I said to myself, 'I'm going to learn to fly and buy a plane if I get enough *delayed compensation* from Reggie.'"

"You might have taken *his* plane."

"I didn't want to set foot on that plane again. And he had an obnoxious, alcoholic pilot I would have had to deal with. When he wasn't flying for Reggie, he ran drugs to the U.S. from Colombia."

"When you finished collecting your 'compensation' from his house and the foreign accounts, you came back here?"

"Yes. When I left you on the seaplane, I had about $300 in cash I had put away, often dollar-by-dollar, snitching it from

Reggie. A couple of months later I came back to Hope Town as Jennifer French and I had—I know it down to the last dollar—$442,572,487—in three accounts in banks in New York, London, and a place in Europe. Plus what I was carrying—some change. About $70,000 in cash. I opened a new account in Marsh Harbour with $20,000 cash to start my bar. I had plenty of money to open the bar, but I was scared to spend it. The bar was successful from the start, and I lived on its earnings, not counting my boat and plane. My foreign accounts kept growing. . . . End of the financial side of my story. . . . Where were we?"

"You were about to buy a plane and make us an offer."

"I have the plane. When I came back, I started flying lessons by taking my boat over to Marsh Harbour every couple of days. The day I qualified two months later, I flew commercial to Miami, bought a five-year-old Cessna 172, and flew back to Marsh Harbour. I adored that slow prop plane."

"Did you use it much living here?"

"Constantly. I loved flying low over these islands, all the way south to Turks and Caicos."

"Ever fly to the U.S.?"

"Yes! I first flew to Teterboro Airport in New Jersey near New York City. One of my banks is in Manhattan. Now I have an apartment there, on East 68th, a block from Central Park."

"We're Manhattan neighbors!" exclaimed Lucinda. "My apartment is only a block or two away."

"Great! After business and a few days of theater, museums, walking, and a very little shopping, I flew on to Boston where one old friend from my years at Wellesley had settled. Coming home I realized that the Cessna 172 was too slow for what I wanted to do. While I built lots of hours flying the 172, I also began to fly to Miami every week for lessons on flying a jet."

"Do you still have the 172?"

"No, I traded it in for my jet, a two-year-old Cessna Citation Mustang that seated six before I swapped two seats for a bed."

"You liked it so much you used it like a vacation cottage?"

"Almost. A couple of months ago, I hired a pilot to go with me, and we flew to Ireland and then England. Another of my banks is in London."

"Where to next?" asked Lucinda.

"That's where you two come in."

"A tour of the Bahamas by private jet sounds good."

"That, too. But I really mean I want to fly you both to Montana when you feel it's safe. I've never been further west than the Cessna Company in Kansas."

"Why do you want to take us west?"

"You told me you were heading back to your Florida cottage and then to Montana."

"It's more likely we'll go directly to Bozeman," I said. "Well, not direct. Marsh Harbour to Miami, Miami to Salt Lake City, and then to Bozeman."

"Wouldn't Marsh Harbour direct to Bozeman be better?"

"Much better. Do you take dogs on your plane?"

"Not unless they're shelties named Wuff. In that case she has a full bed and we three sit up."

"You're going to spoil the three of us, Jen."

"I'm going to try. You're why I'm alive. Montana Whiskey and Gentlemen Jack at 35,000 feet sound good?" she asked.

"Not for you, madame pilot. For us, Yes. But we won't need the drinks to get high," Lucinda beamed.

23

THE FOLLOWING NOON

"KEN, ANY RECENT NEWS ABOUT THE GANG killings?" I asked, mesmerized by the turquoise water seen from the porch.

"Not a word other than rumor and speculation," Ken Rangley replied from his Park County sheriff's office in Livingston. His principal deputy, the diminutive Erin Giffin, was in an uncomfortable straight-back wooden chair facing his desk. She had added a thick pad, which gave comfort to her rear but raised her enough that her feet were an inch above the floor. She does not like me to refer to her as being vertically challenged and alleges she's over five feet tall. Maybe, but only if she wears her hair in some updo bun style.

Rangley put the phone on speaker and set it where they could both hear.

"Macduff, Erin's here, and the phone speaker is on."

"Hi, Macduffy. How's sunny Florida?" Erin asked.

"Sunny," I said, assuming it was.

"Is Lucinda there?"

"I am. Always," Lucinda answered.

"Where is there?" asked Erin. "I'm assuming it's Mill Creek, and you haven't been in Paradise Valley long enough to call us."

"'There' is about 30,000 feet. We're in a plane."

"If you're on a plane, you're not supposed to be on the phone; it should be in airplane mode. Otherwise you may interfere with the aircraft's radios. If you fly over us, I'll have to arrest you when you land."

"First, we're over Oklahoma which is not in your jurisdiction. And, second, we're in a private plane."

"Yours?" Ken asked.

"A friend's."

"Do you have a vehicle at the Bozeman airport waiting for you?" Ken asked.

"We hoped you'd ask. No. Can you meet us and drop us off at the Jeep dealer? I talked to a man there yesterday. He's doing the paperwork for a Jeep Wrangler."

"Two door?"

"Four door. So you two will fit. And have your own doors."

"We'll take you there. It isn't more than a block out of our way. When do you expect to arrive?"

"We're an hour away. Where should we meet?"

"Look for general aviation."

"I understand there's a customs service."

"That's not needed flying from Florida. Maybe it should be."

"We're not coming from Florida."

"Let me guess. Cuba? Transylvania? More likely the Cayman Islands, where you launder your money?"

"I'll ignore that. Ever hear of Hope Town?"

"Sounds encouraging."

"Elbow Cay? Spelled K-e-y to you. Abaco? Marsh Harbour?"

"O.K. You were in the Bahamas. Where Lucinda had trouble a couple of years ago?"

"I did," she answered. "That's where I was confined for eighteen months after my ex, Ellsworth-Kent, abducted me and took me to Hope Town to be confined at Reginald Covington's mansion."

"And Macduff went there and freed you."

"With the help of our pilot, who owns *this* jet."

"Remind me to thank him," said Erin.

"He is a *she*. Name's Jennifer French. Lives in Hope Town."

"I think there are some stories you may want to tell us," added Ken.

"I get to tell you about Lucinda and Macduff," interrupted Jen. "I'm Jennifer. Call me Jen. Have a Kalik ready, and I'll tell all."

"Jen, I doubt that there's a bottle of Kalik in all of Montana. How about Moose Drool?"

"You're kidding. . . . You're *not* kidding. Instead, give me a glass of Montana Roughstock. And one for Lucinda, who's nodding."

"Done. . . . See you in an hour."

"We'll be in a Park County Sheriff's Office car," said Erin.

"Lights flashing?" Lucinda asked.

"You bet."

"Sirens?"

"Only if you crash while landing."

24

THE MURRAY HOTEL IN LIVINGSTON, MONTANA

W E FIVE, LUCINDA AND I, OUR PILOT AND NEW friend, Jen, and Erin and Ken, gathered for cocktails in a quiet corner at the historic Murray Hotel. Erin and Ken had met us at the Bozeman Airport as promised in a Park County Sheriff's Office vehicle, with lights flashing. They were dressed in mufti rather than their usual uniforms.

"Ken, I appreciate your calling me Jen, but I wouldn't mind if I heard you tell people, your wife included, that you were out to dinner with a twenty- to thirty-year-old blond named Candi Treat."

"I'll more likely tell my wife I was with a jet pilot named J. French. . . . Are you staying longer, after having a rest and a few days being guided around by Lucinda and Macduff?"

"She's staying as long as we can keep her," Lucinda responded. "This is her first time in the Mountain West."

"What's on your 'must see' list?" Erin asked turning toward Jen.

"I saw a glimpse of Paradise Valley yesterday on the flight and drive to their Mill Creek cabin. I want to see more, including a drive all the way up Mill Creek to see the gold mine that caused so much trouble last year, and, hopefully, float a day or two with Macduff and Lucinda on the Yellowstone."

"Do you fly fish?"

"I assume I'll have no choice about that. . . . Also, I want to see some of Yellowstone Park by car, and we plan to fly my plane to Jackson Hole so I can view the Grand Tetons from the air as well as the ground."

"Staying with your friend John Kirby?" Ken asked Macduff.

"Probably not. He and Sarah left for Canada after the third guide murder. I need to call John and learn if they're back."

"Macduff, aren't *you* concerned about going to Jackson?" Erin asked. "You're a guide with a reputation for being unable to avoid trouble."

"I'm only a little concerned. The three killings were about a week apart each. It's approaching a month without another. Maybe they've ended."

"Will you float the Snake?" Erin asked.

"I want to take Jen on each of the sections from Jackson Dam down to Moose," I said.

"What have you two heard from your sheriff contact in Jackson?" Lucinda asked.

"Jen," Ken replied, "Huntly Byng's my equivalent in Teton County and that is mainly Jackson Hole. . . . Have Lucinda and Macduff told you about the gang murders?"

"Some, but I'm sure you know more now. You're aware that Macduff and Lucinda came to Hope Town partly because of the murders."

"Ken, I canceled most of my scheduled floats here in Montana after the deaths. I have a few drifts planned over the next few weeks I'd like to do, but I'm going to vet the clients carefully."

"How do you do that without being called a racist?"

"I'll treat all young Hispanics equally. I won't float with *any* of them. When I was teach. . . ."

I was about to say I had close friends in Mexico City when I was teaching and lecturing in Mexico, but I hope I caught myself. Jen knows nothing about my past before Macduff Brooks was created and little about my decade and a half years living as Macduff, most of that with Lucinda.

"You were a *teacher*, Macduff?" Jen asked.

"That's another extremely brief time in my life, Jen," I answered, Erin and Ken both looking at me wondering. They're aware that I had a different life before I moved to Montana, and that it is not to be the subject of questions. I don't think they know I taught. Or where.

Ken's special emergencies phone began vibrating on the table, and a small light was flashing. He looked at it, got up, handed Erin his cell phone, took a few steps away and began to talk in a whisper.

"Emergency," he said a moment later. "I'm going to step out and take this call."

"Have you all known each other long?" Jen asked, looking at Lucinda and then me. "You act like good friends."

"I met Ken when I moved to Montana," I explained. "I was driving south from Livingston looking for a place to stay when he pulled me over, lights flashing and siren screaming. I told him I couldn't have been speeding, and he said it was worse: I was going too slow! Our conversation somehow got to fly fishing, and he never wrote a ticket. We've been fly fishing together ever since."

"I know Macduff a different way," Erin explained. "Macduff and Lucinda were both shot on their drift boat floating on the Snake in Jackson Hole. Their dog, Wuff, was also wounded. They all survived, but Wuff has a limp. Lucinda was in a coma for a week and had amnesia for a year or so. Macduff was unable to deal with it. He didn't eat or sleep regularly and began to deteriorate. I knew them, but not well. I was asked to look in on him and found him on the floor of his cabin. He looked dead and nearly was. I got medical care and then gave him some tough love about Lucinda and Wuff needing him. He survived, Lucinda slowly conquered her amnesia, and we've been friends ever since. They're both the best. . . ."

Ken was back and interrupted our conversation.

"I have to leave. Erin can stay, but I'll probably need her later."

"You look upset," Lucinda said.

"Another drift boat incident. About two hours ago. This time on our turf. On the Yellowstone River between Carter's Bridge and here."

"Who was the dead guide?" I asked.

"Hank Martin. But he's *not* dead, fortunately. He's in the hospital."

"Was his client a gang member?"

"Can't tell yet. He was young. Maybe Hispanic. I shouldn't say this, but the good news is that the kid who tried to murder Martin is dead."

"Do you know how it happened?"

"Not yet. Macduff, do you know Martin?"

"Most all guides know Hank. He donates more time to charities like Project Healing Waters and Casting for Recovery than any guide I know."

"You've worked with Healing Waters, Macduff. What's Casting for Recovery?" Erin asked.

"I know," exclaimed Lucinda. "It's to teach fly casting and fishing to women who have or, like myself, have had cancer."

"Martin sounds like a good guy. Why would anyone try to kill him?" Jen asked.

"Was it *Calle Rojo*?" Lucinda asked at the same time.

Ken tried to answer them together.

"As I said, we don't know yet. *Calle Rojo* may have been involved. The dead would-be murderer had a Hispanic accent. He was in his early twenties. There was a machete in the boat with blood on the blade. But because he was killed, apparently by Martin, we don't know if he planned to kill Martin and cut off his right hand, the gruesome recent trademark of *Calle Rojo*. It also makes sense to think it was the *Calle Rojo* because I don't know of anyone who disliked Martin. He may not have been handpicked; but certainly he was unlucky. . . . I do have to leave. I'll let you know more later."

"What does this mean for us, Macduff?" Lucinda asked, as Ken left. "I see us at risk. I mean you, Macduff. You're the guide. No spouse or companion has been targeted."

"I had maybe a dozen guide trips scheduled over the next few weeks. I've carefully checked *everyone*. I'm not guiding anyone I don't know."

"Are they all people you've guided for in the past?" asked Erin.

"Almost. The few that are not have been recommended to me by people I know and trust. The others I canceled. Period! I'm more concerned with what this does to *other* guides who earn their living guiding and haven't yet built up a clientele."

"Can't the *outfitters* they work for help by vetting each person?" asked Erin.

"How?" I asked. "Most new clients call by phone and reserve a date. Few questions are asked. One not asked is whether they're Hispanic. The guide doesn't meet them until the float."

"If the older, successful guides adopt procedures to eliminate the possibility of booking a gang member as a client, what happens to *new* guides? Will they take risks to earn a living?"

"Maybe new and mostly unknown guides actually don't have to worry as much. Each of the murders, as well as this attempt, seems to have been against a well-known guide. That does create more shock than killing someone not known among the guiding profession, much less the public."

"True," Erin nodded. "Someone like Macduff can afford even to miss a whole season. . . . No early rising to start a drift. He can stay in the sack with you, Lucinda."

"If this isn't solved in the next year, it will be the end of guiding as we know it here and on the Snake in Wyoming," I offered. "Guides who book on the phone without being part of an outfitter's guide staff will try to join outfitters if they're not comfortable with their own booking procedures."

"What about completely innocent people who fly fish and want to book a guide by phone because they live far from here?" Jen asked. "Like me, calling from Hope Town?"

"Many guides will do something different," suggested Lucinda. "They won't give up fly fishing. But they won't want to be on a river or even in a state that's the site of murders or where they may see a boat they become suspicious about."

"Or would they only fish in places that haven't had the problem?" asked Jen.

"Where?" I asked, doubtful about where the conversation was going.

"New Mexico, California. Perhaps the Adirondacks or New England," Lucinda said. "What if you're a Maine outfitter and a young man comes in from Vermont and wants to float with *any* guide? Does distance diminish the danger?"

"Probably not a problem," said Erin.

"*Probably* isn't assurance," Lucinda quickly responded.

"What if he has a Hispanic accent and says his name is Alberto Gomez?" Erin asked.

"The outfitter likely will say he's booked for the rest of the season," I responded, adding, "and off to the nearest plaintiff's law firm goes Gomez."

"Gomez proves to be from Salvador and is a member of the *Calle Rojo* in Jackson?" Lucinda said, only partly as a question.

"If the outfitter has the slightest reason to believe that, he is justifiably scared. Does he assign his new young guide in his first season to guide Gomez? If the guide is murdered, is the outfitter responsible on a 'should have known' basis?"

Before we knew it, three more hours had passed. We were about to break up when Ken walked in, looking serious.

"Any more news?" Erin immediately asked.

"Hank Martin will live," Ken said, slumping into the chair he earlier vacated. "He's in the hospital in Bozeman where his arm was sewed up. I talked to him together with the head of the Gallatin County Sheriff's Office."

"What did Martin have to say?"

"He was concerned when he booked the float because the guy had a strong Hispanic accent."

"Why did Martin accept him?"

"Because when he called he *seemed* nice."

"That's what they all say," countered Lucinda.

25

MORE AT THE MURRAY HOTEL

THE NEWS ABOUT THE ATTEMPT TO MURDER Hank Martin was disturbing. He would live, but the first three guides were not so lucky. The broader question was this: Would the profession of guiding fly fishing floats survive—in the Mountain West or otherwise—if the murders or attempted murders did not stop?

The five continued their dinner discussion, again under the veil of a somber tone.

"Ken, who was the guy who tried to kill Martin?" I asked.

"He said his name was Jimmy Castle, but his proper name was Jaime Castillo. Martin thought he'd be safe. But to make sure, he borrowed a protective vest."

"Protective against bullets?"

"Yes, and Martin assumed a machete couldn't pierce the front the way the other three were killed."

"Did the guy try to stab Martin with the machete?"

"Apparently, he did. But the blade slipped off the vest and slashed Martin's arm," answered Ken.

"How did Martin kill Castillo?"

"Martin had taken a snub nose .357 magnum pistol with him. It was in his left vest pocket. When Castillo pulled his machete from his bag, it momentarily became caught. By the time Castillo had set the tip against Martin's chest, Martin had pulled out his gun, and before Castillo could thrust the blade, Martin fired his first shot. His other arm was slashed by the machete as it slipped off the vest. Martin quickly fired four more times."

"Did Martin say what they talked about on the boat?"

"He said Castillo never focused on fishing. He was visibly nervous, not interested in talking, and gave brief responses."

"To what kind of comments or questions by Martin?"

"Martin asked Castillo what he did for a living. Castillo said he hadn't decided and that he was looking for a job. To a question about when and why he came to Jackson, Castillo said only that he came a few weeks ago because a friend said he'd help him get a job," Ken responded.

"Did he say he had found a job?" Erin asked.

"He didn't say. I guess Martin didn't ask."

"Did Castillo say anything to Martin about why he was spending a day floating on the river or how he paid for it?"

"He said a friend told him that the view along the river was nice and that the friend paid for the float."

"Did he say who the friend was or know how much the friend paid?" I asked.

"Not exactly. He said he thought the payment was something like fifty dollars. Not very realistic."

"Not at all. A full day's float is about $400. If the guide works on his own, he keeps it all. If an outfitter scheduled the float, the guide shares the fee, and may be given a tip by the client. Usually another hundred."

"Did Castillo show any hostility towards Martin before he went for his machete?" Lucinda asked, worried about Macduff.

"No," Ken replied. "Martin described Castillo as cleanly dressed—jeans and a red T-shirt with no lettering on the front or back. He wore fairly new sneaks and a popular green cap that said 'John Deere' on the front. His English was rough, his grammar poor. He used a lot of wrong words and spoke with a heavy Spanish accent."

"Nothing at all unusual in the way Martin described him?"

"Only that Castillo was interested in Martin's family and religion. He asked if he were married. If he had any kids. And if they were good students."

"What did Martin tell him?" I asked.

"The truth. That he was married a dozen years ago and that he had two young honor student daughters."

"You said he asked about religion?"

"Yes," responded Ken. "That was a little unusual. Martin said Castillo asked him if they were married in a *Catholic* church. Martin said it was and that the priest who married them was his brother. Martin said he also had a sister who was a nun. Neither was true. By now Martin was worried and making up answers that he hoped would help him survive."

"Did Castillo ask why Martin himself wasn't a priest?"

"Yes, Erin. Martin said he wanted to be but was rejected because his grades weren't very good. Martin told Castillo he was a poor student and tried to make up for not becoming a priest by going to mass several times a week and working with several Catholic charities.

"That seemed to open Castillo up more and made him appear uncertain about something. He asked what charities Martin worked for."

"That's when Martin said one was to find places for the homeless to stay?"

"Exactly. Castillo asked if any were Hispanic."

"Martin said about half and that one other charity he worked for was a Catholic program to help Hispanics who were in the U.S. illegally to obtain legal status."

"How did Castillo react?" I asked.

"He asked Martin whether he would help Castillo if he entered the U.S. illegally."

"What did Martin say?"

"He said 'yes,' his faith required him to provide that help."

"Did Castillo say anything?"

"Not directly, but he seemed calmer than before and even smiled once or twice."

"Then, what prompted him to stab Martin?" questioned Jen.

"It was after Castillo asked if Martin knew about the youth gangs in Salvador and how they caused so much trouble in Los Angeles and other Southwestern U.S. cities," Ken answered.

"How did Martin respond?" Jen asked.

"He said that he had read some newspaper pieces about gang members illegally entering the U.S. and that the U.S. was likely to stop these entries."

"Did Castillo react to that?"

"He asked Martin if he thought they *should* be stopped."

"Martin said 'yes.' He believed it was a serious problem and that the U.S. had the right to control its borders."

"Castillo's reaction?" inquired Lucinda.

"Martin said his manner changed quickly. Castillo didn't say another word. That's when he went for his machete."

"Do you think if Martin hadn't discussed the U.S. and immigration that Castillo would have tried to kill him?" Lucinda next asked.

"My personal view?" Ken replied. "No. He seemed to be looking for a way out. Martin's link with the Catholic church and charities clearly affected Castillo."

"Was Martin justified in shooting Castillo?" I asked.

"Why do you even ask that? Castillo had a machete that he tried to thrust into Martin."

"But Martin had a protective vest?"

"It's not what we think. It's what a prosecuting attorney thinks."

"And if the prosecutor doesn't charge *Martin* with murder, the Wyoming Hispanic community will be outraged?" Lucinda wondered aloud.

"I hope not."

"Ken, I know you're tired," I observed. "But, what are you going to say to local outfitters and guides who ask what they should do?"

"I'll suggest that they learn about the person—try to see them—who wants to float and, if at all concerned, not to book him. Or her. But we haven't had a female killer. I don't think the *Calle Rojo* accepts women as members."

"And the outfitter or guide responds, asking, 'If the person persons comes into our place and is clean and dressed reasonably well, has no metal or other piercings, no visible tattoos, and seems pleasant, do I accept him?'"

"If there's no other reason to reject him, I'd tell the outfitter or guide he *should* accept him."

"There should be a reason to reject the person," Erin agreed.

"Assume the person is about twenty and speaks English with a strong Spanish accent. Any difference? Good reason to reject?" Lucinda asked.

"I'm beginning to be worried," admitted Erin.

"And if you accept him and he arrives at the boat with a bag that he says has extra clothing, but which could hide a machete, what do you do?" I asked.

"You have good reason to ask to go through his bag."

"Telling him what when he objects?"

"Say that you as a guide and an outfitter you work for have a policy of no weapons on the boat and you have to search."

"And if he swears that he has no weapon, then what?"

"If he won't let you see, don't start the float."

"Next, the Hispanic community in town responds and screams racism. What do you do?" Lucinda interjected.

"I can't believe any credible Hispanic group is going to defend murderous Hispanic gang members," Ken said. "Nor that a prosecutor, knowing the recent past where the *Calle Rojo* is believed to have killed three guides, will want to prosecute Martin. But?"

"But what?" Jen asked.

"As an outfitter or individual guide, I'd quickly raise the matter with other outfitters and guides and try to adopt a policy that on its face is not racist."

"Is not? Or appears not?" Jen inquired.

"You said that, not me."

26

THE NEXT DAY AT MILL CREEK

"TAKE ME FISHING ALONG MILL CREEK?" JEN asked, setting a plate of eggs, bacon, sausage, and toast in front of me and another at her place.

Lucinda shrugged and took a bite of her array of fruit.

I didn't say a word and continued chewing on a piece of sausage.

"If you keep feeding him like that, Jen, you can take him home to Hope Town when you go."

"I'll take him any way he'll come. I didn't think the easiest way would be breakfast food."

Wuff was ten feet away lying in her bed facing us, her eyes following whoever was speaking. Although she looked as though she understood, she was more likely listening for words like "treat," "banana," "supper," "snack," or another familiar diction, probably followed by Lucinda's or my tossing something her way. Anything any one of us was eating would be welcome.

"This kind of breakfast and a few hundred million dollars to spend today might be persuasive, but I'd worry about more than a machete if I angered you," I commented, looking at Lucinda.

"Good," she said, pulling away my plate and setting down a duplicate of her plate with chunks of watermelon, avocado, peach, and pineapple, all surrounded on one side by a skinned banana, a half-dozen strawberries, and one fruit I couldn't identify.

"What's this? Are you trying to hide it between the banana and watermelon?"

"Eat it. It's healthy."

Jen was nodding, meaning either "It is pretty tasty" or "I don't know what it is, but eat it and shut her up."

"It's apricot," Lucinda said.

"You tried to get apricot down me last month, mixed in with perfectly good slightly charred lamb. It didn't work."

"Leave it. I'll give it to Wuff. I'll get some into you sooner or later."

"See what I go through every morning, Jen? Actually not just morning, most every meal."

"Maybe she's trying to tell you she'd like you to take us all out to dinner," Jen said.

"Deal," I quickly replied. "Wuff gets the apricot," which was quickly transferred from my plate to Wuff's bowl.

Wuff ate the apricot and belched.

I didn't say a word, but I did smile.

"You haven't answered my request to fish on Mill Creek?"

"We should, Macduff," Lucinda affirmed. "Picnic lunch or picnic dinner?"

"Dinner is a better time to fish. Also, I need some time to collect our gear and rig a rod for Jen."

That afternoon we drove a mile up Mill Creek to a parking area at the bridge to the Passage Creek Falls trail, an easy four-mile round trip hike. The narrow trail took us past masses of blooming spring wildflowers—yellowbells, sagebrush buttercups, and arrowleaf balsamroots to remember the names of only a few. The creek meandered off to our left while close by to the right the land became a rock wall that rose raggedly three hundred feet.

I stopped our group.

"Jen, this is a good place to start. The stream doesn't look like it would hold many fish, but it does. They're small cutthroat trout up to about seven inches. They have the same wonderful color they share with their older and bigger brothers and sisters."

"Seven inches! Macduff, something that small we'd call bait-fish around Abaco."

"And you'd catch the bigger fish off a boat or surf fishing where nothing was in the way of your cast."

"That's right. There's so much brush around here, I don't expect we can fish."

"This is exactly where we'll start."

"You showed me some basic casts behind your cabin. We can't do those here."

"That's mostly true. Let's start at the pool here where the stream widens and is shallow, just a few inches deep."

"I don't see any sign of a fish."

"Look where there is *likely* to be fish. Remember that, if you can see one, it can see you."

"What do you think of underneath that brush to the right of the pool where it hangs over the water and provides some shade?"

"OK. The pool is ten feet upstream. Walk carefully toward that pool along the bank up past the quiet water and then let out about twenty feet of line, leader, and tippet. Make sure it's loose at your feet and not caught on anything. I want you to reach out and simply drop the fly onto the water and let the current float it down and under the edge of the brush. Pull out some of the line at your feet. Keep your rod tip close to the surface so the line stays under the brush as it floats. Not too much slack or the fish will have time to spit out the fly before you set the hook."

Jen dropped the fly perfectly, but as it floated toward the brush area, she raised the rod tip too much to take out slack, and the line caught the brush. But the fly continued to float for two feet, and a trout hit the tiny #18 Adams fly. Jen jerked the rod. The tippet broke on the brush, and the fish disappeared.

"That wasn't too successful," she said, embarrassed. "Lost my fly and lost my fish."

"It may never happen again in your fishing life!" I responded.

"Maybe for another ten minutes, but I suspect over time I'll feed as many flies to the brush as I do to trout."

"More! That attempt was one reason we use barbless hooks. Let's move on upstream toward the falls to a less disturbed section of the creek."

We hadn't gone thirty yards when we came to another part of the creek where there was some calm water, caused by eddies downstream and beyond a tree limb that had fallen across the creek.

"Let me put another fly on your tippet. Same Adams fly, same #18. Do what you did before, but here you want your fly to float down under the part of the tree trunk that crosses the creek. There are some shadows that may be hiding fish."

She cast it perfectly.

"My fly is floating pretty good, Macduff, and there is no nasty brush to catch my line."

"True, but I bet someday you'll come back to where we were just skunked and challenge that pool again."

"That's exactly what I was thinking as we walked to this pool. Maybe on our way back later," she laughed.

"Set it!" I called out.

She did.

"I've got one!"

"Keep it upstream of the tree trunk so your line isn't caught."

Soon a six-inch cutthroat was in the net. The glow on Jen's face was worth the wait. She took a photo, or five or six, and I carefully returned the trout to the stream.

Jen quickly tossed her line back in the same spot.

"You already fished out this pool," I said.

"I like this place."

"That doesn't mean you'll hook a fish on every . . ."

"Got another," she interrupted, lifting her rod tip and slowly bringing in another an inch longer. "You were saying?"

"Nothing. It's the same fish. It barely was back in the water. You didn't give it a chance to catch its breath."

"How can it be another inch longer in twenty seconds?" she asked, smiling and releasing the trout carefully.

"Beginner's luck. They grow fast in the summer months." I responded.

"You're jealous!"

"Very. I fished here three times before catching anything."

"How about you Lucinda?"

"First time here, three fish."

"Why is it that you teach us to fish so successfully, but you don't catch much?" Jen asked me.

"Pavarotti's teacher couldn't sing as well as he. Babe Ruth's batting coach could hit as well as he. Sometimes the best are saved to train a new generation. I share my best secrets when I teach you fly fishing, either casting or catching. The hard part is when my pupils show me little respect."

"Oh, Oh. Here come the tears. Jen, he can also teach acting. He acted in drama in high school and college, so be careful what you fall for."

I didn't say a word. I was enjoying watching.

"Macduff, I want you to fish," Jen said. "Right now and here. Take my rod. Use whatever fly you wish."

I wouldn't have accepted her challenge if I hadn't been looking past here where she caught her fish. I had seen a rise that I couldn't believe. There are some fairly large fish in the creek. But there was not another rise. I would go to the bottom after it

"If you insist," I said, taking her rod and quickly changing her #14 Adams for a larger white and chartreuse streamer my friend, Dave Johnson, gave me to try. I didn't add any floater to keep it on the surface.

"Watch this carefully," I advised, turning and pulling off about 16 feet of line. I dropped it all in the water in front of me, made a false cast and set the fly down two feet upstream of where the last rise had been. I waited, letting the fly settle what was probably three feet to the bottom, and then, a quick pull on the line caused me to react with my quick follow up that told me a had something on the line. Three seconds later a Cutthroat broke the surface showing its colors, and what had to be the oldest resident of this part of the creek was soon in my net.

"My God," said Lucinda. This creek's too small for that size fish. I'd guess 11 inches!"

"Measure it, Jen."

"A fraction under eleven," Jen soon said.

The fish was soon back in the water. I thought of paying someone to come and feed it daily as a reward.

"I apologize, Macduff," Jen exclaimed, grabbing my arm and patting my back.

"I don't," added Lucinda. "Something's fishy."

"I've always had a student who thought she—or he—was more knowledgeable than the teacher," I said, smirking.

"Let's leave her here," Jen suggested, "while we finish the climb to the top of the falls and have a picnic lunch in honor of your most likely record for this creek."

"Good idea," I said.

"Or you can wait for us here, we'll be back in about two hours," Jen suggested to a nervous Lucinda.

I took Jens arm and escorted her the 15 feet to the parallel path where we continued our hike toward the falls. Two minutes later I turned and saw Lucinda keeping pace, but thirty yards behind. It was going to be an interesting lunch.

Jen and I reached the top and sat on a massive rock ledge overlooking the falls and listening to the water pass by and tumbled down. Lucinda arrived five minutes later and carefully laid out our luncheon tablecloth, napkins, sandwiches, and opened the bottle of wine. She poured glasses for Jen and me.

"Please have some wine, Lucinda," I said, sipping the special *Pouilly-Fumé* Jen had brought.

"Like it?" she asked. "Lucinda told me you love *Pouilly-Fuissé*. Can you tell the difference?"

"To be honest, I don't think so. Maybe if we had both kinds to sample at the same time. The *Fumé* is based on *Sauvignon Blanc* and the *Fuissé* on *Chardonnay*. Let's buy a bottle of each when we are in Livingston and have a test at evening cocktails."

"Me too." Came a quite request from Lucinda, who had slowly edged her things up to ours.

"If you behave on the way home," I said.

The conversation turned to the death on the Yellowstone, which captured all the water of Mill Creek, which, in turn, captured all the water of Passage Falls Creek not more than fifteen feet away from where we were sitting.

"Three murders and a fourth attempted in three different states—Wyoming, Idaho, and Montana. I'm confused trying to choose the best approach to a resolution," I commented.

"The murder in Idaho was in a rural area near no significant city. That meant there was no population center that felt as strong about solving the case as in Jackson. The attempt in Montana failed and ended in the death of the putative murderer. That meant the fear in Paradise Valley and Livingston was somewhat tempered by the success of the guide's action in both saving his life and ending the life of one who didn't deserve to experience any more of it."

"Do you mean that your guide friends in Jackson, like the John Kirby you often refer to, are *more* concerned than guides are at the Henry's Fork or here along the Yellowstone?"

"I mean that guides in Jackson are more likely to get together and take collective action. Not that that's right. After all each of the four perpetrators was young—late teens through their twenties, each was Hispanic, each was. . . ."

"Wait a minute," interrupted Jen. "Is it certain each was Hispanic? The first three got away; it's only the fourth who is *known* for certain to be Hispanic."

"But each of the first three scribbled *CR* on the drift boat with the blood of the victim. That probably means *Calle Rojo*."

"Probably," I repeated, with no proof to offer."

"*Calle Rojo* means Hispanic!" Lucinda asserted.

"Not literally, but true. Is there any opinion about the identity of the first three murderers?" Jen asked. "They could have been done by the same person. Maybe by Castillo."

"Wait a minute," Lucinda said. "I think it's fine to be investigating each of the first three separately. But maybe the focus for the authorities should be on breaking up the alleged responsible *group*, the *Calle Rojo*. What do we know about it?"

"Have you ever seen one name of an admitted *Calle Rojo* member?" Jen asked.

Lucinda and I looked surprised. Neither of us had thought about that approach. The search should start to identify *any* member.

"Should we walk around Jackson and tear open the top of any shirt of a person who looks or sounds Hispanic?" Jen asked.

"You said it, not me," Lucinda and I responded at the same time.

27

BACK AT THE CABIN ON MILL CREEK

WHEN WE REACHED OUR CABIN, A CAR WAS parked near the foot of the steps. Erin Giffin from the county sheriff's office was sitting on the porch reading some official looking papers.

"Where have you all been?" she asked, looking up but not moving.

"On Jen's first trip to Passage Creek Falls," Lucinda responded.

"Did you fish?"

"Of course," said Jen. "I asked them to take me. They taught me how to fly fish for small trout on small creeks. I loved it, but it was frustrating. I caught several trout and lost twelve flies!"

"What brings you here?" Lucinda asked, walking up the steps and leaning over and hugging Erin.

"Excuse me, but I'm exhausted," Erin said. "I called around noon but, as usual, you were in one place and your phones were in another."

"Lucinda and I will ignore that," I said. "Any developments with the Martin case?"

"Only that Martin's out of the hospital and recuperating at home. He'll make a full recovery. He must shudder when he thinks how close he came to be joining the three other guides who died on their drift boats from machete stabs."

"Anything further about the dead creep, Castillo?" Lucinda asked.

"We've asked about him throughout Paradise Valley and Livingston. We showed people a photo of his face taken from his dead body."

"Anyone recognize him?"

"No. We think he's from Jackson Hole, and Sheriff Byng is helping there. These are strange cases. Byng said that no one in his valley wants to admit publicly knowing anything about *Calle Rojo* or specifically about someone named Jaime Castillo. Anyone asked seems scared when you mention the gang, especially if you ask a guide or person—customer or employee—at any outfitter's shop."

"Erin," asked an uneasy Jen, "do you have gangs here in Montana, especially in Livingston?"

"We do. In several places: Billings, Bozeman, Helena, Great Falls, Missoula. . . . I could go on. Even Livingston has a problem with them. But not like *Calle Rojo*. Here in Montana the gangs have been mainly Anglos, thirties and older, and they're bikers. A few years ago, a nationwide search located one of the worst leaders of one of the motorcycle gangs—called the *Bandits*—in Livingston."

"Are they as dangerous as the *Calle Rojo?*"

"So far, no. There are a lot more motorcycle gangs, and the worst, including the *Bandits*, are involved in murder, extortion, narcotics, weapons transactions, and more."

"How do you distinguish good bikers from bad?"

"What they do when they're together in packs of bikes. How they look, how they dress, what their tattoos say or express, their manner. Like defining pornography: I'll know it when I see it. One way to get an idea is the small patch some bikers wear that says '1%er' and relates to a comment made decades ago after the famous Hollister, California rally. There, 4,000 participating bikers caused a riot. They were relatively mild compared to more recent biker events. The head of the American Motorcyclist Association allegedly said '99% of motorcyclists are good, decent, law-abiding citizens.' Members of the more difficult gangs responded to make it known they were in the 1% and wanted to be viewed as bikers who were *not* law abiding. The *Bandits* fits that group nicely."

"I assume the *Bandits* don't get along with the *Calle Rojo?*" asked Lucinda.

"It may be better to say that neither group gets along with anybody," responded Erin.

"It wouldn't surprise me if at this very moment the *Bandits* are meeting to decide how to match or trump the publicity recently given the *Calle Rojo*," she added.

28

THE SAME AFTERNOON AT AN OLD BUILDING BY THE RAILROAD TRACKS IN LIVINGSTON, MONTANA

THREE YEARS AGO THE OWNER OF A BUILDING no longer used to make railroad cross ties for Burlington Northern rented the poorly maintained two stories to a local group that was described on the lease agreement as the "Foundation for the Furtherance of the Use of Bike Trails." The building's owner was led to believe that the foundation was a charity that assisted communities in designing and building new bicycle trails.

Not one bicycle powered with pedals has ever entered the main floor where railroad ties were once made. This afternoon, the oil-stained concrete floor had become the cooling off place for six hard-driven Harley motorcycles. Each had brought a governing committee member of the Foundation for a meeting on the second floor in what once was the board of directors and general business meeting room for the railroad tie fabrication business.

The room did not look like a board of directors' suite except for a large table in the middle where a dozen persons sat. This day six thirty- to fiftyish-year-old men were sitting around the old board table. All dressed alike the way a board of directors might, but they were not wearing dark suits, white shirts, ties, and polished shoes, but rather wrinkled jeans, ankle-high leather boots, and black T-shirts that said in white letters "BANDITS mc"—meaning motor club—above a white skull with what looked like phallic symbols crossed behind the skull. On the back of each chair hung a black leather jacket with "BANDITS MAKE THE RULES" across the back and a triangle framing "1%er" on the chest and above the words "Montana Bandits."

All but one of the six men had some form of facial hair, from a modest moustache to scraggly, erratically trimmed hair that reached partway down his chest. Two wore no hats, but the four others had mostly black head wear—a Stetson with the front brim rolled up and pinned, a baseball cap that said, "Dames Devour Bandits," a red and black head-bandana, and an old scuffed leather aviator's cap.

Not one arm was lacking some tattoo bearing letters or crosses or fists with thrusted middle fingers or female names or the overused "1%er."

The air was strong with marijuana and two dozen empty beer bottles, half-standing and half turned over, embellished the table.

It was fair to believe this group was not discussing the funding and construction of a bicycle path through Paradise Valley. The conversation indeed was quite different.

"We can't let this happen," said the one with the aviator's cap. "Goddam spics from one of those little pissholes below Mexico. I think the country's called Saveador or something stupid like that."

"We gotta teach those kids to stay outta Paradise Valley and Livingston," said the hatless one who bore the small moustache.

"That boat was floating on the Yellowstone River not far from here in Livingston when this dumb kid—I think named Costelo—tried to kill that fishing guide," added the one with hair hanging to his mid-chest. "That's *our* turf."

"Some guy told me Costelo had a machete and tried to cut the guide. The machete had *CR* painted on the handle? What did that mean?"

"It meant *Calle Rojo*," said the one at the end of the table, who seemed the only one with an education beyond sixteen. His companions probably made only infrequent appearances in school before that.

"I'm gonna tell you about them," he continued, relating what he had collected from local online newspapers. There was nothing new.

"The first three machete killings took place in Wyoming and Idaho, on rivers a long way from here," interrupted the one with no facial hair other than about four days' unattended growth. "The attempt here was a bust. Why should we worry?"

"Because we don't want any other gang members even walking through our territory," said the one with the Stetson.

"That's right," cut in the aviator capped one, "*No one.* We own Paradise Valley and Livingston. But the SOB spic is dead. So be it. Let's get on to business."

"That incidence was our business," said the more-or-less educated one. "We have to let the *Calle Rojo* know to stay outa here."

"I got an idea," said the one with the head-bandana. "We got a lot of members here and more in Bozeman. And a few hundred in Idaho Falls. We ain't got no chapter in Jackson. I say we hold a rally in Jackson of the three chapters. My kid, the smart little bastard, looked up Jackson on the computer he stole at school. He shows me a picture of a town square with hundreds of animal horns in arches at the four corners. There's a bar facing the square."

"Man, I like this idea," interrupted the quiet one with the baseball cap. "I figure we can get 1,000 bikes here 'cause we invite every chapter within maybe 300 miles of Jackson."

"We take over the Goddam town," said the one with chest-length hair. "Show them rich bastards who we are. They even got a former president that lives there."

"I think it were a Vice-President, not a President," said the one who seemed to be leading the discussion. "His name is Rick Chainey. Or something like that."

"No, it ain't. You act so smart," said the one who had removed his aviator cap to show a badly scarred head.

"Then, what's his name?"

"I don't know, but it ain't Chainey. Whatever his name is, I always liked him because he shot some Goddam lawyer guy he was hunting with."

"I want me one of those rich Jackson divorcees, or—ha ha—widows."

"They'll be lined up at the bar just waitin' for us," someone responded.

"I got another idea," said the quiet one. "I don't mean to change the plan for the biker rally. But I was thinkin' about what we could do to irritate that *Calle Rojo* group. They been killin' fishing guides. We got a bunch here. We pick the one most prominent in Paradise Valley. I'll do it and make a file on him. There's a guy who lives somewhere down near Pray or Emigrant. Mac something or other. Had some trouble over the years with some killings he wasn't charged with but that he was around when they happened. If we took him out the *Calle Rojo* would be really pissed. I'll get his name and where he lives."

"Do it," said the one with the red bandana as others nodded.

"This is great. We gonna *cause* trouble." asked the one with a long beard.

"We *are* trouble," replied three in unison.

29

MILL CREEK CABIN

JEN HAD BEEN HAVING THE TIME OF HER LIFE. Fishing Mill Creek was followed by a day on the Yellowstone River beginning at Emigrant—a long eleven-mile float to Loch Leven.

Jen talked the entire time on the float and the drive home, especially about how the view changed with every bend on the river that presented a different version of the valley that truly delivered on its name: Paradise Valley.

I had Jen sit in my guide seat, Lucinda was behind her. I took the bow seat facing Jen and taught her the basics of rowing a drift boat. She learned quickly.

"This is as much fun as flying a plane!" she exclaimed. "And I don't have to worry about crashing."

"Don't say that," I warned. "There's a part of this river about fifteen miles south of here that is called Yankee Jim Canyon. It's one stretch of rapids after another. Rubber rafts float it, but not many fishing boats."

"You're a smart pro guide, Macduff, couldn't you row it?"

"If I'm smart as you allege, I wouldn't attempt it."

"Could we do it in a rubber raft?" She asked.

"Yes, and that's a promise. But I've got the next two days booked on two different rivers. Then we'll do the Yankee . . ."

"Macduff! A fish hit your fly. I saw it rise. It was beautiful; I could see reds and silver."

"I've still got it," I exclaimed, "I'm amazed the cutthroat trout set the hook all by itself. Give Lucinda the net and keep the boat facing the fish."

The trout made two runs trying to escape, but there was no place to go. This stretch of the river was straight and there were no downed trees along the river to act as refuge for the trout. Within a few minutes Lucinda had netted the fish which we quickly photographed behind Jen rowing and carefully returned it to the river.

"For a minute I thought we were having trout for dinner," Jen exclaimed.

"It was a cutthroat and has to go back. The fishing regulations say so. We could keep and eat a rainbow. But I don't keep any trout. Period!"

"Why?"

"I caught my first trout, a six- or seven-inch brook trout, on a Royal Coachman fly. I was fishing in a small stream in Northwest Connecticut and was so overwhelmed with the idea of catching something so beautiful and full of life, and on a fly I had tied, that I carefully put it back in the water. In all the years since I've never kept a fresh water trout."

"What do you mean 'fresh water trout,'" Jen asked. "You keep salt water trout?"

"Sometimes."

"What's the difference. A trout is a trout is a trout."

"Not to me."

"Jen," interrupted Lucinda, "You have a lot to learn about his idiosyncrasies."

"I learn some of that every time we eat out. He seems to have a restricted diet. Medical mandates?"

"Mental obstructions," Lucinda said, avoiding my frown. "You'll understand better when we have all our meals in Yellowstone Park in a few days."

"Shouldn't you be concentrating on your fishing," I said to her. "Jen's rowed you past three rises in the past five minutes. It may be the last of the Mother's Day hatch."

"And you didn't tell me! What fly did you put on Jen's rod?"

"A stonefly nymph. But now I'll change it to something for the hatch."

"You didn't tell me the stoneflies were working. What do I have as a fly?"

"Something I found on the floor of the boat by my feet.

"Jen, you can have him!"

"The stonefly nymph?"

"No! Macduff."

"Do I get Wuff too?"

"No. She stays with me."

"Then what do I get? An old fly fishing guide who doesn't help both his beautiful clients," Jen said, with a wink to Lucinda I couldn't see.

"You've got an hour to accept or reject him. We should finish the float about then," Lucinda declared.

"If I catch more trout than you before we get to the takeout, Lucinda, I'll take him. If not, he's yours."

"I don't think I like this," I said quietly.

"Just be quiet and take back the guide's seat. I want to be where I can cast and make her work to keep you."

The last hour of the float was like the finals of an NBA basketball playoff. The score jumped back and forth. I had never floated this section of the Yellowstone with as much activity. As we came within sight of the take-out ramp the score was tied at five each. Within thirty yards both hooked onto another trout and I didn't know whether to favor one or the other by positioning the boat. Then they crossed their lines. At the last minute, Lucinda took her small knife and reached over the side and cut one line. Jen's fish swam off trailing the line.

"Lucinda, I have to say your love for your man showed itself today. You had a choice of which line you cut, mine or yours. You chose to cut my line and keep Macduff."

"Could you tell which line was your's and which was mine?" Lucinda asked, with a grin.

"They were so twisted I couldn't tell. They were both yellow lines. How could *you* tell?" Jen asked, tilting her head showing a questioning, curious look.

Lucinda sat smiling and didn't say a word. Not one of us mentioned it again the rest of the day.

~

We floated the next day on the Gallatin down from just above William's Bridge, sliding off the rubber out of a borrowed pontoon boat whenever we wanted to fish or had to drag the boat past shallow areas. Part of the land flows through Ted Turner property. I wish he owned more, he is a fly fisherman and maintains his properties to avoid the damage done breaking down the banks by thirsty cattle grazing on so many ranches along Montana rivers.

There are times when you wonder how you can be floating this unblemished river—until the diversion dams begin near the old, closed Gallatin Gateway Inn.

I rowed the full way this time, I didn't want to put Jen into rowing on narrower, shallower, and more rock strewn than the previous day on the Yellowstone. One may wade and fish the Gallatin. And one may float the Gallatin, but due to the shallow areas and large rocks, drift boats give way to rubber pontoon boats. Most important, one may not fish this section of the river from any kind of boat.

With dozens of previous ventures down the same stretch of the Gallatin, Lucinda and I have come to know our favorite places to stop, slide off the rubber pontoons, and wade fish.

"Jen, have you ever waded to fish?" I asked.

"No. What should I worry about?"

"Falling, because of the rocky bottom where the current keeps you from seeing very clearly. Would you like a cane?"

"What do you think I am? Ninety?"

"Your choice."

Lucinda took her cane, preferably called a wading stick. And I took mine. We didn't tell Jen that the wading stick made us each a tripod of two legs and the stick, which is far more stable than only two legs.

Jen learned fast, she worked her way slowly fifteen feet off the bank, several times having to stop and regain her balance. Then, ignoring her unstable position, she began to cast.

She had a 7 foot bamboo rod and I tied on a #14 Royal Coachman dry fly. The 7 foot rod is easily explainable with the narrowness of the river, but the fly is my preferred starter every time I'm on the Gallatin. My first time, after a dozen flies brought nothing, a #14 Royal Coachman tossed off a bank presented me with a 19" Brown trout, my best to date on the river.

I always start with the same fly and tied it on both Jen's and Lucinda's line as well as mine. Maybe tripling my first-time luck.

It quickly proved to be Jen's first hook-up on the Gallatin, followed by what brought forth some language she hadn't used since we met.

Her unstable position, lack of a wading stick, and quick strike by a trout that leaped out and seemed to stare her down before falling back and taking off for safer places, caused Jen to tumble head long into the water, which I later measured at 52 degrees.

I offered Jen a hand. She refused, expressing frustration with more four-letter words than I thought could fit into a sentence.

Fortunately, I always place dry clothes in a waterproof bag. I gave it to Jen who was back on the bank trying to get her cold, soaked clothes off. She put on mine, rolling up the sleeves and pants legs, got back into her waders, picked up her rod, took my wading stick, and in another minute was back in the water casting from the spot where she had fallen."

"Got one, Macduff!" Jen called, no more than ten seconds after her Royal Coachman landed softly at the river's edge off the far bank. It was an eleven-inch trout glistening with the color variations that made it a Brown.

"Was it worth the soaking?" I called out.

"You bet! Look at that color," she said, looking over her shoulder smiling at me. I was hanging her wet clothes on the fence that separated the river from a large field where new, tiny leaves were sprouting from some crop I couldn't identity. I arranged her clothes by a fence post so they looked like a scarecrow, arms thrust out to each side from a sweatshirt with Captain Candi's Bar across the front, and a cap that said Hope Town resting on top of the post. Jen took photos of it when we finished fishing and decided to move on.

"Are four fish worth the immersion?" I asked Jen as we started downstream again on the pontoon boat.

"What immersion? Tripping when your guide doesn't properly outfit you isn't an immersion. I admit to a little dampness."

"I offered you a wading stick."

"You offered me a cane!"

"And you refused."

"Of course. I'm not a cripple old woman."

"And you fell in?"

"Yes."

"Up to your eyebrows?"

"Well, almost."

"Would you like your cane when we stop again?"

"Only if you stop calling it a cane."

"Would you like my wading stick?"

"I already have it."

"What am I going to use," not telling her I had a spare.

"That's your concern. You're the guide. Now put another. . . . *please* put another fly on my line."

"You lost the Royal Coachman? I spent hours tying that fly."

"I gave it back to you, sort of."

"Meaning?"

"Look at the back of your cap."

I pulled off the cap. A #14 Royal Coachman was stuck in the back of it. A foot of tippet hung down from the fly.

"Did you do that, Jen?"

"I admit it. My back cast was a little off just before we got out of the water. Since you missed it so much why don't you keep the Coachman and give me something else to try."

"OK. I'll tie on a Yellow Humpy. It's on a barbless hook. If you complain I'll cut off more than the barb. I'll cut off the hook. Then you can cast at will and I won't be ducking all the time."

"I'll pay you back. No tip for the guide."

"But at least I'll be alive. You're a menace on the river."

"I had a good teacher."

~

The next day we drifted on the Madison River down to Ennis, the quintessential fly fishing town with a life size bronze fisherman at the north entrance.

Jen asked to row and learn about placing and maintaining the boat about thirty feet off the bank. I sat in the rear, from where I could comment on her rowing. She learned quickly.

"Jen, do you like rowing," I asked a few hours later as we loaded the *Osprey* on the trailer after we pulled out at Ennis.

"I do. With more instruction I could become a guide."

"How would you like to go to the Orvis guide school in Jackson?"

"Will you recommend me?"

"Of course."

"Do they take women?"

"They do. Maybe Lucinda would go with you."

"She's too advanced."

"Not as a guide. She's very good at casting and OK at rowing. She needs to have someone other than me who teaches guiding, not just casting."

"We can room together," said Lucinda to Jen.

"You're on. When do we go?"

"I'll make some phone calls tomorrow," I offered, "and see when their next classes are scheduled, and if they have openings."

"Lucinda," Jen said nodding at Lucinda, "if we become guides we won't need our current guide anymore."

"We'll guide you!" Lucinda said. "You sit up front and fish. You've always said when you become a guide you fish less yourself."

"We'll make it worth your while," explained Jen. "Lucinda and I will wear as guides what we wore when we were Lucinda and Candi Treat living at Reggie's place in Hope Town. Which was very little—short shorts, thin T-shirts and no underwear. One of us will row, the other sit in the back, preparing drinks and snacks. Every hour we'll swap places."

"How will I concentrate on fishing?" I asked.

"Oh! You plan to fish?"

~

"Lucinda, when are you two going to take me to Yellowstone Park?" Jen asked that evening sitting on the log cabin porch watching Mill Creek flow past. I love Mill Creek and Paradise Valley, but I have to see our great national park and watch Old Faithful erupt. And I want to at least cast a fly somewhere in the park."

"I heard that," I called in from the Mill Creek cabin porch. "Are you ready to fly down over the park to Jackson? I can call John Kirby and tell him we're coming. If he and Sarah are back from Arizona."

"I didn't mean going to Jackson—yet. First, I want you two to show me Yellowstone Park from the road. Do the full loop from the entry at Gardiner to Mammoth, Norris, Old Faithful, Fishing Bridge and the lake, Canyon Village, the top of Mount Washburn, Lamar Valley, and back to Gardiner."

"Do you want to fish in the park?" Lucinda asked.

"Absolutely. How long is the loop?"

"To drive with few stops, except to let bison cross the road, between five and seven hours."

"Can we stay over one night?

"If we can get rooms. The park's usually full. I can call about rooms. Ideal would be to overnight about half-way. That means staying a bit past the mid-point, hopefully at Lake Village where the Yellowstone River comes out of Yellowstone Lake."

"Macduff," Lucinda suggested, "you call while I fix some lunch. Tell the lodges around the lake we want two rooms for one night as soon as something is available."

I called. At the Lake Lodge and Lake Hotel every room in every cabin was booked solid, with one exception—in two days there were two rooms for one night. I took the rooms and gave them a credit card and contact info.

"We're in! We have one room overlooking the lake in the old Lake Hotel, and another room behind the hotel in what they call the Frontier Cabins."

"Soon?" Lucinda asked.

"The day after tomorrow. Jen should take the room in the hotel and we'll use the cabin."

"Are they far apart?" Jen asked.

"The hotel sits at the edge of the lake and the Frontier Cabins are immediately behind the hotel."

"The hotel sounds more glamorous," Jen suggested. "Why don't you two take that room?"

"It's yours, Jen. Everyone should stay in the hotel once for the experience. It was built around 1880. Our Frontier Cabin was built almost a half-century later, sometime in the 1920s."

"Macduff, on the park map is a place on the lake called Grant Village. Is it quaint? Less formal than the Lake Hotel?"

"Grant's an embarrassment to the Park Service," Lucinda noted, opening a *National Geographic Yellowstone Country* edition of the magazine to a sordid description of Grant Village.

"It's an ugly complex with a beautiful lake view," I added. "A last resort, mostly filled with people who can't get a room anywhere else in the park. . . . Lucinda and I drove in once to look at it and drove right out. It even gets terrible opinions from park rangers. Listen to this from *National Geographic*, quoting a ranger: 'I regard it as an obscenity, the most obtrusive development on the lakeshore.'"

"The Lake Hotel sounds better with every word about Grant Village," Jen said. "Do we need to dress to eat at the hotel?"

"Compared to how most visitors to the park dress, yes. But not really *formal* dress. Just avoid short shorts—better avoid any shorts. And no T-shirts and the like. But you'll see some there."

"If I take the hotel room, will you two be my guests at dinner?"

"Accept," I responded immediately.

"Agreed," Lucinda added. "Maybe I should insist that I sit between you two."

"Probably a very good idea," I said, with Jen nodding and smiling.

We left our Mill Creek cabin two mornings later after feeding Wuff and leaving her with Mavis Benton, our loyal Mill Creek housekeeper who has her own priority list for protecting the household. The list begins equally with Wuff and Lucinda tied at the top and ends with me alone at the bottom. In between are the *Osprey,* our drift boat, and the house. But I *am* on the list. I may be dropped a place when she gets to know Jen.

I sat in the back of the Wrangler as the tour guide. Lucinda outlined the park tour rules which were truthfully *her* rules.

"Your role as tour guide, Macduff, includes *never* to criticize the driver about her driving."

"May I comment on the driver's record of receiving tickets for her driving?"

"Never."

"About her past cryptic verbal comments to park visitors who blocked the road to view animals a half-mile distant?"

"Never."

"Jen, this may be a very dull tour."

"Macduff, you can fill me in when she goes to the rest room, pumps gas, or checks in at the lodging."

"All of which Macduff will do himself, except the peeing part. And, Jen, when I head to the rest room, you have to follow. I don't want you two conspiring."

"Or eloping," I said, a comment I would pay for later.

"May *I* criticize your driving and take the wheel when I want?" Jen asked, looking at a surprised Lucinda.

"Yes, as long as when we fly on your jet to Jackson Hole next week, I can criticize *your* flying and takeover the jet."

"Macduff! How would you like to live in an historic house on the harbor at Hope Town? I promise never a word of criticism about *anything* you do will fall from my mouth."

"And food?"

"Burgers, fries, milkshakes, sausage, ice cream, and key lime pie daily."

"Sounds fair. I acc. . . ."

"Macduff," Lucinda interrupted, "you need to start guiding again. Specialize in only taking clients who are young Hispanics from El Salvador."

I shuddered and ignored her, looked at Jen and frowned, and continued my tour commentary.

Lucinda and I agree Yellowstone is the most astounding national park in the country. We hope everyone in the U.S. feels that way about one of the national parks. But we also agree that it's often overcrowded, given the number of free days granted liberally without regard to the thought of there being "too many." Maybe there's truth to Noel Coward's *Sail Away* song that starts with "Why do the wrong people travel, travel, travel, while the right people stay at home?"

"We are close to Gardiner, which is where the park begins," I said, passing the small roadside airport. It's where we took you earlier, Jen, when we flew your jet from Bozeman here to store it inside a hanger and closer to us at Mill Creek.

"Once through the center of Gardiner you can see the famous entry to the park called the Roosevelt Archway. Beyond the arch we will show our park entry passes, and then we're officially in the park. The road rises, following the Yellowstone River, and we soon enter the Mammoth Hot Springs Historic District."

"How is my guiding, my love?" I asked Lucinda, when she pulled off at the inspiring travertine terraces that extend up the hillside from Mammoth's center.

"I'll grade you when we get home tomorrow evening," Lucinda answered.

30

YELLOWSTONE NATIONAL PARK

I HAD PRAYED THAT THE ELEGANT FEATURES OF Yellowstone National Park, when combined with my brilliant, stimulating descriptions of park history, geological phenomena, flora and fauna diversity, all overlaid with subtle humor would suppress further threats—idle or otherwise—by Lucinda. I knew I had succeeded when she went into the restroom at the Norris Geyser Basin after my erudite commentary on the walk among the thermal features, and not only didn't insist that Jen accompany her but also after a brief tour of the small Norris museum, she handed me a large Almond Joy bar, my favorite.

Chocoholic? Yes. Nut freak? Yes. Combine them and you understand the use of "joy" in the name. Had Lucinda forgiven me for whatever she alone thought I had done? Was the candy forgiveness? If I asked, she would say "conquest."

We returned to the car and I opened and held her door while taking a bite of the candy. She nodded and flashed her "I won" smile.

"Where to next?" Jen asked when we reached where the Firehole and Gibbon rivers meet and become the Madison.

"Jen, next is Old Faithful. When we get there, we'll check for the time of the next eruption. They're about every hour. . . . But a few miles before we get there, we'll stop at a place called Fountain Flats and fish on the Firehole River."

"Will the Firehole be too warm," asked Lucinda, who fished there with me at least once or twice a season.

"It may be too warm from the summer's sunshine and scalding geyser water flowing into the river from the banks. If it is, we'll walk up along Little Firehole, where the Brown trout flee for cooler waters at this time of the year. We'll fish the cut banks."

"What's a cut bank?" Jen asked.

"These rivers sometimes have strong currents, especially during the spring runoff. The water, especially on the outside of bends, scours under the grass-covered banks, making what becomes the favorite hiding place of Brown trout."

"How do we get a fly inside the cave-like depression?"

"I'm not good enough to do an accurate sidearm cast or skip a hopper into where the trout are," Lucinda commented, "so I cast across the river and upstream, setting the fly down onto the grass bank. I gently pull the fly, often a grasshopper pattern, until it falls into the water at the edge of the bank. As it floats, it may get sucked under the edge and be attacked by a hungry Brown."

"I can't wait," Jen said. "Do we find a good place along the Little Firehole and keep tossing flies until we get some fish? Or run out of flies left hanging on bushes?"

"It's different here as you'll see. More open. Cast once and watch your fly float along the bank. If a Brown doesn't hit it soon after the fly lands, move on."

The Firehole proved to be too warm to expect much action, and we walked upstream along part of the Little Firehole. It might not have been a good day for catching trout, but we all had a chance to work on developing more accurate casting to an opposite bank.

"Disappointed?" I asked Jen as we got back in the Wrangler.

"Let's say I'd rather catch a fish than not. But qualify that by adding that catching or not isn't what makes a day to remember. . . . Being with friends on this twisting Firehole River, with geysers spitting smoke and hot spray, is the best way to spend the day here. As you both keep telling me, fly fishing is much about 'being there.' There are a lot of 'theres' I have yet to see. I need to start a long fly fishing bucket list."

Twenty minutes later we parked the Wrangler and walked to where Old Faithful was due to release another spectacle. Lucinda and I had traveled the road past this legendary geyser many times, and we haven't once failed to stop and been awed by one more eruption. We're always thankful that the park belongs to all of us and not the few who would develop and exploit it. Lucinda and I are adamant that there is no room for a McDonald's in the park. Or Burger King or Domino's or Starbucks or whatever quick eatery in forgetful and monotonous architecture can be found polluting the view entering most every town and city in America.

From Old Faithful, where we enjoyed lunch at the inn under wall and ceiling logs larger in girth than each of us, we soon drove twice across the Great or Continental Divide. The Old Faithful waters drain not behind us to the Pacific, but northward to exit the park near its northwest corner, and then flow nearly a hundred miles further north through Paradise Valley, turn east at Livingston, and merge with the Missouri, then the Mississippi, and finally spill into the Gulf of Mexico. For only a few minutes—in between the two Continental Divide crossings—we were in the Pacific watershed where waters flow through Lewis Lake and River, into the Snake and south. After passing through Jackson Hole, the waters turn west toward a Pacific Ocean destination. It's one of the wonders of the park.

"This Yellowstone Lake is huge," exclaimed Jen soon after we reached the junction at West Thumb and swung north to run the rim of the lake, turning to conclude our day at the Lake Hotel. We all agreed to unpack and enjoy an early dinner. Lucinda, as expected, ordered an organic beet and goat cheese salad, followed by Alaskan sockeye salmon. Jen more or less followed Lucinda's entrée with a poached pear salad and then, to show non-discrimination, she joined me having bison tenderloin. I omitted an entrée, saving room for and being the sole one to order dessert—a warm chocolate truffle torte with a molten middle—called the Yellowstone Caldera.

I thought I had ordered the desert, but the waitress—notice that it was not a *waiter*—placed the sole desert she brought to our table between my two companions, each of whom produced a large spoon and immediately devoured the torte. *My* torte. I called back the waitress, but by the time she returned with *my* spoon, the torte was gone.

"You two planned that! I'm ordering another."

I did and got up from the table as it arrived and took it and my spoon upstairs to a single, isolated easy chair by a window overlooking the lake. I don't remember enjoying it because I had to keep an eye on the two while I ate, and I ate too fast.

Lucinda waved me back to the table. I assumed it was to apologize, but when I sat down, she handed me the bill, which included two deserts.

The sun gave us a half-hour of light to enjoy a walk along the shore on the more rustic side of the lake complex, which includes the Lake Lodge Cafeteria where we planned to have breakfast, but not together.

While Lucinda was showering the next morning, I slipped out of our cabin behind the hotel and jogged to the lodge cafeteria. Sitting by myself at a window watching the sun rise, I consumed two scrambled eggs, six slices of bacon, three sausage links, home fries, and a biscuit.

Lucinda and Jen never showed up at the cafeteria. Jen invited Lucinda to have breakfast in the hotel dining room. Later that morning I heard them talking about their chilled cranberry juice and poached eggs on sautéed crab cake, along with rainforest dark roast coffee with organic vanilla almond milk. Ugh!

Back on the road we stopped for gas at Fishing Bridge and then walked across the bridge where the Yellowstone River flows north from the lake.

"Jen, if you tossed something that would float into the river here, in a few days it would pass the confluence where our Mill Creek enters the Yellowstone River."

"I don't think I believe you."

"And a month or more later, it would flow past New Orleans and into the Gulf of Mexico."

"Could we start here in your drift boat and end up around Thanksgiving at a dock at New Orleans and walk to Galatoires for breakfast?" she asked.

"You wouldn't make it. You'll see why in a half-hour."

Ten minutes later Jen learned firsthand that this part of the river would be too challenging for drift boats, which are not permitted on *any* water in the park. We passed the wild, tumbling LeHardy Rapids, where even bank fishing isn't permitted because of the danger of falling in. But soon after the rapids, the river widened, and in a few miles it was shallow and a wader could cross at appropriately named Buffalo Ford.

When we first met, Lucinda and I often fished at Buffalo Ford, part of which is now called Nez Perce Ford picnic area, but the introduction of Lake Trout into Yellowstone Lake two decades ago caused what some insist has been a ninety percent reduction of the Cutthroats in the river below Fishing Bridge. Few fly fishermen now fish Buffalo Ford, where dozens might have been seen two decades ago.

"Lucinda, pull over at the Sulphur Cauldron parking area. Let's see the fizzy, bubbling pool and then go down behind the pool to our former favorite fishing location."

We watched the fermenting muddy pool fizz and bubble, and then hanging on tree to tree, we carefully struggled down the steep slope behind the steaming pool to the edge of the river.

"Jen, before the Cutthroat numbers dropped, this was also a prime fishing location, partly because the river is down a steep bank behind the cauldron, discouraging people from climbing down. Also because it allowed fishing on the river immediately before the water flowed through Hayden Valley, which is a fishing prohibited area. Not all the fish remained in the valley. "

"Why is Hayden Valley closed.?"

163

"So as not to disturb wildlife on one of the park's favored habitats for bison, elk, grizzlies, coyotes, and smaller mammals. We'll soon drive through it."

The heavily forested area we had driven through since the lake ended and the landscape changed abruptly, opening to the broad plain of Hayden Valley, a favorite place for herds of bison to convene on the road.

Past the valley the landscape changed again, and the Grand Canyon of the Yellowstone began. We were awed watching the drama of the 100 foot drop Upper Falls and only a mile or so downstream the 300 foot drop of the Lower Falls.

Lower Falls put us at Canyon Junction, where we could choose to continue north on the main loop or turn west to cross the middle of the park and come out at Norris Junction, which we passed the previous day. I suggested the latter route, but only to within about a mile short of Norris where we turned off and doubled back to peaceful Virginia Meadows along the part of the Gibbon River that is only a few feet wide.

"This is breathtaking. And no one else is here," Jen whispered as we parked. "I hate to disturb the peace. How did you find this divine afterworld?"

"By accident, taking the one-way byway a few years ago and stopping here because it's where the Gibbon completes its winding run through Virginia Meadows. People come on this unexpectedly and don't realize it's the same Gibbon River that soon enters Gibbon Meadows and follows close to the road, then tumbles down and over Gibbon Falls on its way to the Lower Meadows to join the Firehole River and become the origin of the Madison River."

"What's special about *these* meadows?"

"For me the Gibbon River system is magical. Years ago, I caught a Brown on the Gibbon in the Lower Meadows not more than 200 feet from where it joins the Firehole. More than a decade later I came across Virginia Meadows and caught some Brook trout, not realizing that I was almost at opposite ends of the Gibbon. It comes out of Grebe Lake as a tiny stream that flows into Wolf Lake and then into Virginia Meadows.

"Before we have our picnic here, where the tiny Gibbon flows toward us across the meadows, we'll walk upstream east along the banks all the way—more or less a mile—to where the meadows begin. We'll turn around where the creek flows out of woods and feeds the meadow grass."

"What are we fishing for? The Gibbon here is at most only a dozen feet wide."

"Remember Passage Falls Creek?"

"That was about the same width, but in a dense forest rather than a meadow, and it had faster water than here."

"Same size fish, not more than seven to eight inches. They're as colorful as the adults. Some are Cutthroats, some Brookies. . . . I have special rods for you."

"A 7 foot bamboo?" Jen said, reading the label on the rod case.

"That's right. Seven feet because we don't need anything longer, such as the 9 footers we use when floating on the Yellowstone and other substantial rivers. The 7 foot rod usually helps to make short casts here. The bamboo isn't needed, and a modern graphite rod casts better. But this rod lets you cast with something historic; it was the favorite for decades before fiberglass, graphite, and modern tech took over."

"You're a traditionalist!"

"I try to be when it feels right."

"Are we using old flies along with the old rod?" Jen asked.

"We can. I have some with me I tied when I was a teen. The difference is now we use a lot of artificial materials."

"How about using sheltie fur?" Lucinda asked, "thinking about Wuff's long golden hair."

"Sometimes I'd like to. I looked at an old Herter's catalog I've saved from 1953. It looked like pictures from an endangered species book. Much of what Herter's lawfully sold in the 1950s couldn't be sold today."

"Such as?"

"Herter's listed for sale fly tying materials such as 'Imported Genuine Mandarin Duck Skins, Jungle Cock Necks, Sacred African Monkey Skins, and Siberian Red Fox fur'. . . . Times have changed! Is Wuff an endangered species? . . . I think she's nodding."

"I'm hungry, Macduff," Lucinda whined. "Let's get fishing and then have lunch."

"OK. OK. I've put a small #20 Adams on one rod, and I'm tying on a slightly larger #18 Yellow Humpy on the other. Take your pick, Jen."

"What would you use?"

"I don't give away fishing secrets."

"You do want to fly back to Florida in my jet, don't you?"

"Ms. French, bar owner and illustrious fly fisher, I would choose the Yellow Humpy because I want some color. It's a little overcast. Also, I think #18 will work better than #20. I would use easy, short roll casts even though it's all grass behind us. Try to drop each cast about four feet further upstream and especially look for deeper pockets."

"Macduff," interrupted Lucinda, "you don't give me this much detailed advice. You just hand me a rod and box of flies and say, 'I'll meet you in a half-hour. Good luck.'"

"You don't have a jet. . . . Furthermore, if I tell *you* everything about what *I'm* going to use, you'll copy me and catch more fish."

"You're so sweet."

"It's all luck, anyway."

"Not so sweet."

"Jen, Lucinda and I have fished this part of Virginia Meadows a couple of dozen times. The first time was when I was teaching her, and she must have caught more than both of us together on all the trips since. I guess it was a combination of beginner's luck, after incredibly skilled teaching, and—to be fair—one of those days when the fish will attack anything."

"I'll tell you the truth later when Macduff's not present," Lucinda called as she stopped on the trail and made her first cast.

Each made a dozen casts before landing a fish, first Lucinda and less than a minute later Jen. Probably a small school.

We didn't lose or change a fly over the next forty minutes as we continued upstream across the meadow. Jen and Lucinda stopped counting after the first half-dozen. Nearly all the trout were found in small groups at two-foot depth pools.

At the end of the meadow the two fisherladies, who were fifty feet ahead of me, began to walk back toward me.

"Have you two quit?" I asked.

"This may be a light rod. We're using tiny flies and catching nothing more than seven-inch trout. But I'm exhausted," claimed Lucinda."

"Me, too," added Jen.

"And I'm still hungry," whined Lucinda.

"Me, too," added Jen.

167

"OK," I said. "We'll eat and get on to the next park attraction. We're having a late lunch, and we have only about four hours of light left."

We retraced the short drive to Canyon Junction and turned north.

"If the wild LeHardy Rapids didn't persuade you, did the Upper and Lower Falls this morning convince you that a drift boat trip on the Yellowstone River is out?" I asked Jen as Canyon Junction disappeared in the rear-view mirror.

"Can it get any more dramatic than the two falls," Jen replied, "or more pastoral than Hayden Valley and Virginia Meadows?"

"From here to where it finally vacates the park into Paradise Valley, there's a lot of rough river. We won't see much more of the river until we're all the way back to the park entrance at Gardiner. Then, with the exception of Yankee Jim Canyon—a brief white water stretch a little north of Gardiner—the river meanders more or less passively through Paradise Valley—with water added by our Mill Creek. It turns east at Livingston, and flows beyond Billings to join the Missouri and later the Mississippi, which, in theory, takes us the rest of the way to New Orleans and Galatoires. If we arrive at the latter after 5 p.m., inside the front door is a rack of blazers for me to meet their dress code."

"Is there a dress code for us?" asked Lucinda.

"Of course—dress, stockings, jewelry, and pumps."

"Are they inside the front door like the blazers?"

"Scratch Galatoires. And I was dreaming of having *pompano en papillote.*"

"Nowhere on the entire Yellowstone River is there a dam," I lectured, resuming my role as tour guide. "That includes the portion we didn't see from its high mountain Teton Wilderness origin to entering Yellowstone Lake. I mean the kind of dam we usually envision—like Hoover or Aswan—not what exists on the Yellowstone, a half-dozen three- to eight-foot tall diversion dams that turn the Yellowstone River into what more properly should be called the Yellowstone Diversion Ditch. River water is redirected for agriculture at the expense of what must be millions of native fish."

Another half-hour took us over Dunraven Pass and north of the 10,000+ foot Mount Washburn. Dropping back down, we were treated to a priceless view entering the Serengeti-like Lamar Valley, the best location to view the park's elusive wolf packs.

At the bottom of the incline, we joined the east entrance road from Cooke City, wound west back to Mammoth, and again passed under the arch at Gardiner. We were at our Mill Creek cabin as the sun disappeared behind the peaks of the Gallatin Mountains.

"Good two days?" Lucinda asked Jen.

"Yellowstone is the most beautiful place I've ever been. Like so many other such beautiful places, developers must drool at the thought of money they could make if our federal Congress passed legislation to give control of the park to Montana and Wyoming."

"In our lifetime, no. But in the next generation—meaning my daughter Elsbeth's—states' and D.C.'s greed may rule."

"Let's not ruin two wonderful two days talking about greed," Jen said, thankful to part company with a massive logjam of free-day park visitors leaving through Gardiner.

31

THE MILL CREEK CABIN

"MACDUFF, I'VE BEEN TRYING FOR TWO DAYS to get through to you," the voice of John Kirby claimed. "So you still have a cell phone after all?"

"I block crank calls. Sorry. My phone must have made a mistake. John Kirby shouldn't be on my block list. You know I wouldn't do that. Anyway, Lucinda and a friend and I made a two-day great-loop tour of Yellowstone. Including some fishing."

"Did Lucinda skunk you again?"

"I didn't keep track of numbers. That's what some guides I know do."

"Macduff, years ago before you finally married Lucinda, you told me women were better at fly fishing than men. Now that Lucinda has proven that to be true, you seem to do everything you can to downplay the fact that in addition to looking infinitely preferable, she casts better, concentrates on the floating fly better, sets the hook better, plays the fish better, and after netting, gets it back into the water quicker, and . . . what else is there?"

"I'm pretty good at rowing our drift boat *Osprey*."

"I admit you're OK. But when you're rowing, wouldn't you rather be fishing?"

"Of course."

"How much rowing does Lucinda do?" John asked.

"Almost none. She fishes."

"So, you're really not a fly fisherman, but a rower of fly fishermen?"

"And fisherwomen."

"If I rank Lucinda as the best fly fisher but you as the best rower, no further complaints?"

"I'll have to think about that."

"Have you thought any more about the four murders or attempts that involved guides?" John asked.

"Of course," I replied.

"You know I've stopped guiding. Or at least deferred it until after these murders have been dealt with."

"I know," I responded. "And I agree with you. I've canceled all my bookings where I don't personally know the client."

"I'm worried about young guides who don't have many past clients yet," John expressed.

"I worry about them, too. They're the future of our profession. . . . What do you think?"

"Do you and Lucinda have any plans for the next few weeks that include Jackson Hole. Sarah and I miss you."

"Not scheduled, but we'd like to bring a friend down. You know that in a few weeks we'll be heading east for the winter."

"Back to Florida?"

"Maybe not."

"Where?"

"Hope Town, Bahamas."

"Who do you know in Hope Town?"

"Candi Treat, a bombshell blond."

"Macduff, is Lucinda listening in on this call?"

"She's off."

"Where?"

"Shopping."

"Alone?"

"No."

"With who?"

"Candi Treat! The bombshell blond bar waitress."

"Now I'm very confused."

"Would you like to meet Candi Treat?" I asked.

"I don't want her name mentioned in my house."

"What is your image of her?"

"You know."

"Blond hair?"

"Yes. You've already told me that."

"Long?"

"Medium but full."

"Figure?"

"I don't want that on record."

"Intelligence level."

"Cellar dweller."

"Education?"

"Enjoyed school so much she repeated several grades."

"Skills?"

"Do I have to answer with a name like Candi Treat? With that name she's no astronaut."

"Would jet pilot be OK? Graduate of Wellesley College? Successful businesswoman?"

"Getting better. If I believed you."

"Candi owns and flies a Cessna Citation. She flew us here from the Bahamas."

"Did you say she's a *waitress?*"

"She owns a place at Hope Town called Captain Candi's Bar. It's very popular. She's loved by her employees."

"And you've convinced Lucinda you have to help her out financially?"

"I estimate her personal net wealth at something around $400 million."

"From Powerball?"

"No. From what I call her power mind. She benefits from people—like you—who assume she's just another dumb blond. She does have some help. And some luck."

"Can you come here tomorrow?"

"We'll leave late in the morning. Candi, whose real name is Jennifer French, would like to be called Jen and is excited about flying over the Grand Tetons. Let's plan on a 4 p.m. arrival at the Jackson airport."

"I don't believe there really is a Candi Treat. Have you been drinking?"

"Only pulp free orange juice with my eggs and sausage."

32

JACKSON HOLE

LUCINDA AND I HAVE FLOWN INTO JACKSON ON commercial airlines numerous times over the years and, because of prevailing winds, usually have landed north to south, making the window on the right the place to be. The runway parallels the Grand Teton range, and the view is breathtaking.

This trip into Jackson Hole on a private plane was a first for us; we were comfortably settled on Jen's Citation jet. We didn't miss the thrills of commercial flying—abominable offerings alleged to be food that would be rejected at a homeless shelter, restrooms that staff somehow ignore and leave to be cleaned between flights, late arrivals, changed or canceled seats, and disappearing baggage.

Lucinda rode in the right front seat of the jet, and she worried she might accidently hit one of the duplicate controls and send us plummeting downward.

We had hoped to fly lower, but obeyed the rules limiting us to at least 2,000 feet above ground level when over either Yellowstone or Grand Teton National Park, meaning that the best view of Grand Teton was on our final approach until we touched down.

Ours wasn't the only private jet at the Jackson general aviation building; at least twenty others were parked on the ramp. Jackson Hole, according to one poll, is third in the world for private plane landings, behind airports in Scotland and London. I'd always thought Teterboro, New Jersey, a dozen miles from Manhattan, was the most active, but the only top ten list it has made was for the number of bird collisions annually caused, in part, by pilots anxious to get away from Manhattan.

The busy summer season was not quite over, and we couldn't get reservations for our favorite—Dornan's Spur Cabins at Moose. We did get two rooms at the Rustic Inn in town and called John from our rental SUV as soon as we left the airport.

"Where are you?" John asked when he picked up the phone. "Hope Town, St. Augustine, Mill Creek, Manhattan, D.C., or none of the above. I hope it's the last—none of the above—and that you're really here in Jackson Hole."

"We have a rental car and are driving alongside the Elk Refuge. We'll be at the Rustic Inn in five minutes. What are your plans?"

"Sarah's with a patient at the hospital. I'm at home. Can we meet for lunch?"

"At Sweetwater?"

"See you there. Noon. Is Candi with you?"

"Yes. I knew you'd ask. And as I said, she prefers to be called Jen."

"Candi is fine," Jen said from the back seat, "unless Sarah's around."

Sweetwater is three decades old and a favorite. We parked a block off the square and walked another block to the restaurant.

"I've only been in Jackson Hole for an hour, and I'm in love with it," Jen said, as we crossed the town square adorned with its famous elk antler arches.

"Too many people who come here feel that way," Lucinda commented. "They want to live here, but real estate prices are out of sight. Per capita, Teton County is the wealthiest in the country. Half a million won't touch a house, but it might buy you a small condo."

"Maybe I should buy a house," Jen mused. "I can afford it."

"Do it. One on the Snake. With a separate guest cabin facing the river and mountains that only Lucinda and I have keys for."

"I'll sleep on it," she replied, as we walked into the Sweet-water where John was waiting.

"You must be Candi," John said with an approving grin. "Welcome to Jackson."

"I must be Candi since I'm the only person you don't already know here."

"Is Macduff training you to say things like that?"

"I hoped it didn't show. I'm really nice."

"Have Lucinda and Macduff told you about the guide murders here and in Idaho?" John asked Jen after we were seated and ordered. "And the attempt on the Yellowstone River that failed?"

"I think they've told me everything they know. We're anxious to hear what you know and your views about how to deal with it."

"You know I've stopped essentially all of my scheduled float trips. So have dozens of other guides here. From what I read, the cancellations decrease the farther you go from these three places where the incidents occurred."

"You mean some guides *are* canceling trips in Colorado and New Mexico and Utah?" I asked.

"Yes. And add California, Oregon, Alaska, New York, and as far as Maine. I could go on. Float numbers are down all over the country. Especially if *Calle Rojo* is believed to be present in the area."

"Who's hurt most? Guides and outfitter shops?"

"And don't forget good, honest people who want to schedule a float but don't personally know a guide. Especially if those people are Hispanic. And young."

"I know what you're saying," interrupted Lucinda. "If you're between 16 and 35, have a Hispanic name, and especially are from El Salvador, you will find it essentially impossible to engage a drift boat in the U.S. If there is any evidence that you entered the U.S. illegally, went first to Los Angeles, or were ever associated with a youth gang, your chances have dropped from poor to none."

"What if you're a young Hispanic from El Salvador by way of L.A. and you lie and say you entered legally from Costa Rica to Miami, have never been to L.A. or been in a gang, and your name is Ricardo Prentice Gonzalez because your father was Costa Rican and your mother was a Peace Corp member in San Jose when she met your father?"

"Regrettably," admitted John, "I would feel uncertain about guiding that person. But why take a chance? *Don't ever publically say you will not take young Hispanics fishing; find a different excuse.*"

"What about asking anyone who is suspect to prove his or her citizenship, status in the U.S., address, and length of time in Jackson?"

"What does being 'suspect' mean?" asked Jen. "As a guide or outfitter, would you want to have to check the authenticity of immigration documents?"

"And ask 'Are you Hispanic? Are you from Salvador or Honduras or maybe Guatemala? Are you a member of any gang?' We've come full circle. The answer is don't ask the most important questions but ask enough to know the answers to those questions."

"Can we move on to something more pleasant?" pleaded Lucinda. "I'm getting indigestion at one of the best restaurants in town."

"John, when are you taking the two of us in your drift boat on the Snake?" asked Jen.

"As soon as I learn if either of you is a member of a youth gang, especially *Calle Rojo*. Or if you're Hispanic. Or if you entered the U.S. illegally.

"Even if you came from the Bahamas."

33

DRIFT ON THE SNAKE

WE WERE THE ONLY DRIFT BOAT LAUNCHING at Pacific Creek on the Snake River when we arrived at a little after eight the next morning. Pacific Creek is the usual beginning point for a drift south to the takeout at Deadman's Bar. In turn, Deadman's Bar serves as the launching point for a drift further south to Moose.

These two more or less nine-mile floats are the crème of the Jackson Hole floats. They provide both a spectacular view of the Grand Tetons and a full-day float of terrific fishing.

There is another float that has equally attractive Grand Teton mountain views from a different angle—more north—but the float is quite short—about four and a half miles—in distance and duration. It begins at Jackson Dam as the Snake River resumes its journey from Jackson Lake to the Pacific and ends at Pacific Creek. It's often the only float on the Wyoming portion of the Snake that has clear water during the spring snow melt run off.

Where Pacific Creek joins the Snake, where we were putting in for our float, the flow of high, rapid, silt-tinted coffee-colored water means drift boat fishing essentially ceases. Sometimes that discoloration lasts well into July, reducing the length of the season to the dismay of guides who rely on an already short summer season to make their living. But fish have to eat even when the water is cloudy. The trick is to make your fly visible to the fish.

John met us at the Pacific Creek launch.

"Who's going with me in the boat? I know one is Jen. Are you coming with us, Lucinda?"

"Maybe. I want to take photos of the boat on the river."

"I could use it for advertising," John commented. "Especially if Jen or Lucinda is in the photo in the bow seat. So I assume Macduff stays on shore."

"John," I asked, "if you do a drift with a couple of guys who each weigh least 250, that would mean 500 pounds of clients. Right?"

"Yes, that's why it's great to have two 100-pound ladies. Add to that the fact they are both gorgeous, and I have an easy row with a great view all day."

"That's not where I was going. You've floated with two who together total 500 pounds. You've admitted that."

"And?"

"Lucinda, Jen, and I total only 400 pounds."

"And that means four in a boat designed for three with *only* three single seats. Do you plan to stand? My boat has no straps to hold on to like a subway."

"Let Lucinda and I sit in the stern. I fish, and she sits on the floor, taking photos of you rowing and Jen fishing. How's that for good advertising."

"Macduff, you know I've never taken four in a drift boat. Have you ever seen more in another boat?"

"Yes, once when you and I were fishing on this river a little above Moose, where Cottonwood Creek enters the Snake. Remember?"

"Don't remind me. That boat had six people. But remember, it crashed against a pile of trees in the middle of the river and they all ended up in the water, while the boat was breaking apart."

"I'm not suggesting *six* people."

"OK. You win. But if along the way I decide four is too many, you agree to get out and walk the rest of the way."

"That would be a terrible thing to do—leave me on the bank with no way out other than to stumble along the edge of river."

"I recall you making a client named Parker Salisbury walk out several miles in much the same way."

"He deserved it. We floated the Deadman's Bar to Moose section in my wooden drift boat, *Osprey*, and stopped on a gravel bar to fish. I told him no keeping or killing the trout, but as soon as he caught one, he pounded it to death. His wife Kath was furious with him, and she went on the remainder of the float with me. He walked."

"He didn't take that well, did he?"

"Months later he killed Kath and her new husband in Maine and then came after me. He came on *Osprey* again, wearing a clever disguise. Partway through the float, he pulled out a gun and shot Wuff and Lucinda and me before we shot and killed him."

"We!" said Lucinda. "I shot him. You couldn't find your gun."

"That wasn't the first death on your *Osprey*. Tell Jen about Ambassador Anders Eckstrum," John suggested.

"It's not a good story. Anders was a friend. I took him and his high-school-age daughter fishing on the Pacific Creek to

181

Deadman's Bar float. We were almost finished when someone from shore with a high-powered rifle shot and killed Eckstrum."

"Did you learn who shot him?"

"After Park Salisbury shot us some months later and was himself killed on *Osprey*, the police concluded that Eckstrum had been shot by mistake by Salisbury. I had loaned him my hat. The assumption included that Eckstrum's killer wanted me."

"Your boat is dangerous," exclaimed Jen. "I'm glad were going on John's boat."

"All this has nothing to do with today's float," I responded, showing some irritation.

"Let me end this," interjected Lucinda. "Macduff, how many people have been shot and/or killed on John's boat? The one right here that we're going to use."

"Ask him, but he'll tell you that no violence has ever occurred on his boat. I have to agree."

"John," Lucinda asked, "how many people have been killed on Macduff's *Osprey*?"

"The two we've been talking about, Eckstrum and Salisbury. But the question you should ask is how many were shot on or around boats Macduff has owned or borrowed for floats?"

"I sense you can't wait to tell us," said Jen. "Tell me the whole tragedy—I mean story. How many dead bodies?"

John smiled and began his version of the saga.

"There were the three Shuttle Gals murders in Montana when on three different floats on the Yellowstone River the dead body of one of the women was mutilated and strapped on Macduff's trailer to be found at the end of a float.

"A couple of years later, Macduff was involved—at least indirectly—in five deaths on drift boats caused by plastic explosives wrapped across the rower's chest. They occurred at precise intervals—on a solstice or an equinox—on five different rivers here in Wyoming as well as in Montana and Idaho.

"That's only the beginning. Half a decade later Macduff's daughter, Elsbeth, and two of her friends, Sue and Liz, were fishing on the Gallatin using a borrowed pontoon boat to transport them from place to place where they got out to fish. On that section fishing is not permitted from a boat. When they continued, they narrowly missed running into barbed wire strung across the river. Hanging from the wire was a body of a floater who was less fortunate and had not ducked beneath the wire.

"Days later there was a near duplicate repeat of a body found on barbed wire in another location on the Gallatin close by the first. That time Elsbeth was fishing with her dad and with me. I had driven up from here in Jackson to stay at Mill Creek for a few days with the Brookses.

"Another murder happened close to the first two on the same Gallatin. Grace Justice—a dear friend from St. Augustine—was with Macduff, and she was ensnared in the barbed wire and died. Macduff went ashore and called 911 but was shot and severely wounded by a man who for reasons we won't go into, had killed his wife at Jenny Lake a few days before and was determined to murder Macduff.

"Unfortunately, it was Grace Justice who was sitting in the front of the pontoon boat, not Macduff. I should mention that the gunman, within minutes of shooting Macduff, was eradicated by multiple shots from Elsbeth and her friend Sue, who fortuitously arrived as all this occurred."

John sat smiling and pleased with his presentation. I remained silent, looking out at the scenery. I wasn't smiling.

"Shall I continue?" John asked, intending to do so regardless of the answer. But a quick answer came as a resounding yes from Jen and Lucinda.

"About a year later three murders of guides took place, all found with black flies hanging around their necks. All were prestigious Master Casting Instructors—we call them MCIs. One was killed fishing the creek in Cascade Canyon, a wading trip Macduff was first scheduled to guide. He was replaced because something he had to attend to created a conflict. Within weeks, two more died, one on Mill Creek only a couple of miles from Macduff's cabin.

"The second of the three murders was unusual. Not because the victim was a female fly fishing guide, but because the killing occurred in Crystal River, *Florida*, at a fly fishing conference Macduff attended and indeed spent several hours having a casting lesson and talking with the victim over drinks and dinner a few hours before she was killed."

"It's unfair to include these three black fly deaths," I pleaded. "I had been the guide scheduled to take the first victim wade fishing, but I didn't and at the time of death was hundreds of miles away with Lucinda on our annual drive across country to Florida. The woman who was killed in Florida had given me some pointers about several complex casts; in appreciation I bought her dinner. We went our ways to our *separate* rooms, and I left for Gainesville early in the morning. She was killed during the night.

"The third killing was on Mill Creek, at a camp site about four miles upstream from our cabin. I had been with Lucinda all day."

"And all night, I must admit," she added, smiling.

"Granted that the death of the two men was confirmed to have been done by another person, but the death in Florida was never solved," John explained.

"Are we through?" I asked.

"The killing of the MCI in Florida reminded me that there were several deaths in Florida and Cuba that involved Macduff. Do you want me to tell you about them?" John asked.

"Of course," Jen said.

Jen's expression showed disbelief and questioned whether I could have been involved in such horrible murders. Or gotten away with so many.

"I'll do this part quickly," John promised, noticing my frown. "Three guides were found dead wrapped in gill nets in Florida. One in the Southwest part of Pine Island Sound near Sanibel. Another in the Panhandle off the coast outside Apalachicola. It's the third that brought Macduff into the investigations: the charred body of a man wrapped in a gill net was found on Macduff's burned flats boat at the dock by his St. Augustine cottage.

"Not long after the gill net murders, Macduff was asked to investigate the disappearance of a U.S. Senator at a small settlement on the south coast of Cuba, arguably the best fly fishing on the whole island. Macduff fished for one day. Remains of both his guide and the senator were found in a barracuda pen at a nearby marine research center.

"Finally, two murders occurred in Florida on airboats. The victims were tied to the propeller and literally spun to death. One was in Southwest Florida. The other occurred within a mile of Macduff's cottage in St. Augustine."

"And now there have been three murders on drift boats of guides working here in the Mountain West," Jen observed. "But when those occurred Macduff and Lucinda were either in St. Augustine or with me in Hope Town. . . . Macduff, do you have defenses for what John has so eloquently and dramatically related?"

"Defenses as good as my answer to Lucinda's insistence that I proposed to her?"

"Oh!" exclaimed Jen. "That is something I haven't heard about. Tell me."

"Don't say a word, Macduff," Lucinda said, forcefully scowling at me. "Jen, I'll show you the marriage papers. He always tries to worm out of something he promised and then discovers he can't handle."

"This sounds interesting, but let's save it for another story telling session."

"That's a good idea," John said. "We're only half-way to Deadman's Bar, where we end our float."

"And, Jen," added Lucinda, "look off east to your left. On the shore is where the first murder occurred when Park Salisbury thought he was shooting Macduff but killed Ander Eckstrum."

"Just imagine how many stories I wouldn't be able to tell if Salisbury had been a better shot!" Lucinda exclaimed.

34

AT THE DEADMAN'S BAR TAKEOUT

LUCINDA AND JEN SHIFTED OUR GEAR FROM John's drift boat to the Wrangler. John's cell phone rang, and he walked over behind the restrooms to answer in private.

"John, this is Huntly Byng at the Sheriff's Office. Are you alone?"

"I'm at Deadman's Bar. I just finished a float. No one is close to me. Go ahead."

"I hope the float wasn't with a *Calle Rojo* member."

"I had three other people in my boat, against my better judgment. Lucinda and Macduff and a lady you haven't met. Her name is Jen ... I mean Candi Treat. Blond. Beautiful. Bright. Available."

"My wife Susan's here with me listening in."

"She may be available, but *he* isn't," called Susan, apparently from across Huntly's office.

"Candi Treat is my stage name," Jen quickly responded, heading for the woman's rest room and overhearing John and Huntly. "My real name's Jennifer French. John's trying to stir things up. Ignore him. I'm a friend of Lucinda's and Macduff's."

"Huntly, I'm giving the phone to Macduff; my boat's blocking some others," John said.

"I heard the name *Calle Rojo*? Did you solve the murders?" I asked.

"Much worse," Byng commented, "I hope all of you are listening. This morning I received an Associated Press bulletin about a murder of a person, Whitney Stein, on a drift boat on the Delaware River. I've since gotten some more information."

"*Calle Rojo?*" I asked.

"Apparently. *Calle Rojo's* big in Wilmington."

"Guide?"

"Stein was a prominent fly fishing guide, recently highlighted in the newspapers for work with Wounded Warriors."

"Machete?"

"Yes. Mirror image of the killings here in the West."

"*CR* in blood scribbled on the boat's inside?"

"*Big red letters,*" Byng exclaimed.

"Any differences from the killings out here?" I inquired.

"Yes. One. The killer was caught after he murdered the guide. A couple of Wilmington police by chance were fishing from another boat around a bend, and they heard a scream. Before they could react, Stein's boat came around the bend and rammed the boat with the police. The guide, Stein, was bloody and dead on the bottom of the boat. The young killer was rowing toward shore, but the current had carried the boat around the bend. He threw a long knife into the water which proved to be a machete. The water was shallow, and the police retrieved it."

"Has the killer been identified?"

"Yes. Rodolfo Arena. He was scared to death and has been talking his head off."

"What do they know about him?"

"From El Salvador. Seventeen years old. Entered the U.S. illegally into Arizona paying a coyote. Hitchhiked to L.A. Did a little yardwork. He was caught trying to rob a convenience store. A sympathetic judge said it was Arena's first crime, ignoring the record obtained from the U.S. embassy in El Salvador of Arena's history of crime after crime as a juvenile. When he left Salvador, he was wanted for murder of a policeman in Soyapango, which I've never heard of but apparently is the second largest city in that country. Not clear how he got to Wilmington or why he chose Delaware."

"You said he talked," John noted.

"Did he ever! He was barely in handcuffs when he started blaming a Pedro Revuelta for making him kill Stein."

"Was this Revuelta part of the Wilmington *Calle Rojo*?"

"Yes. Arena was required to call Revuelta *Jefe*. He gave the order to Arena, told him the details of how to go about it, and gave him a machete."

"What were the instructions?"

"What Stein looked like, his contact info, and money to hire him—Arena was to tell Stein he always wanted to fly fish and his grandparents gave him the float as a birthday gift."

"How did he explain to Stein how he got to Wilmington?"

"He lied, saying he was able to come to live with his grandparents because his parents died in the violence in Salvador and he was a minor without other relatives."

"Any idea why Stein accepted him as a client?"

"Stein would have to answer that, if he were alive. . . . The head of guiding at the shop where Stein worked told the police that the outfitter had a policy of absolute non-discrimination. Apparently, if Stein wanted work, he took clients who were assigned to him."

"I'm overwhelmed, Huntly. One question. You made no mention about one of Stein's hands being cut off, the way it was in the three murders here."

"It wasn't cut off. Arena killed Stein and panicked. The local police said Stein's right hand was hanging by a ligament."

"Anything more you can tell us?" John asked.

"The *Jefe*, Revuelta, who gave Arena his instructions, told him that he should be honored to be doing this killing, that it was the first of a planned series in *Calle Rojo* chapters all over the U.S., to show solidarity of all the chapters and make *Calle Rojo* known everywhere."

"How many chapters of *Calle Rojo* are in the U.S.?"

"Thirty-seven that we know about. It's the fastest growing youth gang in the U.S."

"Why do you suppose that is?"

"U.S. immigration policy toward young people is soft. Including those with criminal histories."

35

JACKSON HOLE WAREHOUSE

FIFTY YOUNG MALES STOOD AROUND THE MAIN
warehouse room in small groups. Their conversations were
loud and embellished by much gesturing. Most were dressed in
long or short pants that badly needed a visit to the laundry. In
many cases the pants were frayed or torn. All wore old sneaks or
sandals; none wore socks. T-shirts or tank tops were the overwhelming choice. Several of them had removed their shirts to
show *Calle Rojo* tattooed across their chests.

Some had shaved their heads; a few had long hair that was
in most cases uncombed. The odor the group brought to the
room confirmed their lack of attention to periodic bathing.

A side door opened and in walked a different appearing man
who was not as young as most of the group. The youths parted
to allow the new arrival to pass to the table at the front, where
there was a single chair that leaned against the table to show oc-
cupancy.

The single man wore cuffed, pressed khaki trousers, held up
by a leather belt with a Western motif buckle. His short-sleeved
shirt had muted gold stripes. It was the only shirt in the room
that had a collar. On his feet were new Nike sneaks.

If the youths in the room saw the person in town and were asked who he was, most would answer with a look of surprise and exclaim "That's *Jefe.*" But, they rarely if ever saw him except for the occasional meetings in this room. When they heard him call out "Take your seats," they responded immediately.

Jefe didn't speak immediately. He looked around the room at each person until the person looked away. When he finished, he waited another minute or two and only then began to speak to an increasingly nervous group.

"Our recent planned appointment here in Jackson of a candidate as a member of *Calle Rojo* failed. Failed because he was weak. Being weak, he could not carry out the order I gave him. I have learned that, as the day progressed on the drift boat floating the Yellowstone River, he was increasingly doubtful of his mission and lost his determination to kill his assigned target. He weakened during his day on the Yellowstone River and gave the guide the opportunity to fight back, using a pistol to kill our candidate. He brought shame upon himself and upon us. I won't even say his name.

"Even more recently there was another failure, this time at our brother chapter in Wilmington, Delaware. But that was worse. The candidate became scared and decided not to carry out his assignment. Worse, he survived and willingly told everything he knew about the *Calle Rojo* and what he was instructed to do.

"We will not let those experiences delay or discourage us at this chapter. For those of you who are candidates for membership but have not yet received your assignment, are you ready to do as ordered?"

There was an immediate and overwhelmingly positive loud vocal response.

"Are all of you ready to kill?"

Again, the response was unanimous and even louder.

"When you are a candidate, are you ready to return to this group with the right hand of your victim and be inducted?"

Not one person in the group failed to raise his fist and scream some form of agreement.

"An assignment will be made to be carried out this week. But first we need to adopt measures that will assure us of success."

Heads turned from one to the other and nodded assent.

"We are going to follow practices that will not cause our chosen victims to reject our candidate. With each of the past initiations, it became increasingly easier for the guide to refuse our candidate as a client. Questioning may have disclosed our intentions.

"Each of our candidates will disguise himself as a refined young man who, although he admits and shows his Hispanic character because of his accent, also shows why his rejection would be a racist act against all Hispanics.

"Here are the changes we have adopted. To show them to you, our next candidate, Antonio Salazar, will demonstrate how future candidates will appear and act when with their guide."

Antonio Salazar was listening outside the door behind *Jefe's* desk. He walked in to the applause and whistles of the group. He did not look anything like anyone in the group.

Salazar was wearing a pale-blue light-weight long sleeved shirt with "L.L.BEAN" embroidered above the breast pocket. He had a clean pair of khaki colored cargo pants with large pockets, held up by a belt embellished with dozens of images of tiny rainbow trout. On his feet he wore black sports socks and a pair of gray and black ankle-height hiking shoes. On this cool evening he was carrying a light-weight Patagonia fleece jacket.

But it was not only his dress that changed his appearance. Salazar's hair was moderately short and neat around his ears. He was clean shaven. In all ways he appeared to look like a conservative Jackson Hole multimillionaire couple's son—like he was an Eagle Scout and a private school student-athlete.

"Antonio is our next candidate for membership. He was prepped the past few days about how to act when he books a float trip tomorrow for this weekend anywhere on the Snake, which will be close to the end of the season, and how he will act on the drift boat until it is time to strike.

"He will play the role of the son of a wealthy family that lives in Mexico City and has recently bought a vacation home on the golf course at Teton Pines Country Club. Antonio has been told to speak politely and only when spoken to. If his guide is considerably older, he will say 'yes sir' and 'no sir.' He will apologize profusely for his poor English and say he is working on improving so he will be fluent in both languages.

"He will tell the guide that he has a steady girlfriend in Mexico City a year older who has begun to study law at the elite Escuela Libre de Derecho and has encouraged him to do the same next year and upon completion to return to the United States and study for another year to receive a coveted LL.M. He will say they both want to practice law and live in Mexico City.

"For the float, alongside Antonio's right lower leg will be strapped a small version of the standard machete. After killing the guide, he will use it to cut off the body's right hand. The machete will be disposed of in the river, and Antonio will write the letters *CR* in the guide's blood on the side of the boat's hull.

"Antonio is our first candidate being carefully prepared to face guides who might be reluctant to accept *any* Hispanics. They will no longer be dealing with how we routinely look and act. We are assuming that the guides and outfitters are not anti *all* Hispanics, but anti the kind of Hispanic we reflect by our appearance and manner.

"If any one of our candidates is rejected by the outfitter or guide, our lawyer will immediately file civil charges of discrimination and press the local state attorney to initiate a criminal action," *Jefe* concluded.

"Are you ready to face your guide, Antonio?"

"I am. . . *sir*," Salazar answered with a smile that a grinning *Jefe* returned.

36

THAT EVENING AT JACKSON HOLE

JEN, LUCINDA, JOHN, AND I SAT ON JEN'S CABIN porch at the Rustin Inn talking and watching Flat Creek flow in nature's curves through the manicured grounds. Walking the edge of the creek were two Canadian geese challenging each other. Their screams were enough to disrupt our conversation.

"Long day, John?" Lucinda asked. "You look tired."

"Rowing all three of you for seven hours was a *killer.*"

"Don't say that," said Jen. "In this town it could come true."

"John," added Lucinda, "go on home. Sarah should be waiting for you to have dinner. She'll tend to your wounds."

"It will be leftovers tonight. But I agree; I need to go. I need Sarah's loving touch. Never again will I take three guests on a float. *Never.* I should have known better. I do not have the strong back and shoulders of a thirty-year-old."

"We were easy. No arguments. A few lost flies. Big tip," I recounted.

"Big tip! You bought me a beer at Dornan's."

"A full pint. *And* draft. *And* imported. *Plus,* I left the bartender a dollar. I shouldn't have bought you that; you're driving."

"I forget you're a Scot."

"It's why Scotland has no debt. Well, not much. . . .You should be happy, John; you still have your right hand. The three of us could have overpowered you."

"Was it a good day on the Snake for you three?" John asked, knowing the tip issue was closed and not wanting to discuss the *Calle Rojo* murders. But he couldn't help again thinking that there were not many boats on the Pacific Creek to Deadman's Bar section today. Were guides that scared?

"Days on the Snake floating are always good with you," praised Lucinda, "and it's special when we float down to Deadman's Bar alongside the Grand Tetons."

"Macduff," asked Jen, "was our takeout named Deadman's Bar after your days with Eckstrum and Salisbury?"

"Don't even think of that," I replied. "It's a very old name."

"I'm leaving," John said getting up. "Tell them about Deadman's Bar, Macduff. You're a guide; you should know about it."

"Go home. I do know about it. In 1886," I began, "one of four mining partners, John Tonnar, allegedly killed the other three, two by axe blows to the head, the other by shooting. It may have actually happened not where the drift boat takeout is, but across the river and somewhere upstream. . . . Tonnar was tried for the murders—and acquitted—and the legend began.

"*My* involvement more recently on that section amounted to only two deaths. Eckstrum was shot by Salisbury, and Salisbury was later shot by someone on my boat."

"Macduff," Lucinda exclaimed, "*I* shot Salisbury several times and killed him. He shot me, you, and Wuff before I killed him. When I shot him, you were still trying to find your gun. I agree you finally got off a shot, which probably hit some passing raptor. I was taken to the hospital in a coma, Wuff had a leg wound and still limps, and you were in the outpatient room for a few hours dreaming up stories about being a hero."

"I helped you out of the coma and after more than a year cured your amnesia."

"And to reward you, I promised to marry you. I felt sorry for you."

"I wish I could write fiction. I'd use your versions of our experiences over what seems like a lifetime, and I'd make a fortune."

"You married a fortune. Don't complain," Lucinda replied.

"I'm glad you don't go with me when I'm guiding. You'd correct all the exciting stories I tell my clients."

"They should be called wild tales or, better yet, memory-challenged fibs."

"All three of us are staying here," I noted. "I'm bushed from fishing. I'm going to leave you two to do what you wish this evening. Please behave."

There was no objection from either Lucinda or Jen, and I left for bed.

"Now that he's gone, what do you want to do?" Lucinda asked Jen.

"Show me Jackson after dark. The hot spots. Bright lights. Loud music."

"Eligible men?"

37

AN EVENING IN JACKSON

JEN AND LUCINDA WALKED THE FEW CROWDED blocks from the Rustic Inn to the square and stepped through the door into the El Sabroso, the first tavern where they heard lots of noise and saw scores of people standing along a large bar and even more at tables covering the rest of the spacious room.

The music was live; it was classic country night. A good female voice was singing Shania Twain's *Whose Bed Have Your Boots Been Under?* The two chose a table whose unsteady occupants were showing signs of leaving, picking up their belongings and standing sipping the last of their drinks. The table was in a corner, and Jen and Lucinda sat so they could watch the people moving about on the floor and listen to the song Twain made popular.

Don't look so lonely
Don't act so blue
I know I'm not the only
Girl you run to.

"There are a ton of guys here," observed Jen. "Let's rate them on a 1-10 scale."

"What gets points?" asked Lucinda.

"Whatever turns you on."

"Macduff turns me on."

"Pretend there's no Macduff. Let's keep it to rating the guys who are here."

Over the next fifteen minutes, not one got more than a seven. But, curiously, about the time both women had finished three bottles of Snake River Ale, the ratings began to climb. Then a thirtyish guy walked in.

"A nine, maybe more," Lucinda whispered to Jen.

"If he's not a solid ten, I've never seen one before," Jen replied, a little too loud and drawing his attention, a nod, and a smile.

The guy was close to 6'5", a full head above most of those around him. His hair was short and neatly combed. He wore new, tight jeans and a Wrangler shirt with a Western yoke and pearl snaps. He ordered a single malt Laphroaig whiskey and when he picked up his drink at the bar, he turned, nodded, and held his glass up in Jen's and Lucinda's direction. They both smiled.

As soon as he had set down his glass, a slim hand slipped around his waist, and he turned his head to see a girl who was too young to order her own drink grab his with her free hand and take a sip. He leaned over and kissed her lightly on her lips. She handed the drink back and rubbed her hand down his chest and moved it below his belt. He grabbed her hand, leaned over, and said something in her ear that made her scowl. She walked off, and he went to say "hello" to Jen and Lucinda.

"Want some company? You two look alone."

"We are," Lucinda responded, "but I need to get on home or my husband may walk through that door with a double barrel." She got up and kissed Jen on her cheek.

"Enjoy each other," Lucinda said and was gone.

"We're alone," he said. His English was very good, but there was a slight Hispanic accent.

"Are you two friends, or did you meet her in here tonight?"

"If we can be old friends after an hour, I guess we are. We met outside, both alone, and came in together. You know—safety in numbers. She seemed nice, so I joined her. You seem safe as well."

"You're safe inside this place. It's a favorite of locals. . . . Are you a tourist?" he asked.

"Yes, but I wish I weren't. I like this town. I could easily live here. . . . You?"

"Been here a few years and no plans to leave."

"Doing what? I hear it's hard to get a good job here, much less buy a house."

"I'm enjoying myself."

"And doing what to afford that?"

"Odd jobs."

"How odd?"

"Service industry."

"That covers a lot. . . . If we're going to talk, let's use names. Mine's Candi Treat."

"You're kidding."

"My parents didn't want kids. Or at least if they had them they didn't want them to have an easy life. Like in the Johnny Cash song *A Boy Named Sue*."

"Why not change your name?"

"It grew on me. . . . It's a good way to get a conversation started. . . . Is yours as insane?"

"No. It's actually Juan Ignacio Palacio Hernandez. You know how Hispanic names are. I use only half of it—Juan Hernandez."

"I know something about Latin America, mainly Mexico and Central America. A brief era when I was a model for Victoria's Secret and we flew to exotic places to take fashion photographs. . . . What about *your* background?"

"If we must, Candi. I was born and raised in Merida, Mexico. Know it?"

"A little. Went there with a friend after a photo shoot at Cancun. We stayed for a long weekend. Saw some ruins. Drove north and played on a Gulf beach. . . . When did you move to the U.S.?"

"About five years ago."

"From Merida?"

"Before you think I snuck over the border, I was *legal*. I waited patiently to get the proper docs to enter."

"Why come to Jackson, Wyoming?"

"A family friend skied and came here—to Teton Village— every year. It sounded intriguing. I'd never seen snow, never been bitterly cold. Thought I'd try somewhere and experience both. I came here, helped by enough money from my family to last a year. . . . It lasted six months."

"You must have found work?"

"Yes. My English was better than most Mexicans who come to the U.S. Fortunately, my parents insisted I learn the language. I even took an English literature class at the University of Merida—that's the main public state university in Yucatán. After graduation I decided to come here. I came early one summer and was running low on money by September. My first job was helping to get the ski resort at Teton Village ready for the winter season. That carried me into late October."

"Then you were running out of money again?"

"Yeah. I worked hard and was offered seasonal work at the ski resort at Teton Village helping people on and off a chair lift. The next summer I had a job with a maintenance crew at the ski resort. It wasn't long before I applied and got my current job with the city."

"So the 'enough money to live on' problem was solved?"

"I saved as much as I could. I'm not complaining."

"What do you plan for the next few ye. . ."

"Enough about me," he interrupted, telling Jen her inquiry had become prying. "Tell me about you."

"Raised in Sioux City, Iowa. Big house. Lots of money but little love. I wanted out. When I was in high school, I started modeling. A couple of good photo shoots and I was picked up by Vicky C's. Made my own money. After a few years I got bored with modeling and being told to take off enough pounds to drop two sizes."

"You don't need to lose weight."

"Thanks. I wanted to travel. I liked my photo shoot time in Mexico and Central America. A friend told me he was driving to Costa Rica to work and asked me to go with him. See places. Take a month. We did. Nothing developed between us, and he paid my way home. I landed in Texas and was waiting for a plane to Iowa when the agent at the gate announced that the flight after mine was to Jackson, Wyoming. I canceled mine and came here. I like it."

"I know places you visited," he remarked. "I drove with a friend from Merida into Guatemala, crossed into Honduras, then Salvador, back through a part of Honduras, and our last stop was Managua, Nicaragua. I didn't like the lack of freedom with the Sandinista government. And knew it was time to head home."

"You went south a different way," Jen explained. "We stayed on the Inter-American Highway that runs along the coast of Guatemala and Salvador into Honduras just after a good size city named San Magnus."

"The Inter-American Highway doesn't run along the coast," he corrected. "It goes inland through San Salvador. And the only significant city between San Salvador and Honduras isn't San Magnus. It's San Miguel."

"My mistakes," Jen admitted. "I'm not good at remembering roads or place names. . . . Juan, I need to meet a friend in twenty minutes."

"Can I see you again, Candi Treat?"

"Tomorrow?"

"Day after. I'm hiking with a couple of gals into Cascade Canyon at eight in the morning."

"Seven p.m. right here day after tomorrow?" she offered.

"See you then."

"Enjoy your hike tomorrow."

Jen walked to the door, turned, gave a little wave at Juan, who was still watching her, and left. She walked briskly north the few blocks to the Rustic Inn. There was a note on her door that said, "Come see us. L. & M."

Lucinda opened the door to Jen's knock. We were sitting on a comfortable sofa, and Jen dropped into a deep, soft easy chair next to us.

"Did you like the guy?" I asked.

"Polished. Or better yet maybe slick. Very good English."

"What did you talk about?"

"The usual first meeting talk. Your life history to date. Or a variation. In my comments a lot of variations."

"What was he like?"

"Handsome. Dominant. Maybe a liar. On the other hand, maybe I've found a treasure."

"What did he tell you?"

"That his name was Juan Hernandez, with a couple of more Hispanic names in the middle that I forgot."

"What else?" I asked.

"He was unclear about his background. I don't like accusing, but I sensed he lied about a couple of things."

"Go on."

"He said he was born and raised in Merida, Mexico, and that he studied at what he called the University of Merida. He said it was the main public university in Yucatán. I told him I was once in Merida with a friend. I didn't tell him I had gone to a very small campus of something called the Universidad Marista de Yucatán. I looked it up on my cell phone on the walk here after leaving him. The Marista university is a 2,300-student private Catholic—the Marist link—institution, more college than university. The main place of learning is the public state Universidad Autónoma de Yucatán, with 18,000 plus students. There is no University of Merida."

"So, people make mistakes."

"True, but later I mentioned to him that I had traveled with a friend through Central America by car to Costa Rica. When I finished, he said he knew that area and corrected me on a couple of things that required much more local knowledge about El Salvador than one learned growing up in Merida, Mexico."

"Some people like to study maps as they go through countries. He doesn't need to live there to make the kind of comment you mentioned about Salvador. I'm bad on directions; when we travel, Macduff does some navigating. At least he checks mine because I've gotten us lost a few times driving back and forth across America. . . . I guess I'm jumpy because I worry about Macduff. And Juan. . . . Aside from all this, did you like him? I thought you were going to tell us you had a new hot guy you were going to see again and couldn't wait."

"I did promise to meet him two days from now. Maybe I was swayed by his good looks. He seemed so bright I thought he would know Merida's universities better than I thought he explained."

"Could it be that you really liked a guy who was so taken with you that he's tongue tied when it comes to remembering details about his life?" I asked, thinking I was seeing her emotions control her thinking.

"I'm tired from a long day and probably not thinking clearly. Let's talk more at breakfast. Seven?"

"Good. Any parting comment about Juan Hernandez for us to sleep on?" I asked.

"Yes. I guess any Hispanic I meet is going to scare me," Jen noted.

"That's unfair to a lot of good people," Lucinda noted.

38

MORNING AT RUSTIC INN

LUCINDA, JEN, AND I GATHERED AT SEVEN FOR breakfast in the small upstairs area used for one purpose: a delicious on-the-house morning meal. Since it was a buffet and I'm so polite, I let Jen and Lucinda fill their plates with fruit and whole wheat toast, and after they were seated, I chose sausage, bacon, pancakes, and two toasted English muffins. If Jen hadn't been present, I would have heard about my choice from Lucinda. She remained silent but with a scowl.

"Jen, I couldn't wait to hear more about your Juan," Lucinda said as soon as I sat down.

"Don't call him *my* Juan. He may be an Adonis heart breaker. Sometimes, when I looked at him, I was so excited I became confused. Other times, I imagined him even to be the *Jefe* in the *Calle Rojo* gang. The one who orders the killings and decides what guide to kill. If he is, Jackson has problems because this *Jefe* may be intelligent and clever, but bereft of the slightest moral integrity."

"If you're worried, why did you agree to a date tomorrow?"

"If I didn't agree to see him again, that might have been the last time I would see him."

"What do you plan to do tomorrow? Do you want to be alone with him?"

"If he's what I hope he is, I envision being on top of him sliding around on a massage table."

"In your bikini?"

"Bikini?"

"Jen! You've spent a couple of hours at most with this guy, and you want to go to bed with him. That's a little premature."

"Is it? You told me a few days ago that when you first met Macduff, that same evening after he had drinks alone with you, then dinner alone with you, and a couple of more hours talking and laughing alone with you in front of your fireplace, you were determined to do anything to marry him."

"Jennifer! That was told to you in confidence," said Lucinda, turning the heads of two at an adjacent table.

"This is a very interesting conversation. I was going to refill my coffee, but I don't want to miss a minute," I said, looking at an embarrassed Lucinda.

"I was trying to prove to Jen that it's possible to make a premature judgment about a person, act on it, and then live to regret it."

"And you were using *our* history. When did you first regret it?"

"Let me butt in, Macduff," Jen quickly said, "before you walk away from the best thing that ever happened to you."

"That would be when I adopted Wuff, but go ahead."

"See what I mean?" Lucinda exclaimed. "I come *after* Wuff in his love list."

"A very close second," I added. Her kick under the table not only hurt but also knocked my plate to the floor and scattered eggs and sausage links. We were now the center of attention. The two at the table beside us quickly got up and left scowling, with half their food left on the table.

"I'm going to have to stay with you two longer than I expected," Jen exclaimed. "You need a referee. . . . Maybe we could take our coffee to my porch, and then the only ones we would disturb would be the Canadian geese that cover the front yard."

We took our coffee and headed to the stairs. I gave the best apologetic nod I could muster to several tables we passed.

"Wow!" Jen exclaimed, sitting down on a porch chair so she would be between Lucinda and me. "Did I cause all that?"

"Absolutely," Lucinda exclaimed.

"Not a doubt. We invite you into our home and look what you do," I added.

I could detect moisture around Jen's eyes. Lucinda and I had gone too far. I got up, stepped past Jen, straddled Lucinda who was in an armless chair, and we kissed long and hard enough to change Jen's self-blame to applause.

"You two! I thought Macduff was going to take a swing at you in the breakfast room, Lucinda," Jen exclaimed.

"No, if he did try, he knows I would have jumped him, knocked him on the floor, and smothered him with more than kisses."

"Are you suggesting I jump Juan Hernandez at my first opportunity?"

"No, but I am suggesting you see him again," Lucinda urged. "You're smitten by him. Play it out."

"It can't hurt. We'll be in public places."

"It could hurt unless you make sure you *stay* in public places," Lucinda added. "Don't go into his house."

"Where are we off to today? What do you want to see?" I asked."

"You told me about your favorite hike up something called Cascade Canyon."

"You saw it from your plane as we were landing. I pointed it out to you. You'll love it."

"Can we fly fish?"

"It wouldn't be a favorite place if we couldn't. Macduff knows all the best places as we hike along Cascade Creek."

"Is it safe?" Jen asked.

"From what? *Calle Rojo* gang members?" Lucinda asked.

"Worse. I have visions of grizzlies, wolves, moose, and mountain lions. And if I avoid looking up, I may trip on a rattle-snake."

"All possible but probably no wolves. Maybe swarms of pikas or weasels or skunks. Swooping hawks and eagles. Mosquitos. Scared?"

"Not with you two along. I assume the creek is too small for drift boats, meaning we're safe from would-be murderers."

"One place we will stop is where a client was killed fishing. He was supposed to be with Macduff."

"Can I change my mind, rent a drift boat, and find some young Salvadorian to fish with me on the Snake?"

39

JACKSON THE FOLLOWING EVENING

JEN WALKED INTO THE EL SABROSO BAR FIVE minutes after 7:00 p.m. She had hesitated twice on the walk from the Rustic Inn, wondering if she were convinced Juan Hernandez was someone she wanted to know better. It wasn't the first time she had been attracted to a man at their initial meeting but realized after a few dates she didn't wish to pursue the relationship any longer.

She could be choosy. She was hardly a beautiful, young, impoverished blond searching for a sugar daddy to give her a comfortable life. The opposite was the case: beware the handsome young man looking for a wealthy woman to give *him* a comfortable life.

Using the name Candi Treat did not seem to Jen to suggest wealth, education, or intelligence. She thought her first meeting with Juan Hernandez must have left him with the impression that he had found an exceptionally attractive companion of reasonable intelligence. She would satisfy his need to have a pretty young thing at his beck and call, serving him without question whether accompanying him to some entertainment where they would be seen by others but not be performing or to some secluded place where they would not be seen by others and she would be performing. Both according to his needs.

She stood quietly inside of the door at El Sabroso, her eyes sweeping the room until they focused on Juan Hernandez talking to a barmaid who obviously was taken with him. Jen was favorably impressed with what appeared to be his polite but distant manner. She walked slowly toward him and reached his side as the barmaid left.

"You came!" Juan said, accentuating his surprise.

"You thought I wouldn't?"

"I hoped I hadn't come on too strong. I liked talking to you the other night. I didn't want to leave. . . . It's noisy here. Does a quiet dinner sound like a good idea?"

"Yes. I was hoping we might do that somewhere we didn't have to shout and repeat."

"I know you're new to Jackson. Let me suggest we walk a block to the Wort Hotel and sample its quiet and casual Silver Dollar Bar."

"Am I dressed appropriately?"

"Perfect. The picture of elegance in Jackson Hole."

Jen had bought some clothes in town that afternoon, an ankle length blue blanket skirt with designs she thought were Hopi or Navaho influenced, plus a Western denim shirt and a thin bolo tie. She tried on Western boots but decided otherwise. She never wore heels and thought she would stumble and be unable to walk more than a block.

"You're not so bad yourself," Jen said. "I like your pearl shirt snaps and the leather belt with old Indianhead nickels. Hardly clothes that came from Merida, Mexico, like a guayabera, oversized white pants, and sandals."

"Your clothes are not from wherever *you're* from, Jen, which I know only is not the Mountain West. Where *are* you from?"

The question and answer period had begun.

"I'm originally from Sioux City," Jen said, "as I think I told you the other night. But once I started modeling, I moved around, and much of the time I shared a Manhattan apartment with two other girls—both models. I made decent money but not what the big stars of modeling make, like Gisele Bündchen."

"Why did you give up modeling?"

"Too much control over me; it took acceptance to college to get me to quit."

"College in Manhattan?"

"No, on the edge of Boston. You may not know it—called Wellesley. It proved terribly expensive, and my modeling money ran out after two years. But I was able to finish after taking on some odd jobs. After graduation I did some traveling and ended up here. End of my life story."

"I think there's more I want to know. But let's order."

Both passed on appetizers, had Idaho pan fried trout, and shared a bottle of Italian *Pinot Gris,* and mid-way through the meal ordered a second.

"Juan," Jen asked, "you're Hispanic. Maybe I shouldn't mention this, but I read about a Hispanic youth gang here in Jackson called *Calle Rojo* that is believed to have killed several people as part of the induction of new members. Do you know about this gang and has it affected you?"

"Every Hispanic person in this county is aware and scared of the *Calle Rojo.* That's what the gang wants. They kill with machetes and cut off hands to terrorize the public."

"They cut off hands? I haven't read about that. What do they want?"

"Extortion. I suspect it won't be long before they are demanding monthly payments from guides and outfitters. Like the mafia does."

"Do you think the killing is over?" Jen asked.

"Maybe here in Jackson. The town is scared. At least for the time being."

"What about other places? One attempt was in Montana on the Yellowstone River a little south of Livingston, where I have friends. Another on the Delaware River in Maryland."

"The dead person on the Yellowstone was a member of the *Calle Rojo* based here in Jackson. The guide had a pistol in his jacket pocket. *Calle Rojo* failed there, but the attempt means the Jackson-based gang is spreading out."

"Why?" Jen asked, sensing Juan was becoming angry about the failure to kill the guide on the Yellowstone.

"If they can control extortion in Paradise Valley north to Livingston and west to Bozeman, the potential revenue is huge," Juan commented.

"Any obstacles to expanding?"

"Yes. There is no *Calle Rojo* gang north of Yellowstone Park. Not in Bozeman or in Boise. But there is a motorcycle gang in Livingston called the *Bandits*. It's a violent gang, but so far not sadistic. The bikers have the extortion racquet sewed up in both Park and Gallatin counties. But their members have to be concerned about the expansion north into their territory by the Jackson *Calle Rojo*."

"What about the Delaware incident? Why Delaware?"

"Details about what's happened in Jackson have spread. Throughout the country *Calle Rojo* wants to be considered the most violent and threatening gang. Being most violent means most feared and easiest to collect extortion payments."

"You know a lot about *Calle Rojo*."

"Ask *any* Hispanic in Jackson. We all are worried."

"Has anything specific happened to you?"

"Yes. Yesterday—while you were enjoying your hike—I was called in by my boss. There was a detective with him who asked if I could name *any* members of the *Calle Rojo*. Even one. I told him I couldn't, that it was my impression they used different names."

"Were you threatened?" Jen asked.

"Not in so many words. But my boss made it clear that he's been asked by suppliers and customers if he employed *any* Hispanics. The implication was that he shouldn't."

"Do you think he might fire you?"

"If the killings go on, yes. . . . He might. He can do it."

"Not because you were involved in the killings but solely because you're Hispanic."

"That's reality."

"What would you do? Leave Jackson?"

"No. Especially now that I've met you."

Jen was embarrassed but tried not to show it.

"Juan, what if an outfitter asked you to work for them and do the bookings? That way *you* can say no to Hispanics."

"You're very observant, for someone named Candi Treat."

"What did you expect from me?"

"As you gringas say 'being good in the sack.'"

"Maybe I am anyway."

"Let's try."

Juan booked a room for the night.

40

RUSTIC INN THE FOLLOWING MORNING

LUCINDA AND I KNOCKED ON JEN'S DOOR TO have her join us for breakfast. There was no answer, and we assumed she was already at the breakfast room. We were soon proved wrong. She was not having breakfast at the inn. She must have been sleeping soundly.

"Where do you suppose she is?" Lucinda asked, dishing up a fruit mixture repeat from the previous morning.

"Still in her bed here. Maybe in the exercise room. Or out jogging in town. . . . Or possibly in another bed—with Juan."

"Macduff! She hardly knows him."

"You said she was very taken with him two nights ago when you three met. We don't know her that well. She may be anxious to find someone to live with. Even marry, but I doubt that because dealing wisely with her wealth could be complicated."

"Could she be in trouble?"

"We've come to learn she's a smart lady. I suspect she can decide who she wants to be with and when."

"I know Jen liked Juan, but I also thought she was troubled by some of his comments about where he lived and even that he was Mexican."

"Give her some time. Here, read the local paper. It was by our door. Have another coffee. Jen can take care of herself."

Lucinda scanned the front page, gave a muffled cry, and dropped the paper on the floor.

"Mac! Another murder on the Yellowstone! This time not near Carter's Bridge. The boat was found drifting at Emigrant!"

I moved my chair, so I could read the article with her and not disturb the other diners, as I did the previous day:

Another murder of a guide occurred on a drift boat yesterday. Ben Casper of Pray, Montana, in Paradise Valley south of Livingston, was murdered on the Yellowstone River. Casper has worked from his home for the past two years, after being a guide for seven years for Fish the Fly in Livingston.

It was the second tragedy within two months for the Caspers. Last month Casper's wife Betsey died from breast cancer after a long fight. The Caspers left two teenage children.

The murder followed the pattern started on the Snake River last spring when a guide named Janice Whittaker was killed by a yet unidentified person wielding a machete. The killer cut off Whittaker's right hand, which was not found on the boat with her body.

There have now been four deaths of guides, plus one unsuccessful at-tempt, on the Snake, Henry's Fork, and Yellowstone rivers, in Wyoming, Idaho, and Montana, respectively.

Police have not solved any of the four deaths, but they believe all were caused by a youth gang in Jackson. Each of the murdered bodies was stabbed to death, had a hand cut off, and the blood of the victim was used to write the letters 'CR' on the inside of the drift boat. 'CR' are the initials of the Calle Rojo gang, which began in L.A. and has spread to three dozen cities between L.A. and Boston.

Ironically, the only information about the identity of the specific killers has come from two attempts that were not successful, one earlier on the

Yellowstone and one on the Delaware River near *Wilmington*. The list of attempts, successful or not, follows:

1. In mid-April guide Janice Whittaker of Driggs, Idaho, was killed by a machete while floating on the Snake River below Wilson, Wyoming, close to Hoback.

2. In early May guide Dan Goodyear of Island Park met a similar fate while floating on the Henry's Fork in Idaho.

3. In mid-June guide Chuck Driscomb of Jackson Hole, Wyoming, was killed under the same circumstances while floating on the Snake River near Pacific Creek in Jackson Hole.

4. In late July guide Hank Martin of Gardiner, Montana, was slightly cut with a machete by a young Hispanic, Jaime Castillo, aka Jimmy Castle. He was an illegal immigrant from El Salvador, believed to be a member of the Jackson Hole Calle Rojo gang. While floating on the Yellowstone River near Livingston, when Castillo showed his machete Martin pulled out a pistol and shot and killed him. This attempted murder is believed to be linked to the three earlier incidents.

5. In early September guide Whitney Stein of Wilmington, Delaware, was killed with a machete while floating on the Delaware River, by a young Hispanic, Rodolfo Arena, an illegal immigrant from El Salvador. Stein's right hand was severed but recovered in a plastic bag in Arena's jacket. Arena was caught by police and identified. He disclosed that the murder was ordered by Pedro Revuelto, an illegal immigrant from El Salvador who is the chief or jefe of the Wilmington-based Calle Rojo.

6. Yesterday's murder of Ben Casper of Pray, Montana, is assumed to have been done with a machete recovered from the drift boat. The incident occurred on the Yellowstone River near Emigrant. The murder is believed to have been done by a member of the Calle Rojo gang of Jackson Hole.

The governor of Montana has closed the Yellowstone River west of Billings to float fishing and urged guides and outfitter shops to avoid guiding any young Hispanics until further notice. The governor of Wyoming is considering closing the Snake River.

Neither of us could utter a word. Our world and that of many friends and persons we respected had been altered by the insanity of a few.

"How is this going to be stopped?" Lucinda asked, throwing this latest murder near our Mill Creek cabin into the chaos that she, Huntly, Ken Erin, John, Jen, and I have been struggling to comprehend over the past five months.

"I know Sarah—without question—will have John stop even listening to potential new clients," I said. "The fly fishing season is over in another week or two, although it usually lingers on if the weather permits."

"And *you*, Macduff," Lucinda added loudly, "immediately must stop listening to *new* clients who ask you to take them on a float. You have one client left next Friday for the Madison, the guy who helped sew back your thumb four years ago after you sliced it open when you fell over a fallen tree while holding your rod by the reel. The thumb dangled from your hand by a ligament. You've taken him on a free float every year since. He's about fifty and Anglo."

"He deserves to have me take him. My thumb functions mostly because of him. . . . But I'm at a loss about *next* year. Is it worth coming for the season if that will mean at most accepting a dozen floats?"

Before we could say another word, Jen walked into the inn, looking like she hadn't slept an hour last night.

"Should we ask where you were?" inquired Lucinda. "We knocked on your door forty minutes ago."

"I was still in bed."

"Where?"

"That's my business, Macduff."

"Sorry. . . . I assume you haven't read the paper. Get coffee and some breakfast and read this."

"I don't believe this," Jen exclaimed when she finished reading, too occupied to even have a sip of her coffee. It was close to your turf at Mill Creek, you two. . . . When will it stop?"

"That's what we were trying to figure out. And we've failed," I said.

"I think we should go back to Mill Creek," Lucinda suggested. "I feel safer there even though it's close to Emigrant. I'd really like to leave tomorrow for Florida. Even better would be Hope Town."

"And it's time I went to Hope Town," added Jen. "I still have a business to check on."

41

MILL CREEK

"I'M PACKED," JEN SAID, WALKING OUT OF OUR log cabin guest room with her bags. "If we lift off within an hour, I can drop you both at St. Augustine by two, and I'll be at customs at Marsh Harbour about three. I know how much you two will miss the five-day drive across the U.S!"

"Never again," I mumbled.

Settled on the plane a few hours later, we passed the last of the Rockies and blessedly watched the Great Plains pass quickly at a little over 400 knots.

Jen had the plane on autopilot and turned to Lucinda sitting in the second row behind me.

"Lucinda, I picked up the current real estate catalog from Sotheby's in Jackson and called and talked to an agent. His name is Rutherford Wentworth. I gave him your name if he can't get in contact with me. I told him I'm interested in buying something on the Snake but not a McMansion behind a dike near Teton Village. I like a place he emailed me photos of that's west of the airport."

"Guest room for us?"

"Lucinda, there will be a separate guest cottage reserved exclusively for you two. Macduff can almost cast from the porch into the Snake."

"Wow! Ten minutes from the airport where we can leave our plane."

"Not until one—or better yet both of you—qualify on jets. Why don't you take courses together?"

"We're already booked, and we start soon."

Landing at St. Augustine meant this was the first year in nearly twenty that I had not driven across the U.S. twice during the year, fall east to Florida and spring west to Montana. We had made only one stop for fuel and a snack somewhere in Kansas.

"I'm glad were here," Lucinda said three hours later sitting on our dock pier, swinging out a few feet over the salt marsh.

"I'm glad were alive and together. It was beginning to get scary along the Snake and Yellowstone rivers."

"I worry about John," she said.

"John will be fine. He won't take chances. He has more sense than me."

"Regardless, Sarah will keep him off the rivers."

"And you believe *I'll* be fine because *you'll* keep *me* off the rivers?"

"Exactly. And it will be easier to do that being here in Florida."

"Did you talk to Jen? Does she want us for Thanksgiving?" I asked.

"Yes, but only if we fly a plane down."

"We're starting lessons tomorrow morning. We can put in several hours a day flying a small prop plane, and we'll be licensed by Thanksgiving."

"Jen suggested we charter a Cessna 172 or something like that to fly to Hope Town."

"Perfect," I said, in approval. "I have a license, but it's thirty years old."

"You should start from scratch. Times have changed the laws and regulations. And you must have forgotten a lot."

"I remember how to taxi to the runway where we take off. All else is hazy until we've touched down and are safely on the ground. Something tells me you're going to be chief pilot, Lucinda."

"You can be in charge of everything on the ground," she said, "like refueling and washing the plane. I'll do the flying."

"Do you remember the woman Navy pilot who flew us out of Cuba?" I asked. "She landed on a highway near Varadero in an old Cessna she was restoring at her base at Key West. I read a month ago that she's back as a full Navy captain and heads the Naval Air Station in Key West. Not yet forty, she's on her way to being an admiral. . . . I think you'll do just as well at flying."

"Only if you don't back seat drive."

"It's called back seat flying, and it's really not the back seat. I'll be up front with you."

"If you swear to keep your hands off the yoke and switches and dials. One mistake and I start doing spins and loops until you stop."

"I've stopped already. No loops. No spins. You know I have a sensitive stomach."

"No promises."

42

ST. AUGUSTINE

W E BEGAN THE FOLLOWING DAY TO STUDY for our private pilot certificates, spending two to three hours in the air and in the evening prepping and testing each other for the written exam.

Within two weeks we passed the exam, soloed, and endured easy physicals. Then we began the mandated solo cross-country flights, building the number of touch and goes, and some training in flying under instrument flight rules—IFR—so we'd be comfortable flying instrument if we encountered unexpected bad weather. For the time being, our flights would be under visual flight rules—VFR.

"Either one of us could fly to Marsh Harbour, but we can't yet do it together," I said after two weeks of lessons.

"Why not?"

"We build time and experience as a solo pilot. A solo flight of each of us might be to Marsh Harbour."

It turned out that we didn't have to fly separate planes to the Bahamas; we both completed all that was required, including forty hours of flight time and final check rides with an FAA examiner, who signed each of us off.

We were pilots, certified for "Aircraft-Single Engine Land."

Thanksgiving was a week away. Jen was expecting us in Hope Town. Lucinda called her.

"Jen, we can leave in two days. Macduff chartered a Cessna 172. That's what we mostly learned on."

"Who can fly?"

"Either of us. Both passed."

"Congratulations. I'm in D.C. I'm leaving here in about four hours and flying straight to Marsh Harbour, where I left my Boston Whaler. Call me when you land at Marsh Harbour. By the time you finish customs, I'll be over from Hope Town to get you. I'll call a taxi service I use. They'll be waiting for you and drive you to the marina. I'll be in the boat—the same Whaler we used when you were here."

Our flight two days later confirmed the benefits of private flying. Beginning with the lift-off at St. Augustine.

"No check-in. No extra payment for baggage. No security line and confronting tired and irritable TSA people. No change of planes in West Palm or elsewhere," I said as Abaco came into view. "Why don't you land us. I took off and did most of the flying."

"You're in the *right* seat, Macduff. That means I give the orders because I'm in the left. And I don't need to be sitting in a plane to give you orders."

"I should have remembered that. *O Captain! My Captain!*"

"You're forgiven, this time. You land."

"Tower, Marsh Harbour, Cessna N6161C, ten miles north-west at 1,400 feet," I called.

"Left for runway 09, report on 45."

I checked the brakes, set mixture at fully rich, fuel on both, 10 degrees of flaps, and carb heat on hot as we dropped and passed 1,200 feet. A few minutes later I called, "Marsh Harbour, Cessna N6161C, three miles out."

"Cleared to land."

A few feet off the ground, I powered back and leveled off. The two main wheels touched and then lifted off. A few seconds later all three touched at the same time.

"Perfect," I said and glanced at Lucinda for praise.

"Easy landing. No wind. No other traffic. But it's not necessary to test the runway and then actually land the second time."

"What would you have done other than land twice?"

"Ten degrees more flaps. Maybe a little less speed since there's no wind."

"Will you ever trust me again?"

"I'll give it serious thought," she promised.

43

HOPE TOWN

CUSTOMS WENT SMOOTHLY WITH MORE SMILES from the agent who checked Lucinda and me into Abaco than from any of the agents who checked us out on recent U.S. commercial flights.

The driver Jen arranged was waiting. In ten minutes we were at a dock and saw Jen waving from a Boston Whaler.

I handed her our light luggage, including a rod bag with three Orvis salt water rigs.

"Fly rods!" Jen exclaimed. "I should have told you. I don't have any, and I'd love to take you out. You know *how* and I know *where* to fish. I can almost guarantee some bonefish for fun and mangrove snappers for a meal. . . . Which one of you flew the plane?"

"When we're together, I sit left, and he sits right," Lucinda declared. "But I let him take the yoke sometimes."

"Jen," I whined, "we got rid of all the problems of flying commercially, but at least when we were seated on a commercial flight, I didn't have someone next to me telling me how to fly."

"I should have warned you," Jen responded, nodding at me. "If you'll feel better, why don't you take the helm of my Whaler?

I won't say a word about your running the boat. You know the way to Hope Town and the dock at the house. Lucinda and I have a lot to talk about."

I slid into the helm seat, and Jen went forward to join Lucinda at the bow.

"Have you talked to Juan?" Lucinda asked Jen immediately, quietly enough so I had to listen carefully over the noise from the motor.

"When we left Jackson, I hadn't told Juan how he could contact me. I wanted to be the one to continue our relationship, and I wasn't sure I would. Nothing has changed since I've arrived back here at Hope Town. . . . Has Juan tried to contact you about me?"

"He doesn't know who I am," Lucinda said. "Remember, when we first met him I left without even giving him my name."

"I don't know the full of it, but the Rustic Inn called me and said a man named Juan Hernandez dropped by and asked about a tall blond named Candi Treat. I had been registered as Jen and not Candi. There weren't many people at the inn because it was entering the light season until the holidays. The gal who called me said she had an idea the caller meant me. I guess from the way I dressed as Candi Treat when I left the inn. She said she told Juan nothing because it was company policy not to give out such information. He went away mumbling something about 'that bitch.' I don't know whether he meant the gal at the desk or me. Or both."

"Nothing more since?"

"No. Maybe he's given up. It's strange, but I liked him and feared him at the same time. Anyway, he's certainly good looking."

"Jen, it would be different if you had no plans to go back to Jackson," I noted. "But you were talking about retaining a real estate agent to look for a house for you. You could run into Juan again. The more time you spend in Jackson, the more likely you are to encounter him. Are you still interested in buying?"

"No," she laughed, "but I'm out of the market only because I closed on a place last week. Before you ask, it does have a guest house. It's on fourteen acres and sits on the east side of the Snake River almost due west of the airport. I'm taking title next week and plan to fly out—at least I'm tempted—for Christmas. I'm selling Captain Candi's Bar to one of my employees. You met her; she waited on you. Sue Lane. She has about $30,000 to her name. I sold the bar to her for $1,000. She reminds me of myself. She asked if she can keep the name. I said 'of course' on condition that we destroy all references in the bar's files to Jennifer French and that she tells people who ask that the name Captain Candi's Bar is fiction and was suggested to her by a friend."

"Why do you want no references to you as Jen?"

"Mostly because of my background with Reggie. Some people made a lot of money when Reggie was in charge but lost it all when he tumbled. They resent me. Most have left Abaco. But not all. I don't worry about Reggie, and I've set up a medical care trust for him so he's not destitute."

"Have you set up one for Macduff and me?"

"No, but Lucinda, if you'd like to sell me Macduff, I'll give you $40 million."

"Maybe I'll take you up on that, but you'll have to give me a life estate in him. If I go first, he's all yours."

"But by that time, you will have exhausted him."

"I'm working hard on that."

"If Juan was serious about finding you, could he?" Lucinda asked.

"I think about that every day. One day I hope he does; the next I get chills when I think of it."

"How would he find you?"

"All I gave him was the name Candi Treat. And he knows I was with you when he first met us, but not your name. He knows I—maybe we—stayed at the Rustic Inn, and I'm sorry I even told him that."

"Did you tell him you were from the Bahamas?"

"No! If he knew that, he might find out about the bar from public records in Nassau. If he went to the bar, he'd have to deal with Sue Lane. I told Sue about him and said she should say I moved away from the Bahamas to—she thought to Costa Rica—where my 'meager' savings would allow me to live safely."

"But you have your house here at Hope Town," Lucinda noted. "If Juan learned about that, he could walk in unexpectedly."

"And find no one, except maybe you two."

"I don't follow you."

"I've put my house in your names. 'Jennifer French' no longer has *any* physical presence in the Bahamas."

"Why did you put the house in our names?" I asked.

"You said you might buy in Hope Town."

"We've thought of spending less time in St. Augustine. Not because we don't like it, but because we sometimes feel that things may be closing in."

"What things?" Jen asked.

"We haven't told you that we have a person from Guatemala trying to find us to kill Macduff. He has tried for close to twenty years. Now he's serving as Guatemala's president. We don't think he'll be a problem until his term is over. And from what we hear, he wants to be re-elected. I hope for life. . . . 'Nuff said. We'll tell you more sometime."

"You two are unusual people. Your pursuer sounds like my Juan. . . . Call the house a transfer payment for future services."

"What are you talking about?" Lucinda asked.

"I'll tell you over a drink on the porch," Jen answered.

"We have some secrets to tell each other," I replied.

When we reached Jen's dock, I throttled back and made a gentle landing.

"How was that?" I asked.

"It'll do," Jen responded, and then untied the two bumpers from the port side and moved them to starboard where they were needed to protect the boat from the dock. Not a word was said, but her glance told me what she politely didn't say. She looked at Lucinda, and both smiled.

Carrying our bags and the fly rods, I followed them up the pier and walkway to the house. Lucinda and Jen—each having an arm around the other—chattered about something I couldn't and probably shouldn't hear.

"We get one drink each on the porch and then walk to dinner a few blocks from here," Jen announced. "The usual to drink?"

"The usual."

"One Montana Roughstock Whiskey and one Gentleman Jack. And for me a bottle of Moose Drool."

"You brought some home!"

"A benefit of having your own plane. Try carrying a six-pack of Moose Drool onto a commercial flight. Or a long tube with fishing rods. . . . So, what have you two been up to for the past six weeks?"

"Most of it we blame on you," I alleged. "We flew and flew and flew some more. We're closing in on being certified to fly multi-engines, and maybe not too far off, jets."

"What have you heard from friends in Montana and Wyoming?" Jen asked. "Not much news filters from there to these islands."

"Nothing new. I'd like to hear that there have been no more murders on drift boats," Lucinda responded.

"Most drift boats are parked for the winter on trailers or in garages," I added. "No floats means no murder attempts."

"Do you think *Calle Rojo* will murder people doing something else?" Jen asked. "Like murder on a ski lift?"

"Too public, too hard to get away from, and too many around the lift," I suggested.

"What about killing a lone cross-country skier?" Jen continued.

"Possible, but harder to plan than a drift. And, most significant, not as dramatic. . . . I have it! Murder on a *snow mobile*," Lucinda proposed.

"That makes more sense," I said. "but I think there won't be any more incidents until next April and floats begin again. Then I suspect it will come on like a firestorm. The gang has several months to plan. If they begin to extort protection money from outfitters, it will be a bad sign."

"There is one possibility," said Lucinda. "*Calle Rojo* loses some power. I talked to Erin Giffin last week. She said the word in Livingston is that the *Bandits* biker gang is unhappy. Erin said they would be even madder if they knew *Calle Rojo* has been asking Livingston fly fishing outfitters for protection money for next summer."

"Is there any possibility of a serious physical conflict between the *Bandits* and *Calle Rojo?*" I inquired.

"I hope so," added Lucinda. "Erin didn't say anything about that. They are two very different groups. The *Bandits* are older, redneck Americans, insist on being left alone, and, most importantly, have made *no* attempts to injure, much less murder, people who have not done anything to them.

"But Erin did say that if the *Bandits* determine *Calle Rojo* members are taking over the protection racket, there will be trouble. In fact, the Livingston outfitter who complained to Erin about the demand for money made by the *Calle Rojo*, admitted to paying the *Bandits* a modest monthly protection fee for the past two years. *Calle Rojo* wanted twice that amount."

"What do you plan for next summer, Macduff?" asked Jen. "I assume most outfitters and guides are usually booking floats now."

"That's true," I responded. "I've turned down a few more than I've accepted. The ones I've accepted have without exception been past clients. My outfitter no longer books a float without calling me and checking on and approving the person. How many guides can afford to do that?"

I had talked to John Kirby in Jackson the other day. He's had trouble with his back and shoulders for the past two years and thought he might have to give up guiding. Now that it's off season, his back has rested and improved. Anyway, he's decided to limit his floats both in number per week and exclusively to former clients. His excuse for turning down prospects will be bad health.

"Nobody knows me in Jackson other than Juan and John Kirby," said Jen. "And my real estate agent. Juan knows me only as Candi Treat. . . . If I called any Jackson outfitter, other than the one John uses, from here in Hope Town, and said I wanted to float next July for a day each on three different sections of the Snake, what will I be told? Remember that I have a woman's voice and no Spanish accent."

"I'll evade your question by telling you what one outfitter is doing," I said, handing her a form. "Read this. John sent me this booking sheet that has been used for years, but now has a major addition. If the person looks or sounds Hispanic, they are to be told that the only bookings being made until next May are for past customers, sort of like a baseball fan who has bought season seats for ten years has priority for next year to keep his seats."

"Women are not admitted as *Calle Rojo* members," Lucinda reminded me. "That means a woman who wants to fish should be OK. But women guides remain at risk."

"I wish all my clients were women," I said, wrongly thinking Lucinda wouldn't hear.

"No more lone women in your drift boat for *you*, Macduff."

"Spoil sport. Sorry, Jen."

"Your hypos shouldn't cause any problems creating racism charges," said Lucinda, changing the subject back to "what ifs."

"What if next week two guys who are not known walk into an outfitters office in Jackson or Livingston—if one's even open in the winter—and start talking about their extensive experience fly fishing. The outfitter is impressed with their knowledge of fly fishing and the dozen rivers they talked about in detail where they have fished over the past few years. They look and sound Anglo, or Asian, or African American. Do they get a booking?"

"Absolutely," I responded. "In fact, probably in the reverse order. African-Americans with no Spanish accent are a shoo-in. There are many thousands of black Hispanics, but I don't think a lot live in El Salvador. Asians are fine, especially with an Asian accent. Anglos? Not clear."

"Many outfitters are closed during the winter. So what if the same people telephone or email for a reservation?" Lucinda asked.

"If they phone, there may be an obvious Hispanic accent which results in some excuse for turning them down—but not by telling them it's their accent that causes their rejection! They will be told bookings are full and there's a waiting list. And maybe a high deposit even for being added to the waiting list. If the request for a float is by email, the name may give them away. But, remember, one of the murderers named Jaime Castillo booked as Jimmy Castle."

"Erin told me her outfitter friend in Livingston said he will limit telephone bookings to those who are on record as past clients," Lucinda added.

"What if one or both of the same two hypothetical guys Lucinda mentioned call rather than stop by in person?" Jen asked. "They talk and sound almost as impressive as they did in person. No accent. No Hispanic names. Accept them?"

"The outfitter in that case is probably still going to require recommendations. The caller will be told that too many past clients who were not known have damaged the boat or violated rules like killing fish, using alcohol or drugs, wearing cleated boots on a wooden boat, or something like that."

"I know where we're going with this," said Jen.

"Wherever it is, I'm too tired to go there now," said Lucinda. "It was exhausting to fly here having to instruct a novice pilot," Lucinda said grinning.

44

HOPE TOWN THE FOLLOWING DAY

WHEN LUCINDA AND JEN CAME OUT TO THE porch with breakfast trays, I was rigging the three fly rods.

"Are those rods the same as you use at Mill Creek?" Jen asked.

"No. Every one of those at Mill Creek was a lighter weight. When we fish on one of the rivers from a drift boat, Lucinda, and I use mostly a 9-foot 5 weight, and if we're wading small streams, we drop down to a 7-foot 3 or 4 weight."

"This one you've brought has writing near the grip that says it's 9-foot 8 weight. That's a difference of three in the weight. Why?"

"We expect bigger fish here. Tarpon, redfish, and snook. And ones that get madder than trout when they're hooked. Like bonefish. And show bigger teeth. Barracuda. We may hook fair sized barracuda, about five pounds for a thirty-inch fish. We aren't looking for them, but they look for us to catch fish like snappers. The barracuda will steal your hooked fish the same way the shark does."

"Has that ever happened to you fishing salt water?"

"Not more than five miles from here," I said. "I was bringing in a mangrove snapper when a barracuda came and devoured the snapper. Surprisingly it didn't cut my leader."

"Sad."

"Not really, considering the fun it created. The barracuda got itself hooked, and after thirty minutes I boated it. About thirty inches of very mad fish showed me it's extremely large teeth."

"What happens if we use our 9-foot 5 weight here, which we both use for trout on rivers like our Yellowstone or the Snake?" Lucinda asked.

"That rod will bend more, and the fish will take longer time to land, which doesn't help a fish survive. And we won't cast as far. We aren't using small dry flies here. They will be closer to the size of streamers."

"OK for explaining the rods, but why are these three *reels* larger than what we use out West?"

"Right or wrong, I don't worry much about the reel we use in freshwater fishing for trout. The reel simply holds line. But in salt water encountering larger and stronger fish, we may need more backing behind our regular line. A good 200 yards. That means a lot of line to crank in when the fish runs, turns, and comes back toward us. A bigger diameter reel also means every turn of the reel handle brings in a little more line than on a small reel."

"When you caught the barracuda, did it run?"

"It took all the line and probably half the backing. When we fish in the West, we don't routinely see the backing. Here, I don't think I've ever caught a barracuda and rarely a bonefish without using considerable backing."

"What about line?" Lucinda asked. We usually use a five-weight line that's a *weight forward floating line*, called a WF-5-F line. What's on these reels?"

"Same weight forward and same floating features, but instead of a WF-5-F, we use a WF-8-F, matched to fit the size eight rod."

We finished breakfast, loaded the boat, double-checked sunscreen and drinking water, and took off south on the west side of Elbow Cay. There was a chop, so Jen moderated our speed for the sake of comfort, but in thirty to forty minutes we were south and across the water west to a deserted shore of flats and clusters of sprouting mangroves below Snake Cay on Great Abaco. The mangroves reminded us of our salt flats off our Florida cottage.

"I don't see another boat," Lucinda exclaimed. "In Florida no cluster of boats may mean few fish."

"There are lots of places on our flats that are teeming with bonefish and not another person is in sight," Jen responded.

"What about barracuda?" Lucinda asked.

"They're anywhere there's a free meal," I added.

We fished one person casting at a time. Sight casting means seeing what looks like a fish and casting to it. Two can't do that. I deferred to Lucinda and Jen.

"The sun's bright, and that's good," I said. "Unless we cast a shadow and scare the fish. Bones are sensitive to anything unusual. A shadow or a splash or a noise. That's why I turned off the engine and we drifted. Using a flats boat push pole, I can move us where we want to go, trying not to bang the pole against the boat or splash it."

Jen stood at the bow, and Lucinda sat back at the helm with me. I tied a #4 Veverka's Mantis Shrimp on Jen's line. It has a bead-chain eye rather than a lead eye that may hit the water with a fish-spooking splat.

"Jen, Look fifty feet ahead about thirty degrees off to the right or about one o'clock."

"I don't see anything."

"There are two bones moving this way slowly. Cast that direction but only thirty feet. Let it sink. I'll tell you when to give it a slight jerk."

She cast forty-five feet, and the fly landed exactly over the bonefish in about two feet of water.

"What happened?" Jen asked.

"You more or less tried to club the fish to death. The fly landed exactly above one of them, and they were all spooked. Bones spook easily, like me around you two. Let's try again. Look off to the left at nine o'clock."

"I see a shadow about thirty feet away."

"Drop it ten feet this side of the turbulence. . . . It's a small school." She did as I asked, and let the fly settle on the bottom.

"Lift it with small jerks. . . . There!" She lifted the rod, set the hook, and the bone took off.

"Keep the rod tip up, same as for trout," I shouted.

"It's running! My reel is whining!"

"Let it run. When it stops, it may turn and come back so keep some tension. You have a ten-pound tippet, and the fish weighs no more than five or six. You won't break off unless you jerk too hard."

Jen listened and her reaction was good. In a few minutes, we had a twenty-four-inch bonefish alongside. Her first."

"I'm going to have it mounted," she exclaimed.

"Please don't. Lucinda's photographing you with it. You can have a great copy made and save the real fish for another day."

As soon as I had made my suggestion, the bonefish jerked, threw the hook, and was gone.

"Pretty good," Jen said. "I've been in Hope Town for several years and never had this much fun on the water."

"Reggie didn't fish?" I asked.

"Never saw a rod or reel at the house and never heard him say a word about fishing."

"What did he do all day?"

"*Don't! Please*," cried Lucinda. "Don't talk about that. I'm remembering things about what Covington and Ellsworth-Kent did that I've struggled to forget."

I looked at her. She was trembling.

"I'm sorry. Let's go back and have lunch on the porch," suggested Jen.

Lucinda didn't say another word and kept her head down in her hands trembling the whole way back to the dock. She jumped off the boat first and ran up to the house.

"It's my fault for having you to Hope Town, Macduff."

"No, it's mine for asking about Covington. She wanted to come here. I know she was thrilled to see you. I think it best we don't go to your bar where we might see Covington, as weak and simple as he is now."

Lucinda went to bed. Jen made sandwiches, and we sat on the porch. It was a good time for me to talk to Jen. I had never been with her without Lucinda being with us.

"Is this the first bad memory attack she's had recently?" Jen asked.

"Yes, at least when we've been together."

"Do you think you two should leave and get away from the Bahamas?"

"Let's wait until she's rested and see how she's doing."

"I'm sorry, Macduff; she's been so good. She's a different person than the Lucinda I knew, but seldom talked to alone when Ellsworth-Kent had her captive here. I think back often and wonder why I didn't do something to help. The night you arrived and rescued her and freed me was the best day of my life."

"*You* helped when I came with a friend to free her."

"Was that friend from the FBI or CIA?"

"The CIA."

"Do you still have a contact at the CIA?"

"Yes, but not him. My contact stays in D.C. most of the time."

"I wonder if the CIA is involved with the youth gang in Wyoming. They are illegal *foreigners*. Doesn't that come under the CIA?"

"If the CIA views the gang as a threat and links it to El Salvador, yes. But it probably has to be on a larger scale than one gang in Jackson."

"But the *Calle Rojo* is all over the U.S. and expanding. What would the CIA do?"

"Look at the gang's leadership and how they might get orders from Salvador."

"Are you thinking the CIA might know something about the *Calle Rojo* that it isn't sharing and that might be useful for local authorities to know, like Huntly Byng in Jackson?"

"That's exactly what I'm thinking. I'll call my CIA friend in D.C. I owe him a call. His name is Dan."

"Dan what?"

"Just Dan."

I dialed Dan's private number. His secretary answered and said, "He's a bit grumpy today, so beware."

"Macduff, are you in trouble again?" Dan began.

"I've never been in trouble. I have a friend here you know about. Remember Candi Treat from Hope Town?"

"I do. You told me about her. Tall, blond, beautiful, and I understand possibly now quite wealthy. Macduff, I'm a tallish, handsome widower, Candi sounds most eligible to me."

"She's not looking for a mate," Jen interrupted. "I'm here with Lucinda and Macduff. You do have a pleasant voice, and Macduff speaks highly about you. Next time I'm in D.C., could we have lunch?"

"How long do I have to wait?"

"We're all at home in Hope Town."

"What are you doing in Hope Town? That's where Covington still lives, as far as we know."

Jen filled Dan in about acquiring Covington's wealth, his current non-threatening status, her bar, and her preference to live at least part-time in Hope Town.

She then told Dan about her visit with Lucinda and me in Jackson and as much as she knew about the *Calle Rojo* gang.

"While you were telling me about the gang, I pulled them up on our computers," Dan said. "We do know about the gang and should have files on any members we identify. But the Jackson chapter has been elusive. We don't know who they call *Jefe*, and we have only a name or two of possible members. We get info off and on from local police who try to keep us informed. Jen, do you know anything we should but don't know?"

"Maybe. When I was visiting the Brooks at their Mill Creek cabin, we went to Jackson Hole and I met a guy in a bar named

Juan Gomez Palacio Hernandez. I went out with him. He claimed to be from Merida, Mexico, and emphasized that he entered the U.S. lawfully. I spent some time in Merida, and what he said about it didn't mesh with what I knew. Could he be from Salvador, which he knew more about than Mexico?"

"That's not much to go on, but I'll throw his name in the computers and let you and Macduff know what I learn. . . . Where's Lucinda, Macduff?"

"Napping. We went fishing this morning and tired her out."

"I wondered if you traded her in on a wealthy, tall blond?"

"If I tried, I'd be in trouble. You would have heard. Lucinda would have called you and asked you to have me removed from the protection program."

I realized Jen had heard what I had said. She knows nothing about my existence beyond being Macduff Brooks. Jen was looking at me with a stare that suggested questions were to follow.

"I'll get back to you soon," Dan finished. "I think you're in for some explaining to Jen."

I heard his phone go dead and tried to think what to say.

"What did you mean about being *removed?* From some program?" Jen asked.

"I guess he was thinking about my giving him some advice last month about a family in Paradise Valley that's in a witness protection program after giving testimony in a drug case."

"Oh," she said softly, shaking her head slightly.

"Do you think Dan will find out anything about Juan?" I asked to shift the subject.

"If Dan doesn't find anything negative, I'll probably keep in touch with Juan. I expect to start spending time—at least summers—at my new home in Jackson Hole."

"Jen, when or if you do see Juan, don't tell him about your house. Tell him you're at the Rustic Inn again. It's not Juan that I'm worried about you seeing; it's that if *any* suitor learns about your house, he's learning about your wealth, and that may not be what you want to convey."

But it was actually Juan Hernandez who troubled me.

Lucinda came out from her rest feeling much better. She hugged me and said, "Thanks for understanding," and did the same with Jen.

"I'm going to leave you two for an hour or so," I said. "I want to fix the bow thruster wiring on the flying bridge of Jen's trawler. It will make docking here easier. Behave, you two."

Jen made sandwiches that she took to the porch and joined Lucinda on a swing that faced the harbor.

"Feel better?" Jen asked.

"Much. I don't know why this happens. I'm not threatened. My former husband, Robert Ellsworth-Kent, is dead. Reginald Covington is a wisp of his former self and acts as though he's had a lobotomy. Neither one can hurt Macduff."

"Or you."

"Yes, but my only concern is Macduff. And, of course, his daughter, Elsbeth. To me she's like a daughter, sister, and best friend all together."

"The vine has not withered?"

"Not a bit. You've gotten to know Macduff. The sun rose the day we met, and it's never set."

"If he weren't so in love with you, I'd be after him."

"That's what Erin Giffin tells me every time I see her. If she didn't, I'd remind her."

"What most threatens Macduff?"

"Ever since I've known him, it's been the threat from current President Herzog in Guatemala."

"But how can he harm Macduff while he's president? The U.S. government wouldn't tolerate that. Especially Macduff's contact: Dan whoever."

"Herzog's paranoid. He has control over two people who may know . . . they may know things about Macduff you're not aware of."

"Can you tell me? I assume you know."

"I know more about Macduff than anyone. From the day he was born."

"Where?"

"Farmington, Connecticut."

"I know it. My parents wanted to send me to a girls' school there called Miss Porter's. We visited, but I didn't enroll."

"If you had, you might have seen Macduff. He lived on Main Street about a hundred yards away from where most of the school's buildings were. How ironic!"

"If I had, I would have taken him for my own long before he met you."

"He likes you so much he might have gone with you."

"How did he become so devoted to you?"

"I wonder about that. My good luck, I guess. I think he was ready. He had lost his wife El in an accident a dozen years before we met. I believed him when he said years ago that he never spent a night with another woman."

"No old flames from high school or college after him when they learned about his wife's death?"

"I don't think so. He and El had left Connecticut and moved to Florida and lost contact with old friends."

"Macduff's a fishing guide. Did he move to Florida with El to guide in warmer waters?"

"No."

Lucinda knew she was in danger of disclosing Macduff's former life as a law professor. She respected Jen, who had faced her own life-changing issues, but drew the line before bringing Jen into the secrets of Macduff's life.

"They didn't like the cold winters."

"But after a decade in Florida you said she died."

"Yes, on the Snake River in Wyoming," Lucinda explained.

"That was about a decade before he met you."

"Yes. Eleven years and five months."

"Meaning the accident was about twenty-five years ago."

"Yes."

"While we've been talking, I've opened my iPad and have an article in the Jackson paper twenty-five years ago about an accident on the Snake River that caused the death of a woman named Elsbeth Hunt. Elsbeth is not a common name, but it is the name of Macduff's daughter."

"Yes, it's the Norwegian form of Elizabeth," said Lucinda.

"The male involved was Elsbeth Hunt's husband Maxwell."

"Yes," Lucinda admitted quietly.

"It says he was a Professor of Law at the University of Florida in Gainesville."

"Maybe that was wrong."

"Let's say as a widower Maxwell Hunt returned to Gainesville and his teaching position."

"That might be expected. But it has nothing to do with Macduff Brooks."

"I can only conclude that Maxwell Hunt is Macduff Brooks. More accurately, Hunt *became* Brooks. Why?"

"It's very complicated," Lucinda stuttered, trembling. Macduff has to be the one to tell you."

"Will he?"

"Maybe. He loves you for how you helped me escape from Covington. You know so much that he will tell you enough for it all to make sense."

"Only enough? He won't tell me all?"

"I sometimes wonder if he has told me all. And we've been married for going on two decades."

"And you trust and love him?"

"There has never been one day of doubt about either. I hope I live his whole life and not a second more."

"You know he is threatened by *Calle Rojo* and apparently by the Guatemalan, Herzog. What would you be willing to do to assure his safety?"

"Destroy them all."

"You mean that?"

"Try me."

"Erin Giffin is your best friend?"

"Macduff is my best friend, followed by Elsbeth."

"And Erin?"

"She saved Macduff's life when I had amnesia. She loves Macduff. I have always felt that if something happened to me, he would be best off with Erin."

"How does Erin feel?"

"She has known Macduff for as long as I have. She loves him. I believe it's why she's never married."

"Would you be surprised if I told you I feel the same way as Erin?" Jen admitted.

"I have seen that in your eyes."

"Do you think Erin feels as you do about removing any threats to Macduff?"

"Without doubt. Have you actually asked Erin that?"

"I have."

"When?"

"Before I flew home from Jackson, I went to Livingston and Erin and I talked," said Jen.

"And then there were three! What now?"

"I want to meet with Juan again," Jen said, shifting the subject. "That means going to Jackson."

"If he is the head of *Calle Rojo*, he's dangerous."

"I need some final convincing. It can only come from Juan."

"And you're willing to sleep with him to get it?"

"I already have. You should know something about me you don't know. I sold my body to achieve an impossible goal."

"I'm listening."

"You know I graduated from Wellesley."

"Ivy League."

"Not quite. One of the Heavenly Seven or the Daisy Chain or more often the Seven Sisters. A kind of Ivy League of then exclusively women's schools."

"What does this have to do with Macduff?"

"What I would do to achieve my goals."

"Tell me," Lucinda asked.

"I finished only part of Wellesley when my father stopped all financial assistance. I wanted to finish at Wellesley."

"And?"

"I joined a Boston escort service. The most exclusive. I slept with only enough men to pay my expenses. I would sleep with Juan for as long as I thought he could help me protect Macduff."

"You sound like a threat to me?"

"Not in the least. I'm like Erin. In love with Macduff, but even more in love with the two of you together."

"I'm overwhelmed, Jen."

"Don't be. Let's talk about how we're going to save Macduff."

45

A WEEK LATER AT ST. AUGUSTINE

"I SENT JEN A NOTE THANKING HER FOR OUR Thanksgiving stay," Lucinda said, as I came back from leaving some outgoing mail in our box.

"She's become a good friend, like Grace Justice was before she was killed on the Snake by barbed wire strung across the Gallatin."

"Don't even think about that sad time, Macduff. It wasn't your fault. . . . I loved having Thanksgiving in Hope Town, but I missed not being alone with you to celebrate at the place we met—my Mill Creek ranch."

Lucinda was rubbing my back, sore from removing the summer's accumulation of fallen tree branches, cleaning the dock and pier, and moving our flats boat—*The Office*—from storage to its berth at our dock.

"Let's call Dan and see if he's learned anything ab. . . ." I was interrupted by my cell phone playing a newly installed ringtone appropriate for holding on to good memories of Hope Town: *Island in the Sun.*

"Macduff, this is Dan. It's been a week since we talked. Where are you, still in Hope Town?"

"At our St. Augustine cottage."

"Is Lucinda there?"

"Less than a foot away."

"Keep your hands off him for a few minutes, Lucinda," he said, knowing we always joined each other's call by using the speaker.

"How could you tell?"

"Heavy breathing."

"Have you talked to Jen?" Lucinda asked.

"She called here."

"Called you? When?" I asked.

"Yesterday. I didn't know where she was calling from."

"Did you ask?"

"Yes."

"And?"

"Somewhere in D.C."

"Why was she in D.C.?"

"I don't know. Maybe banking."

"Are *you* going to meet with her?" Lucinda asked.

"Yes. Tonight."

"You're seeing her tonight?"

"I am."

"A date?"

"Don't I wish. I've never met her, but from what you say, she's a knock-out."

"You'll soon learn for yourself. By this time tomorrow you'll be in love."

"That's not likely."

"What did you call us about? I don't think it was Candi Treat."

"She prefers to be called Jen. Jennifer French."

"Why does she want to meet with you?"

"It's about someone she mentioned to me on the phone, a person named Juan Hernandez. What do you two know about him?"

"Only that Jen and Lucinda met Hernandez at a bar in Jackson," Lucinda said, nodding but wondering how much she would tell Dan. "I sensed Jen might be interested in him and begged off to go home. Jen talked to Hernandez for a couple of hours and made a dinner date for two nights later."

"And?"

"Jen had the dinner and spent the night with him! She didn't say much more other than that she had some doubts about him being Mexican and wondered why he seemed to have such a detailed knowledge about Salvador."

"Two dates and she's in bed with him?"

"Yes. Sometime I'll tell you more about her background and you'll understand. . . . Have you checked on Hernandez?"

"It's a common name. Maybe adopted."

"Meaning you don't have a file specifically about him?"

"That's correct. All I know is that there is a person in Jackson Hole by that name. I believe Jen. His background is suspicious. He told her that he was admitted from Mexico after properly applying. We checked and have no record of a Juan Hernandez born in Merida, Mexico and later being admitted to the U.S."

"Does that tell us he's an illegal?"

"That's how we're treating him until we know more."

"Do you have an agent searching for him in Jackson?"

"He begins a search today."

Dan hung up. Lucinda and I walked to our dock and sat on the double swing. I pumped a few times and turned to her and asked, "What do you think Dan will learn from Jen?"

"That someone named Candi Treat or Jennifer French—using either name—is a magnetic blond with a knockout figure and is exceptionally bright and has an engaging personality."

"Dan's a widower. Will he be attracted to her?"

"Love at first sight."

"Will he be able to help us when he concentrates on Hernandez?"

"He must think so because he's starting a search in Jackson for him."

"Assume he finds a Juan Hernandez in Jackson who Jen or you identify as the man you two met. What then?" I asked.

"We ask Huntly Byng—Dan's contacted him—to question him about his history, where he lives in Jackson, and what he does both for a living and for pleasure."

"If he's involved with *Calle Rojo,* the questioning might scare him and cause him to stop whatever plans the gang has for the moment. He'll get an attorney if he's personally threatened with a crime or expulsion. He can't tell an attorney what the *Calle Rojo* has been doing without implicating himself. Of course, he may not have enough money for an attorney, anyway."

"There's usually some money-grubbing lawyer who will work for the prestige he hopes will come with publicity from his association," Lucinda said, looking at me for comment.

"Save that for later."

"Wouldn't it be better for Byng to follow him without making contact?" Lucinda wisely added.

"What would Byng learn that he might not from a questioning session?"

"Where Hernandez truly lives and, of more help, his patterns, such as where he goes. That might lead to learning about meetings of the *Calle Rojo*."

"The last murder shows that the fourth and fifth killings—where the murderer was captured or killed—were conducted in a way that needed change. Once again—in the sixth murder—the guide, Ben Casper, was killed, and the *Calle Rojo* killer got away. This sixth murder takes us back to having to decide how to stop the *Calle Rojo* and restore confidence in fly fishing in drift boats, if we are to have a successful season next year."

"Is that wishful thinking on your part?" asked Lucinda.

46

EVENING IN WASHINGTON, D.C.

DAN CALLED THE WILLARD HOTEL AT FOUR. HE was told there was no Jennifer French registered or with a reservation. He went back to work at his desk and assumed Ms. French had other plans. At 5 p.m. his private cellphone rang. Few had access to the number. Could Lucinda have told her?

"Dan Wilson?" a pleasant voice asked.

"Yes."

"Jennifer French. I have a reservation for two at Fiola Mare in Georgetown, on the Potomac River. Please be there at 7 p.m. and ask for Christina Smith. I'll be there when you arrive. Carry a file folder with a few odd papers. Come to my table and sit. No hugs or kisses. Act as though I'm an old business associate. If you can't make it, leave a message for Christina Smith at the Willard, and I'll call you tomorrow morning."

Dan heard the phone click off the same time his secretary set a brief decoded message on his desk. It was from Stuart Freeze, the agent he had assigned to search for Juan Hernandez in Jackson Hole. He took the message, leaned back in his chair, and read:

There is a Juan Hernandez living in Jackson who works for the county court as a file clerk. I obtained his personnel file from the Clerk of the Teton County District Court, one Miriam Hofstra. Call me anytime. Stuart.

Dan called Stuart Freeze at his temporary lodging in Jackson. He was finishing reading the last page of the county's personnel file on Juan Hernandez.

"How did you get the clerk of the court to give you a copy of the file?" Dan asked.

"Our Agency—even more so than the Lord—works in mysterious ways. Ms. Hofstra is joining me for dinner tonight. There's more to what we know about Hernandez, mainly from talking to Hofstra."

"Fill me in."

"Hernandez started hitting on Hofstra at her office a couple of weeks ago. That caused her to carefully review his file. After she finished, she wondered why he'd been recently hired. . . . I think she was ready to fire him *before* she reviewed it. He listed Mexico as where he was born and grew up. Then there's a gap of nearly a decade where he makes reference only to 'various jobs, including tire repair, messenger, and airport baggage handler.' No signs of attending any college; came to U.S. at about the age of thirty. His file says he claimed he had a temporary agricultural worker visa—H-2A—but U.S. immigration records I checked don't have him listed as entering in any lawful way. I think he was an illegal entrant."

"What did he list as his specific job history in the U.S.?"

"Says he worked at an avocado farm in California. First picking fruit and then as a maintenance worker repairing farm machinery. He then allegedly became a file clerk at the avocado farm's office. Surprisingly, there's no listing of working at the Teton Valley ski resort."

"Did you check with the farm?"

"He listed a farm that doesn't exist. The clerk's office doesn't seem to have investigated his *alleged* past."

"After the avocado farm, what did he do?"

"What shows up next in his record is a move to Arizona and work at another farm in the office as a file clerk. He appears to be bright and good at finding jobs advertised in other city papers. He may have done some online searches."

"Is searching the want ads how he got to Jackson?"

"Yes. He answered an ad in the Jackson paper for a file clerk in the county court office. He was interviewed and noted as having an 'engaging personality.' I asked the clerk if she remembers hiring him. She said it was a previous senior clerk who did that. That clerk was about to leave for a similar position in Laramie."

"Was his being Hispanic part of the reason he was hired?"

"Apparently so. Hofstra was a little guarded when we talked about the minority issue, but I understood her comments as supporting a belief that his work in California and Arizona, and being Hispanic in an office that didn't have many minorities, led to his hiring."

"What did Hoftra say about his work record to date?"

"His job is easy. He's intelligent. His English has improved considerably since he started. Except for hitting on Hofstra, he seems to have been an excellent employee."

"But you couldn't confirm the accuracy of everything he included in his job application?"

"Little. I have no proof he came from Mexico and no record of any visa, H-2A or otherwise."

"Is Hofstra going to fire him?"

"She wouldn't confirm that. It sounds as though he's on an informal probation with her. But I wondered when she said, 'He looks great at the office. Every female here seems to be in love with him. Maybe firing him would get some of our day dreaming ladies back to focusing on their job and not his abs.'"

"What do you plan next, Stuart?" Dan asked.

"Tomorrow, I'm going to meet with Huntly Byng, the top guy in the Park County Sheriff's Office here in Jackson."

"What do you think Byng can do?"

"We'll see, but I hope he'll commit some time and effort to learning more about Hernandez. Especially any link to the *Calle Rojo*. When you called I was working on a report that I planned to share with Byng."

"Have you read or heard anything about local feeling after the last murder that took place on the Yellowstone in Paradise Valley near Emigrant?"

"I've only been here a little more than a day, Dan, and I haven't talked to anyone directly in the fishing business. I will. Likely tomorrow afternoon when I expect to see a prominent guide named John Kirby. You suggested him. Also, I may randomly talk to some fly fishing outfitters. Some are closed for the winter, and their guides are off working as ski patrollers or restaurant workers or whatever will tide them over until the next fishing season. If there is a next season."

"I'll let you go, Stuart, but in addition to investigating Hernandez, try to find out anything you can about the Jackson *Calle Rojo* in general. How big? Where do they meet? And, most important, get *any* names."

"I'll try."

"One last piece of advice."

"Tell me."

"Stay out of drift boats."

47

JACKSON, WYOMING – A FOOT OF SNOW AT THE EMPTY WAREHOUSE SOUTH OF TOWN

"ANTONIO SALAZAR, YOU FOLLOWED WHAT we discussed at the last induction meeting of Ricardo Colon for killing the guide Driscomb; you did all we asked in the way you appeared to the guide Ben Casper and how you lied about your background in Mexico being raised by a wealthy family who had bought a vacation home here at Teton Pines."

Smiling, Antonio stood in front of the rusty table facing *Jefe*.

"I more than followed your orders. I found a week-old Arizona newspaper, which had a front page photograph of a man named Hector Salazar—the same last name as me and who I resembled. He was elected to the U.S. House of Representatives to replace a woman who died. When I first talked to the guide, Casper, I mentioned I couldn't fish for two weeks because I had to attend my uncle's swearing in to serve in the House. Casper looked at the photo in the paper and said, 'You look like your uncle. Maybe someday you'll follow him into the House.' With that I knew Casper would take me fishing."

"I want you all to pay attention. What Antonio did is what every *Calle Rojo* candidate must do these days in killing a guide—use your imagination."

Salazar no longer looked the part he played when he booked the float and the day he arrived to take the float. Now he looked like all the other *CR* members. He had not touched his hair since the killing; it was growing long again. He had a new tattoo on the side of his neck. He wore baggy pants and a sweatshirt with "A Dirty Mind is a Terrible Thing to Waste" across the front. His sneaks had no laces, he wore no belt, and his pants sagged and highlighted his underwear.

On the table were three small stands, each displaying a human hand. The smaller hand had a woman's ring with a sapphire stone set in gold. The second hand displayed a large ring that said "Dartmouth University," and the third had a plain gold ring. On the first plaque was written Jorge, on the second, Hector, and on the third, Ricardo.

"You know why you are standing before me and we are meeting today. You will be voted on to become a member of the *Calle Rojo* of Jackson."

"I understand, *Jefe*," replied Antonio.

By now many members had removed their shirts to show their chest tattoos that said in large letters: *CALLE ROJO*.

"Antonio, it was your task to murder a person you did not know. Did you accomplish that?"

"Yes, *Jefe*."

"Did you kill the person I designated?"

"Yes, I did. I remembered what the others had done on their floats. My guide, Ben Casper, was excited about my phony uncle's induction as a member of the U.S. Congress. I played the role of the spoiled son of a successful Mexican businessman who lives part-time in Jackson Hole. Casper never said a word about the previous murders. I guess he didn't believe I would want to be associated with the *Calle Rojo*.

"Casper was not very pleasant. He said he was quitting guiding after this season. His back was constantly sore, and his skin bore scars from not wearing a hat or using sun screen.

"We were not far from Emigrant when I struck. One moment he was concentrating on changing my fly. The next he looked up to see the blade of my machete plunging into his chest. He screamed but stopped as he quickly bled out. I cut off his right hand, which I got for you now."

Salazar stepped to the table and handed *Jefe* the hand. This hand bore no rings on the fingers."

Jefe took the hand and held it high so the group could see it. Cheers came from every corner of the room.

He signaled them to be quiet.

"If anyone here doubts that Antonio should be admitted to the *Calle Rojo* and receive his chest tattoo, say so now." The room quickly quieted.

"Gracias, Antonio. We have corrected the problems with the first Yellowstone incident and the killing in Delaware, by the way you carried out your challenge. Again, we are a gang to be feared. . . . Are you ready?" he said looking at Antonio.

"Yes, *Jefe*."

"Take my chair and receive your tattoo."

"The group cheered loudly as Antonio was tattooed."

Antonio smiled turning to the screaming members and repeated what Ricardo Colon had called out when he was inducted: "Viva *Calle Rojo*!"

48

MID-DECEMBER AT THE FLORIDA COTTAGE

IT WAS GOOD TO BE BACK TOGETHER ALONE AT the Florida cottage. Thanksgiving was history; Christmas was in our sights.

The morning after we arrived, I slept until nine and woke to an empty bed. I preferred to wake and see Lucinda lying next to me peacefully sleeping. Admiring her contours outlined in the early light brought a good start to a new day.

Regardless of her absence from our bed, I could hear noise from the kitchen and lay back wondering what Lucinda was making for breakfast. It was too noisy to be something simple, like eggs or frying sausage or pushing bread down in the toaster. When I heard the oven door slam shut, I began to worry.

"What are you making?" I asked timidly opening the door from our bedroom.

"It's not for you. I'm cooking for myself and enjoying it. It has eggs, bacon, onions, mushrooms, hash browns. . . . Shall I continue?"

"That's enough. They will be identifiable, won't they?"

"Of course not. It's called the ultimate breakfast casserole."

"The word 'casserole' alone gives me anticipatory indigestion. What's also tossed in the mix?"

"Lots of cheese, red and green peppers, and sour cream."

"All put into a blender?"

"No, carefully cut and chopped pieces all mixed together and baked. In the oven. No mixer."

"I think I smell something rancid burning. I'm going back to bed. Wake me with the lunch menu."

At noon I felt her warm body wrapped around me. There was a delicious aroma.

"I have six minutes until the bison burgers with bacon are ready on the grill," she whispered.

"What can we possibly do in six minutes?"

"Set a record. Only if your indigestion is gone."

"It disappeared as you spoke."

We broke the record and raced to the grill exactly as the burgers were finished.

"They're the best ever," I said, biting into the burger. You should submit how you grill burgers to the *St. Augustine Chronicle*."

"Including what we did the first six minutes?"

"Don't you dare mention that. Only the cooking part."

"But I was on fire for those six minutes."

As the sun passed the mid-day mark, Lucinda's look turned serious.

"Macduff, I thought until yesterday, when we heard about the new murder on the Snake River, that we could relax until spring and maybe everything would go away."

"It hasn't gone away. I thought we were safe. But now I'm doubtful."

"Better here than at Mill Creek. Any suggestions?"

"One, stay away from Jackson. We need to impress that upon Jen as well. I hate to see her so excited about her new house on the river that she takes chances."

"She's not a fishing guide, Macduff. And only John Kirby in Jackson knows that Candi Treat is Jennifer French. And Jen's using an alias for the new house—Christina Smith."

"But she stands out wherever she goes. If she went to the new house, she still has to eat. Albertson's? Jackson Whole Grocer?"

"Maybe we should invite her here to Florida?"

"Should we stay here in the cottage?" I asked. "I'm known as a guide in Montana and Wyoming, but not in Florida. I won't risk being in Jackson, and I'm having doubts about going to Montana in the spring."

"Deputy Sheriff Erin Giffin said her Livingston lease is up the end of this year. That's only weeks away. What do you think of asking her to stay at our Mill Creek log cabin. No rent. If she insists, she could pay Mavis for cleaning. She's known Mavis for as long as you've had the cabin."

"Does that put Erin at risk?" I asked.

"Like me, Erin's not a guide. And even better for her, she doesn't live with one. She doesn't fit the *Calle Rojo* target image."

"My two drift boats are at the cabin."

"Safely locked inside the garage."

"What about next April?"

"Face it when it comes."

"You call her," I suggested. "What reason will you give Erin for our wanting her to have the cabin?"

"I'll tell her that you might be a *Calle Rojo* target because you're a guide and we think we should not be at the cabin."

"Are you going to tell her we'll be here at the St. Augustine cottage through next summer?"

"Yes, I would tell her," Lucinda said, "but I don't think we should stay here anymore than being at the Montana cabin. If the *Calle Rojo* knows your name, which they do, and knows where we live in Montana, they will quickly learn about this place."

"Should we close up this place or rent it to a friend?"

"Perhaps someone in our housekeeper's family—Jen Jennings," Lucinda suggested.

"Where will *we* live?" I asked.

"Hope Town. At least for a couple of months a year, perhaps January to the beginning of April—more or less from the winter solstice to the spring equinox. It is warmer than St. Augustine at that time. Hope Town is a very short flight from here by jet—when one of us qualifies—or a little longer flight in our prop Piper—for which we are both certified now. We have a wonderful place we now have at least a share in, Jen's old house on the harbor."

"Macduff, our life together is threatened," Lucinda commented early that evening. "We've had a relatively smooth existence dividing our time between Mill Creek in Montana and here on the marsh in St. Augustine. Now we're talking about trading St. Augustine for Hope Town and giving up going west at all."

"Only until the *Calle Rojo* murders stop."

"If they have stopped, it may be temporary because the fishing season is over. How can we make any long-term commitment until we know more? There may be more murders when the season opens in the spring, only three months from now?"

"I don't want to wait for months anywhere dangerous."

"I don't think you have to worry as long as you don't do anymore floats. Is it too much to ask that you hold off?" she asked.

"I've taken Henry Waters of Billings out on the Yellowstone for two days in a row every year since you and I met. Are you saying I have to turn Henry down when he calls about next season?"

"Of course not. Henry's safe. But will he *want* to fish if someone might be murdered in a nearby boat?"

"As long as I don't add a third person to the float. Especially a young Hispanic from Salvador."

"Let's not even mention young Salvadorians. We can stay here at the cottage or go to Hope Town. Your call, Macduff."

"You mean that? You're supposed to protect me and that means not passing decisions off to me."

"I'll remember that when we're talking about dietary rules," she noted. "For now, let's remain here in Florida. We can leave at a moment's notice. Put a note in the date book for the beginning of April to rethink all this. That's about when we would be leaving for the summer in Montana.

"There's another reason to stay here," Lucinda added. "Jen was troubled by the idea that some of Reggie's Bahamas friends might go after *you* if they can't find her. Does she know *who* they are—specific names? Or *where* they are—any in Hope Town? And reasons why they might go after you instead of Jen?"

"I can't help with that. But it makes sense if those Bahamians thought their life-style disasters were my fault. I didn't intend that; I wanted nothing more than getting you back alive."

"But Jens's different," Lucinda explained. "They must know she's living well, even if it's not in the mansion. Nice house on the harbor. Big boat. Jet plane. Owned a bar."

"But they have no way to link me to Jen's sudden wealth."

265

"So do we drop it?" I asked.

"No. We owe Jen too much. She's become a close friend. I know she depends on us. She's *deeded* us her Hope Town house and reserved the Jackson guest house solely for us. Jen's a good person. Reggie's big house is going to be donated to some charity. She transferred the bar to Sue for almost nothing. Even Covington won't lack medical care as he ages. She relies on us for advice as she makes important decisions."

"Jen has to deal better with Hernandez, who might be much more than a clerk at the county court," I added. "I'm going to ask Dan to have an agent investigate who might be dangerous friends of Covington. We *might* get some names from Jen. That would get Dan started."

"As usual," Lucinda responded, "you exhaust me. . . . One last question. If you accept any clients to float next season who you know are safe, does that mean we're heading west in April or May? And, if the answer is 'yes,' by foot, by car, or by plane?"

"By plane. If we're not jet qualified by then, we can use a charter or our own prop plane. Maybe Jen will go west at the same time. She might prefer to be with us at Mill Creek rather than in her new place on the Snake River and be who knows how close to *Calle Rojo* members."

"That makes sense. And we can always drive or fly from Montana to visit Jackson Hole and stay at Jen's."

"I bet we don't wait until April to talk more about going west," I commented. "Lots can happen between now and then."

"From experience living with you I've learned that lots *will* happen between now and then."

49

CALL TO D.C.

"BEFORE WE DECIDE WHETHER TO REMAIN AT the Florida cottage, fly to Hope Town, drive or beg a jet flight to Montana and stay at the cabin on Mill Creek, or somehow quietly get to Jackson and hide at Jen's guest house, let's call Dan Wilson at his Langley office and see if he knows anything new we don't know about the drama at the Jackson town square."

"Dan here," the voice from D.C. replied. He had changed his ringtone to the tendresse of a sultry French love song sung by Françoise Hardy.

"Bonjour, mon ami," Lucinda said.

"Hello to you both. I'm having lunch in my office. There's a small group of vocal protesters outside our gate and leaving for lunch today was not an option."

"Happy Ground Hog Day. What have you done now to irritate the public?" Lucinda asked.

"It's what we haven't done here at the Agency—yet."

"Then, what haven't you done—yet?"

"Removed your friend Herzog from office in Guatemala."

"So, you're intending to remove a democratically elected president from a democracy that officially is a friend of the United States?"

"Herzog's in office because following his corrupt election he was removed from but returned to office by a coup. Not exactly what you would call democratically elected. But the country remains a friend to the U.S. State Department because the Guatemalan government keeps socialism or communism at bay.

"I have something to tell you two about Herzog involving his first lady, Nancy Jones—if *first lady* is what we should call her—and also his niece Luisa Solares, the illegitimate daughter of Padre Bueno, Herzog's cousin, whom he murdered."

"I thought Luisa was missing and maybe dead."

"She's not dead. Nancy Jones contacted our mission in Guatemala City and told them Luisa had called her. Jones and Luisa met at a small coffee shop in the Central Market that Jones has come to use for quiet time away from the Casa Presidencial. Luisa was scared. Herzog keeps her in the city and controls her by threatening to wipe out her family. That means Luisa's mother, who is one of Herzog's sisters, and all of Luisa's siblings."

"Would Herzog really kill them?" Lucinda asked.

"In addition to his cousin, we've recorded nine murders Herzog's committed and never been held accountable for. His history suggests he'd wipe out his sister and all her family if they crossed him."

"What did Luisa talk to Nancy about?"

"Luisa's problems mostly. She's walking a tight line by helping the opposition that's planning to remove Herzog from office again, but this time having him 'accidentally' killed in the process. Luisa knows how her uncle operates, his personal habits such as rising at a certain hour, spending nearly an hour bathing, dressing, and having coffee in his rooms, where he sneaks off to a bar for a drink or two with an old friend, always disguised, and the route he always takes to his coffee finca in Antigua."

"Will Luisa help us?"

"She's terrified, but she told Jones she would help the U.S. on condition that she's taken out of the country and, if Herzog hasn't been killed, that she's protected until he's dead. And her family in Guatemala has to be protected."

"Are you going to Guatemala any time soon?" Lucinda asked.

"Yes, and I'll talk to you before I do. I may want you, Macduff, to go with me."

"Oh no you don't," interjected Lucinda. "That's asking too much of Macduff."

"Even if it meant the end of Herzog? Macduff would no longer *need* the protection program. You two could live where you want free his Herzog's pursuit. If Macduff goes to Guatemala with me, it will be in one of our Agency jets. He will have a different name, diplomatic credentials, a concealed weapon, and an armed guard 24/7."

"If he's caught by one of Herzog's men, what will he have?"

"Nothing. . . . Look at it another way. If Herzog is eliminated, Macduff will only have to worry about the *Calle Rojo*."

"And me," Lucinda added, "if he goes with you."

"This is out of hand," I said, listening quietly. "I didn't call to talk about Herzog. There is someone we need help removing here at home. Specifically, from Jackson."

"The head of the *Calle Rojo* gang?"

"Yes. And what's the latest on the *Bandits* gang rally?"

"I was there" Dan announced.

"What do you mean? You were in Jackson?"

"I went to Jackson a few days before the rally to work with Stuart Freeze, the agent I assigned there recently."

"Were you near the square when the body on the drift boat was brought in?"

"I was standing on the far side from where the drift boat was brought in."

"Were you with *Jen*?"

"No. But Freeze and I were keeping an eye on her. We don't know how to read her. I wanted to watch her directly."

"Where did you stay?"

"With Stuart at his temporary apartment. Jen was at her house on the Snake River."

"Did you have any contact with Jen while you were in Jackson?"

"No."

"Have you talked to her since the incident on the square?"

"No. I was busy with Freeze. A few days later Jen flew to Hope Town. I flew back here to D.C. later that day."

"Any decisions by you and Freeze about *Calle Rojo?*"

"Mostly we discussed what might next happen. . . . I decided the Agency needs to infiltrate the gang. And especially find more than suspicion that Hernandez is its head."

"How?"

"Hernandez is a bit of a mystery, but I came to understand that he's enamored of Jen. That might help. If we can work with Jen. I may fly to Hope Town to talk to her."

"Did she see Hernandez while she was in Jackson?"

"Not that Freeze and I could tell."

"Are you going to pursue this?"

"I've instructed Freeze to concentrate on finding Hernandez."

"Are you sharing everything you know with me?"

"Don't I always?"

"Have you ever?"

"I have to put our national interests first."

"Am I part of the national interests? I thought that came with the protection program."

"You're high on the list."

"That's not comforting."

50

GUATEMALA CITY

LUISA SOLARES AND NANCY JONES SAT AT A DIM-
ly lighted corner table covered with a Christmas red and
green cloth from Solola in the Guatemalan highlands. At
Nancy's recommendation they had agreed to meet at the small
coffee shop she favored nearly hidden among hanging textiles in
the middle of the Mercado Central, near the Guatemalan Casa
Presidencial. A marimba was playing in the background the classic: *Luna de Xelaju*. The air was a blend of flowers, food and human bodies.

Nancy Jones wore the same modest dress and blouse, head
scarf, and sunglasses she often wore when she wanted to have a
few hours of private time away from the government buildings,
where she felt like a combination of a kept woman and the na-
tion's first lady.

Luisa Solares also dressed so as not to be recognized easily,
appearing like a poor shopkeeper in one of the craft markets in
the Mercado.

"Nancy, I don't feel comfortable being here."

"I wouldn't have recognized you," responded Jones. "As long as you weren't followed, you're safe."

"I wasn't followed, but I have to be back within two hours. I'm supposed to be at my dentist's office, where I wouldn't dare go dressed the way I am here. . . . Herzog places little value on keeping me alive, but he doesn't seem to know what to do with me."

"Where are you living?"

"In the Casa Presidencial, where you're living. I have a small room in the basement that has one window at street level that is barely high enough to allow me to see out and watch ankles and shoes flashing by. It's adequate, and I'm alive. Herzog checks on me every day. I don't know what he would do to me if I missed a check. I guess kill one of my family. . . . I think he's given up on my knowing anything about who Professor Maxwell Hunt is and where he lives. That's better than my knowing and refusing to tell him—which is the truth. I don't believe he accepts what he learned a few years ago, that Hunt is engaged in work involving fishing. I don't know what he's keeping me for. I have little hope he'll let me go. Every day I wake up believing it may be my last day."

"Why don't you flee?"

"I don't have any proper documentation. He took everything and gave me a Guatemalan passport under a fictitious name. But he keeps it somewhere in his office. If I did flee, I guess I'd go north and sneak out of Guatemala and go on to Mexico City and to the U.S. embassy."

"What if I had you meet a U.S. CIA agent who would take you to the airport here and fly you to D.C. on a private jet?"

"That's what happened to Professor Hunt nearly two decades ago. . . . Could you really do that?"

"A friend could."

"I have family here to think about. You don't. Herzog was furious when I graduated and received my law degree from UF and began to practice in Miami. He had paid for most of my education. I loved what little time I practiced in Miami before my heart outvoted my head and I came here for a family reunion. I tried but wasn't able to hide from Herzog. He had the government cancel my flight out of the country and took my passport. I was escorted from my hotel to the room in the Casa.

"If I fled to the U.S., he's promised to kill my mother and *all* my relatives. Because of his threats, I can't leave as long as he's in power and probably as long as he's alive. . . . I won't flee, but you can, Nancy. . . . Why did you agree to come here with him in the first place? It must be more than living luxuriously as, effectively, Guatemala's First Lady. I hope you know how much the public likes you, especially your two adopted middle names. . . . How long will you stay?"

"If he were removed from office and had to flee the country, I wouldn't go with him."

"What would you do? Live here? Go back to Florida?"

"I love it here. I haven't told anyone, but I'm in the midst of buying a classic 1700s home in Antigua. You can't tell much from the street, which is true of many elegant homes of that city hidden behind high walls and huge, centuries old, wooden entrance doors."

"Nancy, you're not a citizen. Are you allowed to buy an historic home?"

"Maybe not, but Herzog is helping and whatever needs to be waived will be easily done. . . . If I don't stay in Guatemala, all I know is I won't go back to Gainesville. Because of my issues with the law dean, I didn't leave happily. Fortunately, I have enough money saved to live anywhere."

"Rumor has it that you're being paid an enormous annual amount to stay with Herzog."

"I like that kind of rumor."

"Plus, I have to assume that if you tell Herzog more about Professor Hunt, you'll receive a million or more."

"Is that a question?"

"Why not?"

"It's true. I hope I live to enjoy it," Jones replied. "And without compromising Hunt."

"What do you know about Hunt? You worked with him, but do you know his current name, what he does, and where he lives?"

"I don't know his name or where he lives. I do know he's alive or at least that he didn't die from a stroke as announced. And I'm aware that Herzog learned that Hunt is engaged in something to do with fishing."

"If you knew and told Herzog what he wants to know, would he pay you a lot?"

"Yes. I think about that. But I doubt I'd ever tell Herzog—*if* I learned it—what Hunt's name is or exactly where he lives."

"If you told him less, but closer to what he wants, would he pay you and let you leave?"

"I think I can leave now. I'm an American citizen, and I've made certain the people at the U.S. embassy know I'm here and that I'm OK. So far."

"Do you know a man named Dan Wilson at the CIA?"

"Not well. A few years ago I spoke to him once after talking to the UF law dean, who told me she would trade the info Herzog wants—if she knew it and if Herzog would restore his promised multi-million dollar gift to the law school."

"Do you think the dean knows much about Hunt?"

"No, she made that clear. But I'm certain her ears are listening."

"Nancy, how much would I have to tell you about Hunt for you to make a deal with Herzog good enough for you to leave now?"

"There is no way I'll tell anyone Hunt's current name, if I learn it."

"What if *I* told you where he lives? Not his address, but, say, the state he lives in?"

"If it wasn't a huge state, like California or New York or Florida, Herzog might go for it.," Jones suggested.

"Like Montana? Damn!" Solares blurted out and suddenly realized what she had done.

"You're certain?" asked Jones.

"Well, yes."

"Who told you?"

"Someone who sees him regularly. I don't think they know they disclosed that."'

"Who is it?"

"As I said, 'someone who sees him regularly,'" Luisa repeated.

"I understand."

"Are you going to sell your way out of here to a financially luxurious future?" Luisa asked. "Will you tell him I told you? He will insist on knowing your source."

"I won't tell him," Jones promised. "I can make up a convincing story. Already, I have enough to live comfortably. *If* I told him Hunt lives in Montana and confirmed that he works in fishing, and he tried but still couldn't locate Hunt, he might blame me for not being more specific and naming the specific town."

"You don't know the town."

"He doesn't know that. If *you* deal with him, Luisa, to let you go and not hurt your family, you must make it clear that you are telling all you have learned. If he believes you're holding out, he won't shy away from using torture. You're walking a narrow and loose tightrope."

"I know," Solares agreed.

"I've put you in an untenable position. I'm sorry."

"We both are. We know the state Hunt lives in but not the town. And neither of us knows Hunt's current name."

The two stood and hugged for what seemed more minutes than seconds.

"I've stayed here too long," Solares said, picking up her bags. "I'll sound out Herzog for how he might react if I told him I learned the state where Professor Hunt now lives. But every time I think of fleeing, I have visions of my family being brutally murdered. I'll hold off telling him Hunt lives in Montana. I also must think of Hunt's safety. He's never done anything to harm me."

"If Herzog says he must have more information, what will you say, Luisa?"

"That I'm still searching but as of now I don't know his name or address or who he works for in the fishing industry. Convincing?"

"No one can read Herzog's mind," Nancy concluded.

"If we could, we would likely be even more scared."

51

THAT EVENING AT THE CASA PRESIDENCIAL

NANCY JONES WAS FORTUNATE THAT HERZOG had an especially good day at his office. He even smiled frequently when they sat down for a late evening dinner.

"Where did you go this afternoon? I looked in on you about 2 p.m.," Herzog asked, pouring Nancy some *Pinot Gris* from the Casa's extensive wine cellar.

"Last night you poured us a good *Pinot Grigio* that was a little lighter and crisper. How do the two differ?" Nancy asked, to give her more time to think what to tell Herzog about her afternoon.

"As you've said, the *Grigio* tastes a little different. It's from Italy and the same grape as the *Gris,* which is from the Alsace region of France."

"About this afternoon, Juan Pablo, I'm trying to get some exercise walking every day, usually in the afternoon. I circle the plaza and extend the distance a little more each day. I'm learning how big this city is and the variety of shops."

"You need to be careful. Is that why you dress like an ordinary Guatemalan for your walk?"

Jones was momentarily surprised, realizing that Herzog may have someone follow her each day. Had she been seen with Luisa Solares at the Mercado?

"I'm glad you are enjoying Guatemala. You went into the Mercado Central."

"Yes, I like the smells and colors and variety of food and flowers and crafts."

"My man who saw you didn't go into the market. I needed him and called him and said to rush back here."

"It was its usual wonderland. I bought some orchids and placed them in our rooms. Have you seen them?"

"Yes. I wondered where they came from. Gracias."

Jones realized that was the first time she had heard Herzog utter "gracias" in weeks.

"Juan Pablo, what would you say if I told you I may be close to learning where Professor Hunt lives?"

"I would be overjoyed. And very generous. How might you learn this?"

"I had a phone conversation this afternoon with a former colleague at the UF law college in Gainesville. His name is Richard Samford. He taught courses similar to mine, and he also disliked the dean, Rikki Wells."

"Is he going to leave the law college?"

"I don't think he can afford to; he has two children in college. He needed to let off some steam about his problems with the dean. And he wanted one more thing. I personally had bought all the furniture for my office. What the state provided was functional but nothing to feel good about. When I left, I didn't remove any of the furniture. Professor Samford always admired it and asked me if I would sell it to him. I said I'd think about it but was inclined to say yes. I'd let him know in a couple of weeks."

"Does that help me find Hunt? I don't care what goes on between faculty negotiating their office furniture."

"I understand," Jones agreed. "I thought if I gave Professor Samford the furniture he might give me more info about Hunt, if he has or had access to it."

"How did Professor Hunt's name arise?" Herzog asked.

"Professor Samford said Dean Wells treated him much like she did me, testing him for what he might know about Professor Hunt, so she might use the information to get the donation. Samford taught during Professor Hunt's last five or six years, and they were quite good friends."

"Did Samford tell the dean anything specific that you didn't know about Hunt working in fishing somewhere?"

"Yes. Listen to this. He said he told the dean that Hunt had been living in the Mountain West since he left here. I never knew that."

Herzog tried to keep his composure, but his excitement was immediately apparent.

"Where in the West does Hunt live?" he asked.

"He said he didn't know. How many men can be working in fishing in that sparsely settled area of the country? Except perhaps Denver. There's no coastline with an ocean or gulf in what I consider the Mountain West."

"True. Meaning he works some way in *fresh* water. That narrows the search compared to his living along the coast, such as Oregon or Florida. Do you think this Professor Samford knows Hunt's current name and maybe a more specific address?"

"I don't know. He didn't offer it if he does know. I need to be nice to him. Perhaps agreeing to give him all the furniture would help."

"If you do, I'll transfer $100,000 immediately to whatever bank you wish," Herzog agreed.

"That's a kind offer. Use the same bank and number you used the last time. I'll call Samford tomorrow and tell him the furniture is his. . . . You're pleased?"

"Thrilled!" Herzog said getting up without finishing his meal and grabbing Jones' arm and jerking her toward the bed-room."

"It's a little early, don't you think," Jones asked, pulling away.

"Don't try to get away from me," he yelled in a voice that was losing the surprising gentleness expressed when they had their first sip of the *Pinot Gris*.

"You're hurting my shoulder," she said, trying not to fall.

"Be quiet. Be glad you live here with me. You're here to assist me, not complain."

He stripped her of every stitch of her clothing and began to remove his. Jones wondered if it was all worth it.

How different Jones and Solares were to Herzog. Solares was never sexually assaulted by Herzog. She could flee, but her family would face Herzog and surely suffer terribly. Perhaps even death at the hands of her own uncle.

With the help of U.S. contacts, Solares could flee from Gua-temala and return to Miami. She thought Herzog believed she didn't know any more about Professor Hunt and wondered why he even bothered with her. . . . Daily, Solares thought of fleeing and also of the possible consequences.

Contrastingly, Herzog thought Jones knew or had access to information about Hunt, as she proved by disclosing to Herzog that Hunt lived in the Mountain West, a decision that would cause her repeated sleepless nights, both when and after she told him. She could leave Guatemala at any time, and she remained a

U.S. citizen. It would be unwise of Herzog to stop her if she tried to leave. What he had to do was keep her happy. That was linked to the growth of her numbered accounts.

After disclosing Hunt's location to be the Mountain West, for some months Herzog would be especially nice to her, hoping further details would be forthcoming.

Meanwhile, Herzog would not cease his demands for sex. He admired much about Jones, but nothing more than what she offered in the bedroom. She worried that her body might not last until her foreign accounts reached the level she hoped for.

The disclosure of Hunt's current likely residence brought her a bit closer.

52

THE COTTAGE IN FLORIDA

DECISION DAY WAS UPON US: SHOULD WE STAY in Florida or go west? By early April I had carefully scheduled forty-six floats on the Yellowstone or Madison for the forthcoming summer season, about three per week. It would have to be the Madison until the Yellowstone cleared of fast flowing, silted water. That was likely not to happen until halfway through June.

Never had I experienced such turmoil in deciding who to accept and who to—acting most politely—turn down. Thirty of the scheduled floats were to be with fly fishers I had guided in the past. They were males and females ranging from their early twenties to one scheduled to float on his 85th birthday.

I was helped by my card files, now on a flash drive. After my first guide trip nearly two decades ago, I came back to the log cabin and on a file card wrote down the client's name, the date and weather, and where we fished including where we put in and took out. I added the name of any third person in the boat, generally what we used for flies, what we caught and what we lost and why, and how well the client could cast. I also made comments on his or her background, who had recommended me as a guide, what I provided for lunch, and an overall opinion as to whether I would like to float with the client again or not. A few years ago, I converted this information to a flash drive and arranged it so that I could look up a name and see all the floats we did together.

Sixteen of the forty-six people I had scheduled I had never taken on my drift boat. Six were direct calls from people I did not know, and ten were from outfitters. I rejected six after a few minutes of talking, for various reasons, such as every date suggested was filled. But three of those had Hispanic accents, and one also had a Hispanic name. He said he was from El Salvador and had spent two years in Los Angeles. I asked him if he were a member of *Calle Rojo*. He became abusive and threatening, and I hung up.

Another caller among the forty-six was generally unpleasant and rude; I told him I was fully booked the week he wanted to float. He said he knew I could call someone already booked that week and tell them I "had to" cancel but offered no reason. I said I didn't act that way with clients I booked, and he said he'd pay me double. I declined. Next, he asked me what I wanted in return for a float that week, stating that everyone has a price. I told him my price was to be rid of him permanently and I wanted him to hang up. Then he became irrational, and I hung up. He called back and warned me never to hang up on him. I looked at my phone's settings and found how to permanently block a caller. I had never used it—until then. It felt good to press the "block" key.

One caller insisted on bringing his dog on the float; he alleged that it was tame. I asked what kind of dog. He said a mix of Rottweiler and pit bull. I didn't ask if he—the caller not the pit bull—were from El Salvador, and before he said anything further, I pressed the "block call" feature once again.

Five of the ten *outfitters* who called me for a booking said their inquirer was a previous client of mine, but I had no flash card entry for them. Four said their applicant had never booked through an outfitter. I leaned in favor of learning more about the first four, but Lucinda struck them all. She said she suffers enough with me not to add another worry.

The last call was an outfitter I knew and admired. The applicant who had called the outfitter was a young Hispanic female about to graduate from Dartmouth who had received a Rhodes scholarship to study at Oxford for two years. I checked the names of the Rhodes grantees and found her listed. I booked her and congratulated her on the Rhodes. I wondered if I had a list of all U.S. *Calle Rojo* members how many would be Rhodes scholars. Or graduates of Dartmouth. Or graduates of anywhere.

"Are we going west this season or staying," Lucinda asked as I scribbled figures to determine what we would forfeit in shares of the float fees and tips if we canceled.

"A quick calculation suggests we'd lose about $15,000 if I canceled all the floats. One choice would be to cancel the first month's bookings and wait and see if there were any more murders as the new season progresses."

"I have to calculate whether I want to lose $15,000 or you," she said, grinning.

"A month ago, you told me one night in bed that I was irreplaceable. Now I may not be worth $15,000?"

"I remember that night," she said. "At *that* moment you weren't replaceable. That night I didn't have any clothes on, and you were lying on top of me. I might have had a one-track mind at the time. Right now, I can think more clearly."

"Don't you believe it's time for a mid-day nap?" I asked.

"Napping will not solve whether or not we should head west. And I want to finish the download of the Jackson paper. There's a piece about a big motorcycle rally next weekend in Jackson sponsored by the Livingston branch of the U.S. *Bandits* gang."

"You pick strange articles to read," I noted.

"Do you think the Jackson town square can hold 100,000 bikers?"

"If Sturgis can approach a million and Daytona close to that, maybe."

"The paper here has an article and a dozen or more welcoming ads by local stores, mostly bars, about the first of what is planned to be an annual biker gathering."

"Isn't it pushing things to hold it in April? Jackson may have snow in April," I said, taking the article from her and beginning to read.

"Most won't drive their bikes here but tow them on trailers. Jackson clears its streets of snow quickly."

"Why did Jackson agree to this? Large numbers of bikers or even large numbers of sweet little sixty-year-old grannies can get out of hand. Where are thousands of motorcycles going to be parked? Or, for the grannies, their walkers?"

"Along the streets, starting in the center at the square and radiating out block by block. Don't plan on getting into town in your car. . . . The Chamber of Commerce didn't think this up. Apparently, it was planned by the *Bandits* gang in Livingston and the Chamber caved in."

"Why not do it in Livingston?"

"This article suggests it was started here because the *Bandits* gang members in Livingston are mad at the *Calle Rojo* gang members here for starting to invade the protection racket in Livingston and Bozeman."

"Then the Jackson police must be worried."

"They are. They will have police coming from hundreds of miles to help keep order. Considering the number of motorcycle fans, these rallies are usually controllable. There will be excessive drinking on the streets, sex on park benches, and inevitable fights. Hopefully, that will be it and in a couple of days, it will be over, and the bikers will go home, leaving behind a lot of money in the cash registers of the bars and shops."

Macduff finished reading the article and noted, "I'm glad we won't be in Jackson during the time of the rally. Lots of loud drunks. But it may only be, as Shakespeare insisted, 'much ado about nothing.'"

"The merchants of Jackson may not agree. Lots of sales aren't 'nothing.' But let's call John and later Jen and see what they know."

We dialed John. He answered.

"John, are you polishing your bike for the rally?"

"Sarah sold my Harley the week after we were married. I haven't sat on a bike since."

"What do you know about the rally?"

"Nothing more than the article you two have probably read. I'm planning to say a little prayer that the event will be peaceful enough to leave the town richer in the cash registers, but trouble enough with drunken bikers that it doesn't encourage making it an annual event and trying to compete with Sturgis for numbers attending. . . . Sarah and I aren't much interested. In any event, we're planning to be in Arizona over that weekend. If we learn about anything, you'll hear from us in another week when we're back in Jackson.

"Will Jen know anything more?" Lucinda asked after John hung up. "I assume she's in Hope Town, even further from Jackson than we are."

"I hope she's not in Jackson planning to attend the rally," I added. "Let's call her next week and tell her that to avoid trouble she should avoid the rally."

"That's a feel-good call, Macduff. She'll ignore the call but not the rally."

53

A WEEK LATER

LUCINDA AND I HAD MORE THAN ENOUGH TO worry us without including a biker rally a couple of thousand miles away. The online Jackson paper had more ads promoting the rally and how it would be regulated, than articles about any trouble expected by the police and town officials. When we did talk about it, we focused mostly on the underlying conflict between the Livingston *Bandits* and the Jackson *Calle Rojo*.

"Macduff, I hope Jen wasn't in Jackson for the biker rally. She doesn't answer her phone, and I have a suspicious feeling."

"Let's try her again. It's past her breakfast if she's in Jackson, and it's the same time as ours here if she's where we hope she is—at the house we share in Hope Town."

Jen answered quickly this time.

"Lucinda! We haven't talked in weeks! I'd hoped you would be here in Hope Town more. It's *your* house; I'm just a squatter using the guest room."

"When you're in Hope Town, it's still *your* house, Jen. You may not have been watching when you transferred the house, but Macduff convinced your lawyer to add a provision that retained for you a life estate in the whole property, including the house and dock. When you're there, *we're* guests, not you."

"Whatever. I miss you two. Are you going to Montana soon and calling to see if you can mooch a free ride? That is unless you two have your own jet licenses and bought the Cessna Citation you talked about."

"We're deciding right now. We both have boosted our hours on prop planes. We've made a deal with Cessna to buy the jet, and they have chartered us a trade-in Piper M500 single turbo prop that we're using until we qualify on jets and take delivery of our new Cessna Citation. We haven't flown the Piper west yet. It flies at about 300 mph and the range means two refueling stops with no more than the two of us aboard. Plus, of course, Wuff, the flying sheltie. The M500 is a huge leap from the Cessna 172, meaning we're that much closer to being able to qualify on the jet."

"I feel like I pushed you toward the jet. I'm shouldn't have."

"Don't be. Flying makes our life going back and forth all the easier."

"But now you're having to decide if you're safe making that trip regardless of it being by plane *or* car."

"We're planning on the *Calle Rojo* issue being settled not too far in the future so we feel free to go west. . . . Are *you* heading to Jackson to use your new house on the Snake River for the first time?" I asked.

"Actually, I've flown out there twice since I saw you last."

"Not for the *Bandits* gang rally, I hope."

"Yes, I went to it—I knew you wouldn't want me to—and arrived back here at Hope Town late yesterday. The motorcycles were beginning to leave Jackson when I left. I saw lines of them on the highway below when I lifted off from the airport. I was planning on calling you after I finished reading today's online

Jackson paper about the mayhem last weekend. Have you read about it yet?"

"No, our computer has been down again without warning. Got it back an hour ago. Lucinda has it running again. She's looking. . . . Lucinda's downloaded the article and is shaking the paper at me and pointing to the front-page headline. My God! 'Murder on the town square'?"

"It was gruesome. Can murder be an extravaganza? It happened *before* the body was brought to the square. I had a front-row, standing-room-only place to watch. Don't worry. I was well disguised."

"What did you see?"

"Lots! I went as Candi Treat—the only name Juan Hernandez knows me by. I tried to look like a Jackson girl and wore dark green leather cowboy boots, a low cut and very short thin and almost see through white dress, a big silver belt with turquoise accent, a cowboy hat with a band of turquoise beads, and several bracelets and necklaces of silver and turquoise.

"I was at the square standing with Juan alongside one of the elk antler arches. The square was filled with clusters of different biker gangs' members; there must have been thousands of them."

"Any young Hispanics?"

"Not with any sign of being *Calle Rojo*. The most noticeable indication of anything was trash and the stink of beer and vomit. I assume there were some well-behaved bikers in town, but they were not at the square."

"Jen, we understand that the Livingston branch of the U.S. *Bandits* gang promoted the rally because the *Calle Rojo* was invading the *Bandits'* turf in Livingston. Any sign of this?"

"Signs and more signs all over town. On telephone poles, building walls, bench backs, and some license plates, saying

'Spics Stay Out of Livingston.' It obviously offended Jackson Hispanics who were present, and there were some scary fights close to where I was."

"Were the signs the reason for the mayhem you mentioned?"

"Yes, they caused the fights. After the body was brought into the square, the fighting got worse. The police called in the Wyoming National Guard. . . . You didn't know about the mayhem until now? It was constantly on Jackson TV."

"We don't watch much TV unless we hear of something specific that's worthwhile. And that's not every day."

"Would another murder on a *drift boat* be specific enough?"

"Of course. But Jen, drift boats aren't floating on the rivers. It's still much too cold and the rivers are high and dirty, at least according to the local outfitter websites."

"Wait 'til you hear what I watched at the square! While I was at the arch, I heard a vehicle approach with a horn blaring. Apparently, the crowd opened for the vehicle; we scattered away from the center of the arch. A small, old car pulled a drift boat painted all over with big blood-red *CR* letters. In the front seat a body was propped up. It was an Anglo dressed like a biker, but it was missing a hand and had what must have been a dozen machetes stuck from neck to waist. The body was still bleeding."

"Did anyone recognize the dead person?"

"Not immediately. But then whispers began to circulate around the square. It was a male about fifty, unshaven and wearing a sleeveless, black jacket that showed arms covered with tattoos. On the back of the jacket was written 'BANDITS MAKE THE RULES,' above a triangle framing '1%er.' The guy was bald and had a baseball cap with a phallic symbol and next to it the words 'Dames Devour Bandits.'"

"Was he a local?"

"No, apparently he was from Livingston, according to a wallet the police found. The wallet had a driver's license issued to a 'Wino Willie Warner'—that was his real name."

"What a story! What was the reaction of the crowd?"

"I thought the overwhelming number of bikers would go on a rampage in town killing Hispanics."

"It didn't happen?"

"No. Thanks to Huntly Byng's preparations and the National Guard. There were hundreds of heavily armed police and guardsmen in town. Plus, the U.S. *Bandits* gang branches from around the country were heavily represented, along with members of a half-dozen other infamous biker gangs present in large numbers—*Outlaws*, *Hell's Angels*, *Mongols*, *Vagos*, and *Bandidos*—and they stayed in clusters of their own members. Until the biker body was brought to the town square, they distanced themselves from the *Calle Rojo* gang. The visiting gangs seemed ready to clear out of town, which they started to do as soon as the police and guardsmen took over the town square."

"Jen, are you sure you're in Hope Town?"

"I knew you'd ask. I'm not so dumb that I'd stay in Jackson. I abruptly told a surprised Juan I had to go, slipped out of the crowd, went back to my house west of the airport, and called the general aviation office to get my plane ready to leave ASAP. We were in the air a few hours after the commotion on the square. What I learn now will be from the Jackson online and national news. . . . Turn on your TV. CNN's going to have a special program on the murder and gangs in America in general. Eight o'clock tonight."

"You said, 'We were in the air.' Who was with you?"

"Did I say that? I'm still not sure what I'm saying."

"Let's talk again soon and share what we hear and think about all this," Lucinda suggested.

"Promise me you won't go back to Jackson for a month or two," I pled.

"Sorry. I'm packing right now. I'll be on the first morning ferry from Hope Town to Marsh Harbour, and lift off for Jackson by 8:00 a.m."

"Why?" Lucinda and I called out simultaneously.

Jen's phone went dead. Not for long. I opened the cellphone expecting Jen again. It was a shaky female voice asking for Lucinda. I handed her the phone and headed for our bathroom.

When I returned, Lucinda was sitting at the kitchen table staring out the window at little more than pine trees. She looked lost in another world.

"Bad telephone call," Lucinda whispered. "The gal sounded weak and frightened. Not surprising, she has a month to live."

"Someone we know?"

"Someone I know. Mary Snyder. I worked with her in New York before I left to live with you. She's the one person I've kept in contact with these years. Mostly emails about once a month. They kept me up-to-date with the investment firm and reminded me how lucky I was to meet you."

"Is she ill? Now *you* look distressed."

"Cancer. Remember when I had cancer and went to New York for the mastectomy? Mary was the one who took care of me."

"I think you're going to New York."

"Thank you. As soon as possible. I'd like to leave here early tomorrow and drive to Jacksonville for the first flight to New York. I'll stay for a few days and hope she stabilizes. I'll miss you."

"I'm glad we have the Manhattan apartment. I'll know where you are when you're not with Mary. Pack and join me in bed."

Lucinda packed and put her suitcase next to the front door. I was sound asleep. But Lucinda didn't join me. Immediately she went to her computer and sent an email to Hope Town.

Jen, please stop by the St. Augustine airport tomorrow morning. It won't disrupt your trip to Jackson too much. And don't tell Macduff about this conversation if you talk to him before I see you. Lucinda

After pressing "send," she joined me in bed, snuggling close and gently placing one leg across mine.

An hour later Lucinda was still awake. She hated lying to the one she loved.

54

JACKSON, WYOMING

JEN LANDED HER JET AT ST. AUGUSTINE WHERE Lucinda was standing with a suitcase. She loaded her bag and joined Jen taking the left front seat.

Jen looked at her smiling. "I'm glad you asked me to take you. Take over. You've had some jet lessons."

"I'll lift off and get us to flying altitude. But you put us on automatic pilot, and we can talk. Don't expect me to land the plane at Jackson."

"Why are you here?" Jen asked.

"I'll explain to you as we fly."

"Is it about the *Calle Rojo* and *Bandits* gang issues?"

"Yes, but I'm still so upset about the biker rally death and the fact that no one, including Erin and Ken in Livingston and Huntly Byng in Jackson, has been doing anything in stopping more murders. I know the FBI is involved and to some degree the CIA, but I can't live month after month with Macduff at risk."

"What do you plan to do when we reach Jackson? Take the air out of motorcycle tires and boycott eating tortillas?"

"That and more. What "more" is I hope you'll help decide."

"I'm glad I'm on your side."

At the Jackson airport they took a cab the ten-minute ride to the house west of the airport and close to the banks of the Snake.

"Stay with me in the main house. Someone to talk to and safety in numbers."

"Good. But I want a full tour. This is fantastic!"

Both dropped their bags in their rooms. Lucinda headed to the kitchen to get some water. Jen stayed in her master bedroom, closed her door, and dialed a number on her cellphone.

"Bueno?" said the pleasant voice.

"Juan, it's Candi."

"Where have you been? Have you read any more about the drama at the square? I haven't seen you since then. You ran off."

"I've been right here at home. You know I do my business from my home office. I was behind in my work with all the excitement about the biker rally. I'll catch up on reading the papers tomorrow."

"We need to talk," Juan said. "I have some things to discuss with you. I'd like to hear what you have to say; you have good judgment."

"Thank you. Take me to dinner tonight?"

"Fine. And after dinner?"

"Your place."

"Do you have your toothbrush?"

"That's all I need. I have it."

"Pick you up at seven? Give me your address."

"Better would be for you to meet me at *Il Villaggio* at Teton Village. Seven."

"Seven."

Whether or not playing the role of Candi Treat, Jen loved Jackson. A little quiet old money and a ton of brassy new money, all imported and shouting, "Look at me!" She might even enjoy playing games with Juan.

"Lucinda, I'm about to go out," Jen said.

"I'm tired, the flight was a little rough. I'll get used to it. Don't wake me when you get back if I'm sound asleep."

Jen drove her old Jeep Wrangler to the airport from the house and parked it on the far side of the lot from the terminal doors. Then she took a taxi through Jackson center, across the Wilson Bridge over the Snake and to Teton Village and the *Il Villaggio* restaurant.

Jen liked *Il Villaggio* and would have gone there by herself if the invitation hadn't arisen. She remembered having an exquisite spinach pasta that she would ask about. . . . She arrived first and asked to be seated at a corner table.

Juan arrived ten minutes later, saw her across the room, waved, and walked across, stopping a moment to hug a striking redhead.

"You have a friend here? I'm jealous."

"I did a favor for her two days ago, Candi," he said with no further comment.

"OK. I'm having a Gentleman Jack on the rocks. I didn't want to order something you didn't want."

"I'll have the same," Juan said to a waiter who had followed him a few paces behind.

"What have you been doing the past couple of days while I was working," Jen asked.

"Thinking," Juan replied. "The body in the drift boat on the town square bothered me."

"It had to be work of the *Calle Rojo*. That gang overreacted to the bikers' rally, which was working its way almost to the end without serious incident. Do the police know who the dead guy was?"

"Yes, he was known as Wino Willie Warner, from Livingston. As best as the police are aware, Wino Willie was the head honcho of the Livingston *Bandits* gang. He was much liked and one of the milder guys in the gang. No crime record. Not even a traffic warning."

"So what comes next? *Bandits* come down here and beat up *Calle Rojo* members?"

"A quick, deadly, and brutal response, I predict."

"From what I overhear around town from people talking in the streets, if the *Bandits* gang came down and wiped out most of the *Calle Rojo*, only a few Jackson Hispanics would yell for arrests."

"You don't know what you're talking about, Candi. People here don't like biker gangs. They're crude, dirty, dress awful, foul-mouthed, drink, use drugs, and make too much noise."

"All I know is what I hear, Juan, and it's that people are terrified by the *Calle Rojo* gang because they killed innocent fishing guides and cut off their hands, even if it was after they were dead. When I first came, I heard a lot of 'Hispanic this' and 'Hispanic that'; now it's 'spic this' and 'spic that.' Whatever they're called, people want them out of Jackson.

"That would mean I'd be thrown out, Candi. *I'm* a spic."

"Don't go before I've had you a few more nights."

"Beginning with tonight?"

"That's what I'm expecting."

And trying to avoid, she thought.

The two finished their meal and headed to the parking area.

"Do you want to follow me, Candi?" Juan asked, hoping he might get a license plate number that he could use to find her address.

"A friend who was heading over the Teton Pass to Driggs dropped me off. He was so thoughtful."

"He?"

"Yes. Good looking, considering our thirty-year age difference. I helped him get his wheelchair into his rear deck. So, I have to go with you."

The drive to Juan's rented house south of the hospital was one of quiet anticipation. In Juan's living room, Jen went to the bar and poured herself a double. Along with two drinks before dinner and sharing a bottle of wine, she planned to keep drinking until whatever Juan did to her would pass quickly and not be remembered.

He also poured a double, and over the next two hours Jen managed to help him down almost enough to deaden his desire or ability when he finally grabbed her hand and pulled her to his bed. But Juan had such a passion for Jen he managed to overcome her escape maneuvers in bed before he fell sound asleep.

Even sharing the large bed the rest of the night was unattractive if she could avoid it. And she was determined to be gone from the bed and hopefully the house when Juan woke in the morning. She slipped out from under the covers and tiptoed toward Juan's second bedroom, which he used for an office. She would have preferred taking a shower in the master bath, but the noise might wake him.

She sat at his makeshift desk and without knowing what to look for carefully went through his papers. It was the usual pile she might have expected: papers from work and household bills. She felt frustrated. She thought she should get dressed and leave. Then she kicked something under the desk. She noticed a liquor size carton on the floor against the wall up under the desk, pulled the carton out slowly, and opened the top. A folded sweater lay on top. Removing the sweater and a gray hoodie, she saw a black three-ring notebook which had seen most of its usable lifetime pass. Lifting it carefully, she opened the cover and was shocked!

There were ten sheets labeled "*CR* Members." Each sheet had a dozen entries that included the person's name—all appeared to be Hispanic,—address, phone—if any, date admitted to membership, and in a few cases the name of another person—non-Hispanic—followed by the word "muerto." There were notes after some of the member's names.

Jen flipped through the pages and noticed a familiar name —Janice Whittaker, the murdered guide—at the end of the entry for the name Jorge Castaneda. After Whittaker appeared the words "hand plaque." Jen knew from discussions with Lucinda and Macduff that this was the first of the drift boat killings.

She was shaking. If Juan caught her looking at these papers, she would be dead in minutes. There was no way to copy the records and put the originals back. She kept the notebook, closed the box, tossed the clothing on top, and slid it all back under the desk.

Her watch read 3:12 a.m. She had to dress and leave before Juan woke. After setting the notebook by the front door, she returned to the bedroom where Juan remained in a deep sleep from the alcohol. Dressed within two minutes, she went back to the front door, picked up the notebook, and stepped outside into three inches of new snow. The door swung closed and locked behind her. She had left her jacket in Juan's house. The snow was one of those unusual but not unexpected events Jackson people suffered to enjoy living in a paradise.

Jen was on a street in the older part of Jackson; the night was suspiciously muffled by the falling snow. It was unlikely that a cab would drive by looking for someone in need of a ride. Her Jeep was at the airport.

She shuffled three blocks on the road toward the center of town, kicking uselessly at the snow, and falling twice in the slippery mess before she saw a vehicle approaching. She ran directly at a slow-moving pickup, which skidded to a stop not more than ten feet in front of her.

"Lady, you're crazy! You'll get yourself killed doing that."

"I'm desperate. I need your help to get to the sheriff's offices," said Jen, thinking that it would be easier to convince the driver to help her than take her to the airport for her car at this time of the night. And she wanted to get rid of the notebook, which felt both foolish and like a death warrant in her hands."

"Hop in. It's not far. Are you OK?"

Jen climbed into the passenger seat, tightly holding the notebook.

"I'm a heater and air conditioning repairman. I had a call that turned out far worse than I thought. I had to stay until I could fix it, at least temporarily, because the family had three kids under ten and this isn't the kind of weather not to have heat in your house."

"I'm so lucky you stopped. Thanks. And I'm OK, better in this heated truck."

"An attractive woman, wearing what looks like a cotton blouse, hair soaking wet, carrying a big notebook at three something a.m., running down the middle of a slippery street looking for the police, is a new record of strange events for me. But, you don't look like you have a gun, and if you do, you're shivering too much to shoot straight. Any story you want to tell me?"

"If I could, I would. You wouldn't believe it. And you might be visited by a very bad man who is probably out looking for me right now."

"I assume he would like to have the notebook back?"

"He *needs* the notebook. He'd trash me in an instant if he found me with it. And you, too."

"That's not good to hear. The building up ahead, where you can see a couple of sheriff's department vehicles parked, is where you get off. Want me to come in with you?"

"No. Well, yes. Come in and tell the first officer we meet how you found me and then please go home to your family, unless you're asked to stay and provide and sign a report."

The first officer looked surprised when the two walked in. Before he could speak, Jen handed him the notebook.

"Don't lose this," Jen said.

"What's in the notebook?"

"Names and info about the *Calle Rojo*. I'm sure it's the only copy."

"Lady, please sit down and tell me all about it."

"First, please call Huntly Byng—I've never met him—and ask him to come down here right now. Tell him it's a close friend of Lucinda and Macduff Brooks, two of my best friends who I share a house with here in Jackson Hole. They're away vacationing on the East Coast."

The officer called, and Byng arrived in fifteen minutes. After Jen mentioned how she knew Lucinda and Macduff, he said she needed to stop shivering and stuttering and use the office's facilities before they talked about the notebook.

Jen took a long restorative shower while Byng called his wife who brought Jen some warm clothes. Then she and Byng were ready. She started relating what happened earlier that night and soon realized she had to go back even further to her first meeting with Macduff, when he flew to the Bahamas to retrieve Lucinda from her months of captivity.

Byng enjoyed hearing it because he learned more about two good friends than the Brookses themselves were likely to disclose. As Jen's story progressed to her involvement with Juan Hernandez and the *Calle Rojo*, Byng understood what Jen's acquiring the notebook cost her and what it meant to finally get a hand on the *Calle Rojo* gang issues.

Near the end of her tale, Byng interrupted. "I need to wake a couple of deputies and get them out to Hernandez's house to arrest him."

"Maybe not," Jen suggested. "When he wakes, and that may be any time after he sleeps off the alcohol, he's going to find it hard to remember this past night and to recover from the drinking before he does much."

"Do you think he'll first look to see if the notebook's in the box?"

"No, but I think you have to assume he might. If he finds it missing, he could be gone in a matter of minutes. The notebook doesn't seem to cover planned events, but I didn't look carefully. Once I knew what it did disclose, I started trembling, and I'm sure I wasn't thinking straight."

"I'd say you thought straight the entire night. But I can't let him get away. I need to arrest him."

"Please wait until I leave town."

"Do you want to stay here? Or with my wife and me? I don't want you alone in a house Hernandez could break into."

"He knows me not as Jennifer French but Candi Treat, the name I used the time in the Bahamas I told you about. I have a house here, not listed in my name but a Panamanian corporation with my Brooks friends listed as officers under different names."

"I can't, in fairness, let you go home *alone*."

"You win. Drop me at my house and, if you wish, come in with me and check it out. A friend's staying with me. We're flying east on my plane after I rest and deal with a few things. It may be a couple of days."

Byng agreed. He dropped her without going in and arrived at his home at eight in time for breakfast. Over coffee he wondered if the past twenty-four hours really happened.

Juan Hernandez woke with the sun and stumbled about trying to make some coffee, finally giving up and opening the morning paper. Suddenly, had a terrible thought and hustled to his office, reached under his desk, and pulled out the liquor carton. The notebook was missing.

He didn't show up at work at the county court clerk's office. He was trying to plan what belongings to take and where to go.

And how he might kill Candi Treat.

55

TWO DAYS LATER IN MONTANA AT THE MILL CREEK CABIN

"MACDUFF, IT'S ERIN IN LIVINGSTON. I HAVE discouraging news. Is Lucinda listening?"

"No, she's in New York with an old friend dying of cancer. I don't know when she'll be back. We've only talked once a day and very briefly. Is it important?"

"Very. Is there any way to call Lucinda and have a conference call?"

"I'll try."

I used a cellphone Dan provided for such times. It worked, although I didn't understand the technology of why.

"Hi, Erin." Lucinda said as she joined the call.

"Bad news, but fortunately no bodies," Erin explained.

"Tell me."

"Your housekeeper, Mavis, called early this morning and was hysterical. I couldn't understand her and rushed down to your log cabin."

"Was Mavis injured?"

"Mavis wasn't injured, but she was sitting on the porch crying. In front of the house was one of your drift boats on its trailer. Not your wooden boat, *Osprey*, but the unnamed plastic one. I didn't know why it was in the yard and not the locked boat storage."

"A canvas maker from Bozeman was going to come by and measure for a new cover," I said. "Two weeks ago, I called a friend in Emigrant who has a truck with a trailer hitch and asked him to come over and pull the boat out into the yard."

"I assumed the worst on the drive to the cabin. At least there were no bodies in the boat or strewn around the yard," Erin responded.

"Thank God for that," I said. "I can live with some vandalism. What happened?"

"We're investigating. The cover was off and tossed on the ground by the boat storage garage. Sitting in the middle guide seat was a mannequin like you see in department store windows. It was dressed as a fishing guide with waders and boots, a long-sleeved flannel shirt and a fishing vest. On the head was a baseball style cap with a triangle shaped patch loosely sewed on the front with '1%er' in the middle of the triangle."

"Any more?"

"Yes. A strange, out-of-place name badge was on the breast and said, 'Macduff Brooks, *former* fly fishing guide.' A machete was rammed into the chest and the right hand of the mannequin was cut off and lying on the floor. That's it."

"What's next! Why Macduff?" Lucinda screamed. She was standing by a window in Jen's Jackson guest house looking at a moose move slowly along the edge of the Snake. The news caused such trembling that she dropped into a chair and put her face in her hands to hide her emotions.

"I'll kill every Goddam *Calle Rojo*. And every redneck *Bandits* bastard," she added, and crumpled in a chair in convulsions.

"Do you think she's OK, Macduff?"

"Give her a minute, Erin. At least she's safe in New York. Not many know about our apartment there."

"Sorry," said Lucinda, two minutes later. "Go ahead."

"Erin, only yesterday Lucinda and I finally agreed to leave for Montana in the next few days. We agreed to stay away from Jackson because of the biker rally murder. Lucinda's trip to New York to help her friend postponed those plans. What you're telling us may affect what we do in the next few days."

"I expected you'd say that. Ken and I are concerned about you two. You know the Jackson gang is operating here in Livingston. On the Yellowstone River they first tried to kill a guide and failed and later tried another time and succeeded. With the boat and mannequin occurrence in your Mill Creek yard, they are clearly after you, Macduff. I'm not surprised; you were too much in the public eye to be forgotten about."

"Erin," I responded, "if the *Calle Rojo* gang wants to learn more about me and Lucinda, coming onto our Montana property and finding us gone—as they did—may sooner or later lead to their attacking us here in Florida. We've never hidden this address."

"We have to leave Florida, Macduff," Lucinda declared, still shaking.

"Where to?" Erin asked.

"I can join you in New York, Lucinda," I said.

"No, you can't. What I mean is that it's hectic here. My friend's elderly parents have come from Nevada, and I've put them up."

"We'll let you know as soon as we decide," I promised Erin. "Wherever it is, our cellphones are with us. . . . Since the Mill

Creek log cabin is out, as is this cottage, it doesn't leave much. Maybe Lucinda's ranch a mile or so north of the cabin."

"Tell her about Hope Town and Jackson," said Lucinda. She felt strange watching a moose outside the window walking toward the Snake River while Macduff believed she was in Manhattan, probably looking out onto 67th Street and watching a homeless person searching for a corner to sleep.

"Don't pass this on to anyone other than Ken," I suggested to Erin. "We more or less have a place in Hope Town, Abaco. It's an historic house on the harbor that we seem to have been given."

"I'll ask what 'more or less' having a place in the Bahamas means later," Erin said. "But Jackson? What do you own in Jackson? That's the territory of the *Calle Rojo* gang!"

"We have exclusive use of a guest house adjacent to a large estate on the Snake River west of the airport. It's quite hidden. Our name isn't on any property records because the house is owned by a friend who we did some work for. She felt beholden to us. She also owned the Hope Town house, which she transferred to us. Actually, both were transferred to a Panamanian corporation, which the records say is owned by Gregory and Susan Grace. For your information only, those names are in reality Macduff and Lucinda Brooks. I'll explain that to you and Ken someday over a drink."

"Or two," chimed in Lucinda. "Erin?"

"Yes?"

"We're in the middle. Between a biker gang in Livingston and a youth gang in Jackson. We've avoided them but we may be drawn into the fight. I hate to even imagine that. We have enough trouble with Macduff's problems with the Guatemalan who has been searching for him for nearly two decades. At least that seems to be on hold, we believe, as long as the Guatemalan is serving as president.

"Mac and I have dodged bullets and barbed wire, airboats, Cuban barracuda, gill nets, Ellsworth-Kent and Covington, and more. I can't live between pond-scum youth and trailer-trash bikers any longer. Are you and Ken, and Huntly Byng, and all the idiot FBI agents sent to Jackson going to do *something*?"

"There is a system in this country that will see that justice is done. You have to be patient," Erin pleaded.

"I have been for too long. The only speedy justice I've ever seen was when I shot and killed Park Salisbury or when Elsbeth and her friend killed Grace Justice's killer on the Gallatin. What have *you* done?"

"I'm sorry, Lucinda. Our hands are tied with procedures we have to follow."

"Then follow your procedures! Otherwise, I'll see that justice is served while you do nothing."

"Don't do anything that will get you in trouble with the law."

"Thanks for the advice. But I prefer to do things that solve problems, not set them aside in some file labeled 'Pending' or 'Cold Case.' If Macduff is dead, being patient and serving justice sounds ridiculous. Goodbye!"

Apparently, Lucinda had hung up.

"Erin, call us if you have some information about stopping these incidents. They really have nothing to do with why we moved to Montana. I came to fly fish. Please be patient with Lucinda."

"Macduff, this is Ken Rangley. I came in a few minutes ago and heard some of your conversation. Don't you or Lucinda do what you may later regret."

"Maybe you should have given me that traffic ticket those many years ago," I said. "We would have parted with no further contact, making it easier to disagree now and act alone."

I set the phone down and blocked further calls from Ken or Erin. And called Lucinda.

"What do you want?" came her angry voice.

"It's me."

"Sorry, I thought Erin or Ken had called back."

"Lucinda, have we ended two decades of friendship with Erin and Ken?"

"Maybe. I hope not."

"But if it means a better chance of spending two more decades with you," she added, "the answer is an easy 'yes.'"

56

THREE DAYS LATER

LUCINDA AND I HAD COLLAPSED EXHAUSTED AF-
ter that long day, which seemed destined to change our lives.
I thought she was in Manhattan, but she had secretly gone to
Jackson. I was in Florida with bags packed waiting for her return
from New York, so we could leave for some destination we
hadn't decided upon.

Sleep had been less easy for Lucinda because she had lied
about New York and been the harsher of the two of us talking
to Erin and Ken.

A few minutes after midnight, Lucinda's cellphone rang. She
heard the ring from the guest bedroom in Jackson and got up
and answered, thinking it was a wrong number.

"Yes?" she stammered, eyes not yet focused from sleep.

"It's Erin. I hate to call. I know it's barely tomorrow here in
Jackson and a little after 2 a.m. on the East Coast. I know you're
in Manhattan and Macduff's in Florida. You can tell him what
we've talked about. I'm calling partly because I can't leave us the
way we did. And partly with some late news you have to hear."

"Erin, I don't want to listen to any more *new* news. In a couple of days Macduff and I are packing and leaving the country. We have passports under different names we've had for years from Dan Wilson to use if there was a need. We both agree that now there's a need. We'll have cellphones, but we've also agreed not to tell anyone except Elsbeth where we are. . . . What's your new news that couldn't wait 'til morning?"

"I've just finished reading a police bulletin Ken passed to me. It's from Jackson. You won't believe this news made public in the past few hours. I'll read it to you and you can tell Macduff about it in the morning.

Jackson News – May 4. The bodies of four young men have been recovered over the past 48 hours from various places in Jackson Hole where they were shot. Police have no assurance that there are not more bodies they have not yet discovered.

Each person has been tentatively identified as a young man of approximately 20-25 years of age. Identification has been found on each, including names, all of which are Hispanic. The words 'Calle Rojo' were tattooed across their upper chests.

Each one had been shot in the head from close range with a 9mm pistol. A quick examination suggests two similar 9mm pistols were used, each one was used for two of the gang members. Police believe the pistols may have had silencers because the killings took place at locations in the town where shots would have been heard and reported.

Pinned to each body was a small triangle inscribed with the trademark of thousands of bikers across the U.S.—1%er. Decades ago the head of the American Motorcycle Association, upset with bad press coverage from biker riots in California, stated that 99% of bikers were law abiding citizens.

Police are engaged in further searches for additional bodies.

"Erin!" exclaimed Lucinda, "The shootings could be taking the gang issues to your turf in Park County. That's too close to Mill Creek. Is there any evidence that Livingston *Bandits* gang members were involved?"

"It was one of the leaders of the Livingston branch of the *Bandits* gang who was murdered and placed in the drift boat pulled onto the Jackson Town Square. That suggests the four shootings were retaliation. By tomorrow noon we'll have a warrant to search the Livingston headquarters of the *Bandits*. It's an old warehouse along the railroad tracks."

"Good luck," Lucinda murmured. "I assume this news adds to your urging us to stay away from Paradise Valley?" Lucinda asked her.

"Of course it does, even though we've been able to keep news of the mannequin incident from the media. Mavis promised not to tell. . . . But the '1%er' patch on the mannequin in your boat suggests it was the work of bikers, and the closest and most obvious bikers would be the *Bandits* gang here in Livingston. Why they even know about us is beyond me."

"So, when I get back to Florida, Erin, we shouldn't leave for Montana?"

"Without question! Nor to Jackson."

"What can we do from Florida?" I wondered aloud.

"One, keep your friend Jen away from here as well."

"We can't do that."

"Is she in Hope Town?"

"No. Jen left the Bahamas for Jackson in her jet five days ago. About the time I came here to Manhattan," Lucinda said, hating herself for the lie about her location.

"How much does Jen know about *Calle Rojo* and the *Bandits* gang?" Erin asked.

"She'll learn about these killings before the day is out. She was dating the person I think is the head of the *Calle Rojo* gang," Lucinda said. "His name is Juan Hernandez. I haven't told her that was my thinking, but I believe she's reached that same conclusion on her own."

"Why did she go back to Jackson so soon after she had abruptly left there during the biker rally?"

"If you asked me that before what's in the police bulletin happened, I would have said I didn't know. But now I worry Jen's somehow involved. Her dating the *Calle Rojo* head worries me. If the head of *Calle Rojo* even assumed Jen might know about his role, he'd kill her on the spot. But in the West, and especially when she's with Hernandez, she uses the name Candi Treat, not Jennifer French."

"What can Ken and I do, Lucinda?" Erin asked.

"Check our cabin once a day. Call Huntly Byng in Jackson, tell him whatever you know that he doesn't, and ask him to put a guard on Jen."

Neither Erin nor Lucinda knew that Jen had stolen the notebook from Hernandez and that he was missing. Byng already was checking on Jen twice a day at the Jackson house.

"Where is Jen staying?" Erin asked.

"At the house I mentioned that's owned by the Panamanian entity, but really by Jen. It's west of the airport on Snake River Drive. No street number, but there is a mailbox that says only 'G. Grace.' Before you hang up, let me give you the cellphone number we use to reach Jen."

"Do you two believe Jen could be a murderer?"

"No more than I am," Lucinda responded. "She's had a tough life since her first year in college when her parental support dried up. It's for a reason I'll tell you another time and it means you can't push her very far before she'll feel up against a wall where she's forced to take action. But being at the Town Square when the body was brought in on a drift boat does *not* mean she was involved."

"But she was back in Jackson when the four were shot. Does she know how to use a gun?"

"I don't know. I don't think she's ever had to because she has an exceptional mind that seems to keep her out of serious trouble."

"It sounds as though you and Macduff both like her."

"If I were dying," Lucinda responded, "I'd be happy to think Macduff would end up with Jen. Or you, Erin."

"Wow! How's *your* health?"

"I plan on being around a long time."

"I'm not competing with *you*. It's with *Jen*."

"I'm staying out of this. I love you both."

"I know that, Lucinda. So does Macduff, I hope. I'm just thinking about 'what ifs.'"

"What if I took Macduff away to some place we don't tell you about?"

"You wouldn't. If Jen or I can't *have* him at least we can *see* and *hear* him."

"Only if I'm there to see and hear *you*."

57

THE FOLLOWING DAY - EARLY AFTERNOON

THE NEXT DAY I WAS PATIENTLY SITTING AND reading at the cottage, waiting for Lucinda to call about when she would be heading home from New York. I didn't know that she was 30,000 feet above the mid-West in Jen's jet and had not been to Manhattan.

Within the hour Jen dropped her at the St. Augustine airport and flew on to Hope Town.

My phone rang, and I sat looking at it. The ringtone was Stevie Wonder singing "Be Cool, Be Calm (And Keep Yourself Together)."

I tapped the phones receive spot to answer, but Wonder's song remained in my mind.

"Dammit, Stevie, I'm trying to be cool and calm," I murmured too loud.

"This is not Stevie. Do I have the wrong number?"

"Erin? Sorry. It's Macduff. Didn't we talk recently?"

"Yes, but I have some more news you need to know about. Where's Lucinda? Her phone doesn't seem to be working?"

"She may be in the air coming home from New York. Tell me, and I'll pass it on to her when she arrives."

"It's not all good news, Macduff."

"I'm not surprised when *you* call. Let's get rid of the bad news first."

"We don't know if it was quick retaliation by the *Calle Rojo* or what's left of them. It involves the *Bandits* here in Livingston."

"Bodies?"

"Four."

"Same as the *Calle Rojo*."

"Yes, probably retaliation in kind."

"What happened."

"Four *Bandits* leaders were meeting in their old warehouse along the railroad tracks here in Livingston. Some others may have been scared off because of the conflicts, maybe expecting retaliation for the four *Calle Rojo* who were killed in Jackson."

"The four were killed together during a meeting?" I guessed.

"Apparently."

"That's different from the *Calle Rojo* deaths, where four specific members were separately tracked down at their apartments and shot."

"The similarity is that the four *Bandits* were shot with the same two 9mm pistols used to kill the four *Calle Rojo* members! And, like those murders, apparently a silencer was used on each pistol here."

One difference is that whoever the killers were, and I assume there were two because two different pistols were used, they had to deal with four *Bandits* together, not one by one as the *Calle Rojo* were found and shot."

"You're right."

"So you're searching for two killers. Any descriptions? Any ideas what they looked like?"

"Not yet. But we'll find them."

"Are you assuming that it was *Calle Rojo* killing *Bandits* and *Bandits* killing *Calle Rojo*?"

"Not unless they somehow hired the same two shooters. It has to be two outsiders, meaning two who were totally unrelated to either gang. The two pistols being used for all eight killings is a significant link. Macduff, I think it eliminates both *Bandits* and *Calle Rojo* as possible killers. Someone else, at least two, did the killings."

"Who comes to mind first?"

"Frankly, no one."

"Wild guesses?"

"Jennifer French."

"Why?"

"A couple of reasons. First, she was there, at least staying in Jackson at her new house. After killing the four *Calle Rojo* she could have driven to Livingston and killed the four *Bandits*."

"Who was her partner? You said the two guns means two killers. Couldn't one person have used both guns to make you think it was two?"

"Possibly. We're open to any ideas."

"Who had a motive to kill the eight?"

"Remember that both groups were involved with the protection racket. They irritated dozens of store owners."

"Outfitters?"

"Yes. Add to their motivation their anger for what the two gangs did to nearly bring to a halt drift boat fishing."

"Maybe *all* people involved with drift boat guiding. Maybe even you, Macduff!"

"I've been here in Florida at the time of both killings."

"What about. . . ."

"Don't even think about it, Erin. Lucinda has been in New York for a week. I've talked to her every day. You talked to her once."

"That doesn't explain Jennifer French."

"Jennifer's issues were with Juan Hernandez. If she was to kill anyone, it would have been Hernandez."

"Maybe she did that in addition to the eight. He's been missing for several days, ever since Jennifer stole his notebook."

"Notebook? What do you mean?"

"This is the good part of my news."

Erin explained the episode in Jackson when Jen stole the notebook. Huntly Byng had told Ken Rangley all the details, which he shared with Erin.

"God! I don't believe all this. . . . Erin, a car just drove up. It's most likely Lucinda. Let me tell her about the *Bandits* killings and what you and I have discussed. One of us will call you back soon."

"OK. Give my love to Lucinda. I hope her friend in New York is better."

"I will. Thanks."

"Macduff, one more thing. I don't like shootings that happen on my territory. The four are the first homicides in a few years in this county. I take it personally, and I won't let up until I discover who did this. Between you and me, I don't give a damn about the *Calle Rojo* gang. They were far more brutal than the *Bandits*."

"I hear footsteps on our stairs. I'll get back to you."

58

THE FOLLOWING DAY – TO HOPE TOWN

"I'M BACK," LUCINDA SHOUTED AS SHE RAN UP the stairs to the cottage. "Are you here, Macduff?"

I opened the door, and we shared a long embrace. I decided not to ask how her New York friend was because if the news were bad it would only compound her grief. She would tell me when she was ready.

"I hate to tell you before you're unpacked, but I'm packed and ready to get out of Florida. Will it take you long to put away New York clothes and substitute Bahamian?"

"No. Is the Bahamas far enough to go?"

"For now, yes. We'll have the friendship of Jen and maybe Elsbeth will take some time to join us. No one else is to know where we'll be."

"Dan Wilson will have a good idea, but he's the only one. How are we getting to Hope Town?" she asked.

"You're flying us. I called the St. Augustine airport. The Piper is ready."

"If we have to leave Hope Town for somewhere like Europe, can we fly the Piper?"

"No. We'll hanger it at Marsh Harbour and go commercial."

Two hours later we were in the air enjoying the view while dusk greeted us as we prepared to descend to Marsh Harbour.

"Macduff, are you sure we both know everything that's happened in Wyoming and Montana? We were separated for almost a week."

"We also need to know what Jen knows. Can't we wait 'til we get to Hope Town?"

"I can wait. Do you want me to land? It will be dark about the time we touch down."

"I can do it. I've always like night flying. 'White over white, you're as high as a kite; red over red, you're as good as dead.'"

"The lights on the runway ahead are red over white," she noted.

"Just what we want: 'red over white, you're alright.'"

The salt air and warmth of Marsh Harbour were welcoming. A light breeze coming up from the Caribbean had replaced the light cold northwest breeze chilling us at takeoff in Florida .

Jen was standing in front of the arrivals building, waving and smiling. As soon as our propellers stopped, she ran out and first hugged Lucinda as though they hadn't seen each other for years.

On Jen's Boston Whaler there was a silent communication between Lucinda and Jen sitting at the bow that I couldn't follow. They continually looked at each other and grinned as though Jen had just set up for Lucinda who killed the volleyball and won the Olympic gold medal.

"What are you two up to?" I asked to neither in particular.

"Girl talk. We haven't seen each other for at least three hours. I mean three weeks. We're not trying to avoid you, Macduff."

Sitting alone at the helm, I looked at the two sitting together at the bow and occasionally hugging and wondered what they were thinking. We unloaded bags, jokingly debated over who had the master bedroom and who the guest room—Lucinda and I outvoted Jen to give her the master bedroom.

We didn't mix and take drinks to the porch; we took three glasses, a bucket of ice, a bottle of soda, and full bottles of Gentleman Jack and Montana Roughstock Whiskey.

"Can we start with something nice," Jen asked. "I think we each know as much as the other about some things that happened in the Western Mountains involving the *Calle Rojo* and the *Bandits*."

"It can wait for a drink or two while we watch the last glow from the sun, but I don't think we know who shot and killed the four *Calle Rojo* members who did the four murders of guides on the Snake, Henry's Fork, and Yellowstone rivers," I said. "Thanks to Jen and what she's told us about the notebook, we learned their names."

"And where they lived," added Lucinda.

"Secondly, we don't know exactly who killed Wino Willie Warner and drove him onto the Jackson town square," I added.

"It had to be *Calle Rojo* members," said Jen.

"And it must have been *Bandits* who left the mannequin on Macduff's drift boat," said Lucinda.

"Why?"

"The Bandits were threatened by Calle Rojo. Calle Rojo had contracted every outfitter and threatened them. In turn, according to Erin, they had stopped paying money to the bandits and started paying outfitters. I think the Bandits wanted to threaten a guide and they picked Macduff."

"Speculation?"

"I know. But the list of those with motives seems endless. Nothing will surprise me about these two gangs."

"Who had the motive to kill the four *Bandits* members at the warehouse in Livingston?" questioned Jen.

"Who cares?" I said, showing my exasperation. "No one we'll see or meet here in the Bahamas. Let's enjoy it. Let Huntly Byng and Ken Rangley solve it. If it isn't solved, but the murders of guides stops, I can live with that."

"I can live with anything as long as Macduff is safe," added Lucinda. "Jen, one last question. What did you do in Jackson after you took the notebook and gave it to Huntly Byng?"

"Not much. Stayed for a few days. Flew home today."

"When's your next trip?" I asked.

"I don't like snow. I'll wait for summer."

"I think Lucinda and I will miss much of this summer in the West. A chance to do some traveling we've put off year after year. We haven't talked about specifics. We'll be flying in the eastern half of the U.S., building hours and taking more jet lessons. Lucinda's doing great; I have to catch up on the hours."

"I'm looking forward to being here," offered Lucinda. "I feel free to come and go now that Covington's no threat. I'll walk, bike, jog, swim, fish with Macduff, and at the end of each day plop down right here with a drink. . . . Jen, I'm emotionally worn out."

"You, more than anyone, should be," Jen said. "I have only myself. You have Macduff and Elsbeth. And Wuff, who you brought with you now that you're flying your own plane. . . .

Macduff, you're being kept from your love—fly fishing. You're going to miss part of this coming season. Disappointed?"

"Lucinda looks great. So will Elsbeth when she's home from Oxford. And Wuff. I've thought the past few days that it may be time for me to quit guiding. My back and shoulders are weaker than I'd like from rowing. I have enough scars. I could stay right here on this island, at this house, on this porch, and on this double swing feeling Lucinda next to me, and watch the rest of my years go by."

Lucinda began a chuckle, which broke into a convulsive laugh that caused her to choke.

"Are you OK?" Jen asked her.

"Macduff's a sketch. We're not going to give this place up and hope you won't either, Jen. But if you could see Macduff floating Deadman's Bar to Moose on the Snake or walking up Cascade Canyon or Mill Creek or landing even a seven-inch Brook trout or Brown trout or Cutthroat or whatever, you'd know he wouldn't survive long kept away from the West. And now that you have your place on the Snake, which Macduff has dreamed of, I'll have to tie him to this swing to keep him here after a week or two."

"You're partly right," Jen responded. "But it's really you Lucinda. Something messed up his brain when he slipped on ice on your ranch front door stoop years ago."

"I hope you're right."

"Do I get to comment?" I asked.

"We're not finished talking about you," Lucinda replied.

"I need to go to bed. I'm out of it."

"You! What about Jen and me. We flew across the country and. . . ."

"You did *what*? You weren't in New York? You were with Jen in Jackson?"

"I'm sorry. I should have told you. You're right."

"Don't tell me what you did while you were in Jackson, with Jen or alone. I think I know."

EPILOGUE

Elsbeth's Diary

That year isn't one I can speak to from personal experience. I was in England at Oxford in my first year as a Rhodes Scholar. I had little time outside of classes, especially tutorials, and hours and hours in the library. The Spring Trinity Term at Oxford ended in mid-June. Lucinda and Dad visited in London in July.

I hadn't seen Lucinda and Dad for a year, when they arrived by private jet with their new friend, Jen, for a brief visit. They both looked ten years older than when I left for England the previous fall. I soon learned why, including why they were spending more time in Hope Town rather than at the Florida cottage or, at that time of the year—well into the fishing season—at the Montana log cabin.

The story they told about the gangs in Jackson and Livingston and how their lives were altered was hard to comprehend.

Dad was the more visibly affected by those incidents. He felt he was disappointing many of his clients by finally canceling the balance of the season. I'm not convinced he did that because of the uncertainty of the continuation of the Calle Rojo murders or the attack against him by Bandits members.

One matter that was sensitive and slow to include me in conversation was their opinion about who did the final eight killings, four Calle Rojo and four Bandits. But more important to me was their future safety; both gangs still existed although there had been no further murders even though the new season had started the previous month.

Lucinda told me she believed that the murders were exclusively the work of the two gangs, a quid pro quo or tit-for-tat effect. I asked whether she thought Jen might have been the murderer, and she quickly corrected me by pointing out there were almost certainly two people involved. She had no suggestions of who might have joined with Jen. I thought perhaps it was Erin,

327

who was undoubtedly frustrated that her own sheriff's department could not solve the murders. But I remember Erin having an unchallengeable passion for peaceful resolutions of all wrongs, including murder. I wondered, but because Erin was so very protective of Macduff and Lucinda I quickly suppressed that idea.

Macduff was in Florida at the time of the murders, and Lucinda was in New York, so I was relieved of having to even think twice about their involvement.

It was years before I learned what was probably the truth about the murders. I didn't learn it from Lucinda or Macduff. Jen told me her version, which I found hard to disprove. Lucinda was not on New York, she was with Jen in Wyoming. Two people.

ACKNOWLEDGMENTS

To Iris Rose Hart, my editor and friend, who began with the first book, *Deadly Drifts*, as a retained professional, and who has become an indispensable friend continuing to struggle teaching me what is a comma, and why one always has to be inserted where I haven't placed one, and why one often shouldn't be where I have placed one. For Macduff it is more likely that he "eats, shoots & leaves, than he "eats shoots & leaves." (with appreciation to Lynne Truss.)

To Christine Holmes for developing and maintaining my website and designing advertisements.

To the graphic design staff of Renaissance Printing of Gainesville, Florida, and especially Jim O'Sullivan for assistance with the cover, bookmarks, fishing flies beginning each chapter, and posters.

To very special people who have provided quiet places for me to write in Jackson, Bozeman, Livingston, and Hope Town.

To Elsbeth Waskom, Josh Dickinson, and Roy Hunt - continued thanks for the undefinable support that comes quietly with decades of friendship.

To Master Casting Instructors Dave Johnson and Dave Lambert, who struggle with improving my casting techniques. Every time I have adequately performed with what I assumed were all the forms of casting known to man, they unveil another.

M.W. GORDON – The author of more than sixty law books that won awards and were translated into a dozen languages, he wrote one book on sovereign immunity in the U.S. and U.K. as a Scholar-in-Residence at the Bellagio Institute at Lake Como, Italy. He has also written for *Yachting Magazine* and *Yachting World* (U.K.) and won the Bruce Morang Award for Writing from the Friendship Sloop Society in Maine. Gordon holds a B.S. and J.D. from the University of Connecticut, an M.A. from Trinity College, a Diplôme de Droit Comparé from Strasbourg, and a Maestria en Derecho from Iberoamericana in Mexico City. He is a pretty competent fly caster, an average small plane pilot, and a terrible oboist. He lives in St. Augustine with his author wife Buff and their sheltie, Macduff.

AUTHOR'S NOTE

You may reach me at: macbrooks.mwgordon@gmail.com
Please visit my website: www.mwgordonnovels.com

I answer email within the week received, unless I am on a book signing tour or towing *Osprey* somewhere to fish. Because of viruses, I do not download attachments received with emails. And please do not add my email address to any lists suggesting for whom I should vote, to whom I should give money, what I should buy, what I should read, or especially what I should write next about Macduff Brooks.

CPSIA information can be obtained
at www.ICGtesting.com
Printed in the USA
LVHW03s1107060718
582866LV00001B/2/P